Also Available by Frank Leslie

DEAD MAN'S TRAIL

Frank Leslie

A SIGNET BOOK

SIGNET
Published by New American Library, a division of
Penguin Group (USA) Inc., 375 Hudson Street,
New York, New York 10014, USA
Penguin Group (Canada), 90 Eglinton Avenue East, Suite 700, Toronto,
Ontario M4P 2Y3, Canada (a division of Pearson Penguin Canada Inc.)
Penguin Books Ltd., 80 Strand, London WC2R 0RL, England
Penguin Ireland, 25 St. Stephen's Green, Dublin 2,
Ireland (a division of Penguin Books Ltd.)
Penguin Group (Australia), 250 Camberwell Road, Camberwell, Victoria 3124,
Australia (a division of Pearson Australia Group Pty. Ltd.)
Penguin Books India Pvt. Ltd., 11 Community Centre, Panchsheel Park,
New Delhi - 110 017, India
Penguin Group (NZ), 67 Apollo Drive, Rosedale, Auckland 0632,
New Zealand (a division of Pearson New Zealand Ltd.)
Penguin Books (South Africa) (Pty.) Ltd., 24 Sturdee Avenue,
Rosebank, Johannesburg 2196, South Africa

Penguin Books Ltd., Registered Offices:
80 Strand, London WC2R 0RL, England

First published by Signet, an imprint of New American Library,
a division of Penguin Group (USA) Inc.

First Printing, November 2012
10 9 8 7 6 5 4 3 2 1

PUBLISHER'S NOTE
This is a work of fiction. Names, characters, places, and incidents either are the
product of the author's imagination or are used fictitiously, and any resemblance to
actual persons, living or dead, business establishments, events, or locales is entirely
coincidental.
    The publisher does not have any control over and does not assume any responsi-
bility for author or third-party Web sites or their content.

ALWAYS LEARNING   **PEARSON**

Chapter 1

"Yakima, we're gonna get shot so full of lead, we'll rat-tle when we walk!"

"Tell me somethin' I don't already know, Lewis."

A bullet plowed up dirt a foot to the left of Yakima Henry's broad, dark face. Squinting his jade green eyes against the dust, he quickly plucked shells from his cartridge belt and punched them through the loading gate of his octagonal-barreled 1866 Winchester Yellow-boy repeater.

"I believe them dog-eaters got us surrounded!"

"Uh-huh."

Lewis Shackleford glanced at Yakima, powder smoke wafting about his head and ratty canvas hat. "Uh . . . I meant no offense with that dog-eater comment. . . ."

"No dogs around to be offended, Lewis," Yakima said as he punched another round through the Yellow-boy's loading gate in the right side of the brass, or "yellow," receiver that had given the Winchester its nickname.

"I got nothin' against redskins, or even half-breeds

for that matter, as long as they ain't tryin' to take my topknot or eat out my liver!"

A dozen or so empty shell casings littered the bottom of the dry wash around Yakima's moccasins and his friend Lewis Shackleford's mule-eared lace-up boots. Another one clinked onto the collection as Yakima triggered the Yellowboy once more, punching a .44-caliber chunk of hot lead through the right, ochre-painted cheekbone of a Ute brave clad in wolf fur and buckskins and blowing the whooping, howling redskin off his charging paint pony.

Yakima cursed under his breath as he worked the rifle's cocking lever, seating another shell in the Winchester's breech.

Shooting Indians of any tribe didn't sit right with the half-breed. After all, they were his people. But then, they weren't any more his people than the whites were, as his being a "half-breed" meant he had one foot in each of the main two frontier blood pools, so to speak.

Both sides regarded him with equal suspicion, so really about the only folks he could call his own were his now-dead Cheyenne mother and his just-as-dead German gold-prospector father. His loyal horse, Wolf, he considered his "people" at times when he had no one else, though at the moment he'd thrown in with Lewis Shackleford, a white man. Yakima took his friends where he found them, and for as long as they lasted. That was usually never very long.

At the moment, and for the past four months, that friend was Lewis. And while Lewis was a half-mad Irish poet who also prospected for gold, and as raggedy-heeled, smelly, and poison-mean when drunk as your average cavalry sergeant, he did have a solid cabin and a nice-looking daughter, Trudy, who wore her blouses tight enough to make her look even better. . . .

Whump!

An arrow punched into the creek bank over which Yakima was triggering the Yellowboy through a clump of rabbitbrush. The missile fletched with hawk feathers stood at a slant only six inches from his right elbow, quivering. Wrapping a big brown hand around it, ripping it out of the ground, and tossing it away, Yakima said, "Goddamn it, Lewis, can't you shoot any straighter? I don't think you've knocked even one of these damn hellbenders off a horse *yet!*"

"You're mighty shouting right I ain't!" Lewis bellowed from ten feet down the bank from Yakima. "You know I can't hit the broad side of a barn, which means *you're gonna have to!*"

Yakima bit out another curse as two more arrows cut through the brush around him, and then an Indian opened up with a rifle. No, not an Indian. A one-eyed white man in a green top hat, black suit coat, and orange-checked trousers galloped toward the half-breed, whooping as loud as any of the Indians around him. "I see we got us a mixed-blood group today!" Yakima shouted, cutting loose on the white marauder.

The gang leader, Wyoming Joe Running Wolf, was known for his open-mindedness when recruiting killers to ride in his bank-robbing and rustling gang. In fact, Joe was a half-breed like Yakima himself, and his only requirement when recruiting killers was they be "mean enough to sing at their own funerals," or so went the saying. Most of his gang, however, were Utes running off their reservation, and were too mean and deadly for the local army boys to try doing much about them. Yakima and Lewis had gotten crossways with

Wyoming Joe before when, while hunting wild horses, they'd inadvertently crossed into territory Joe considered his own, which Yakima and Lewis must have done again recently, though they hadn't been aware of that fact until just a few minutes ago when they'd seen a rein of riders barreling toward them, yipping and howling like a pack of demon wolves.

The white man currently bearing down on Yakima was jostling around so much atop his skewbald paint mustang's bouncing back that Yakima's lead only found the air around the desperado. And then the rider fired two bullets into the dirt to either side of Yakima before the skewbald crashed through the brush before bounding clear across the arroyo to the other side.

The rider bellowed raucously. The horse whinnied shrilly.

Yakima jerked around as the one-eyed man leaped off the skewbald's back, tossed his Spencer repeater aside, and shucked a stout LeMat from behind his wide black shell belt. Crouching, moccasin-clad feet spread, Yakima triggered the Yellowboy.

Ping!

Empty . . .

Yakima tossed the Yellowboy aside and reached for the horn-gripped Colt he wore for the cross draw on his left hip. He stayed the move when he remembered that he'd emptied the hog leg, too. The grinning, ugly one-eyed marauder leaped into the arroyo and bounded toward the half-breed, the big LeMat in one hand, a bowie knife as long as Yakima's forearm in the other.

As Lewis desperately but with questionable competence continued to trigger his Winchester carbine at the marauders at Yakima's back, the half-breed threw himself to his right at the same time the LeMat roared in the one-eyed man's gloved fist. Rolling off his left shoulder, Yakima reached up behind his neck for the Arkansas toothpick poking up from behind the collar of his buckskin shirt.

With a single, deft flick of his wrist, he sent the five inches of razor-edged Damascus steel toward the one-eyed man. It thumped into the man's right arm, just above his elbow, and the man grimaced in pain as the LeMat fell from his hand to clatter onto the gravelly bed of the wash.

The man looked at the knife embedded in his arm. He jerked his one fury-sharp eye back toward the half-breed and then stumbled forward, growling like a wounded griz and thrusting the big bowie knife forward.

He came hard and fast, crouching.

Keeping his eyes on the knife with its upturned blade-tip intended to disembowel him, Yakima grabbed the one-eyed man's wrist around the knife at the last second. He threw himself over backward and thrust up hard with both legs, sending his attacker airborne.

The man screamed indignantly as he turned a complete somersault behind Yakima and hit the ground with a cracking thump. The knife clattered to the rocks near his thrashing boots. Yakima unsheathed his own wooden-handled bowie knife jutting from the well of his right fur-lined, high-topped moccasin and tossed it at the same time the man lifted his head up.

The timing was perfect. At least, it was perfect for Yakima.

Not for the one-eyed man, who suddenly had no

eye at all. The bowie knife plunged through the remaining one just as it widened in shock and exasperation, turning it to jelly before the big blade rammed hilt-deep in the now-bloody socket.

Phumptt! went the hilt striking the man's skull.

"Yakima, what in tarnation you doin' over there, damn it? This ain't no time to be playin' with yourself!" Now Lewis, his back to Yakima, was triggering two old-model pistols and yelling at the tops of his lungs, "We got 'em comin' up on us fast, son!"

Yakima wheeled to see several men—white men and Indians all dressed in skins and furs against this Wyoming country's December chill—running toward the dry wash from various western points, shooting carbines or revolvers and zigzagging between the rocks. Yakima automatically reached for his pistol, then left it in its holster when he again remembered it was empty and dashed for the Yellowboy. Just then one of Lewis's pistols clicked on an empty chamber.

Then the other one clicked on an empty chamber.

"Rats!" Lewis intoned, flinching as a bullet sliced across the side of his face to ricochet off a rock near Yakima, who was just now picking up the Yellowboy and starting to pluck fresh shells from his cartridge belt and slip them through the rifle's loading gate.

"Ah, ye greasy devil!" Lewis shouted, tossing one of his pistols at a stocky, bearded, sun-leathered white man barreling toward them fast, within twenty yards and closing, whooping and hollering and wielding a war hatchet in one fist, a Remington revolver in the other.

Then Yakima, still loading the Yellowboy, saw two other men come running out from behind rocks, as well, guns blazing, the slugs blowing up dirt and gravel along the lip of the wash. Yakima racked a round into the Yellowboy's breech, and jerked the butt to his shoulder . . . too late. The stocky man had him dead to rights, aiming the Remy at him from ten feet away and grinning down the pistol's barrel.

Bam!

Yakima flinched and then stared in shock as the smoking Remy, its triggered bullet screeching over his head, dropped from the man's hand as the man flew sideways, blood geysering from his right ear. At the same time, what sounded like a cannon blasted in the distance. Lewis was just then throwing his second pistol and yelling at a tall, thin Indian in white war paint and bleached buckskins dashing toward him when the Indian gave a grunt and dove forward, dropping a knife from one hand and a Winchester from the other.

The cannonlike explosion reached Yakima's ears once more.

The tall marauder hit the bank in front of Lewis, who jerked back, covering his face with his hands as the Indian rolled wildly through the brush to land in a heap at Lewis's feet.

There was another thunderous roar, and another marauder—he appeared Mexican, with long black mustaches, a palm-leaf sombrero, and a striped serape— stopped running toward the wash suddenly as a fist-sized gob of dirt blew up near his right boot. He had started to aim his Colt's revolving rifle toward a near sandstone ridge when his hat blew off as though in a sudden wind, and a good quarter of his black-haired skull turned frothy red, blood and white brain matter flying in all directions.

The Mexican stumbled backward, throwing his arms up and out as though in supplication, then hit the ground on his back with a loud thud. A chuff of violently expelled air formed a cloud in the sunny, cold air around his face.

Yakima stared down his Winchester's barrel, swinging the rifle left to right and back again, waiting for a target to show itself. None did. He saw only dead men sprawled amidst the rocks, rabbitbrush, and sage beyond him. The only sounds were dwindling hoofbeats. In the far distance, mare's tails of tan dust rose as several riders fled.

Slowly, keeping his finger curved tightly against the trigger, he lowered the rifle.

To his right, Lewis stared out beyond the arroyo, lower jaw hanging, looking around warily, jutting his prominent chin behind a sparse, gray-salted ginger beard. A thin line of brick-colored blood stretched across his leathery cheek and continued beneath his ear. The broad, ragged brim of his canvas hat buffeted in the breeze.

He glanced at Yakima, one grizzled brow arched over a watery copper eye. "What in tarnation?" he said softly.

Yakima resumed shoving .44 cartridges through his Winchester's breech. When he had eight in the tube, he racked one into the chamber, slipped another through the loading gate, and leaped out of the arroyo and onto the bank.

Holding the Yellowboy straight out from his left hip, he walked forward, glancing around at the several dead Indians and white marauders—rough-hewn men in mismatched winter clothes. Some wore scarves under their hats. They were heavily armed, but now spreading out upon the rocks and dirt of these foothills of the Mummy Range in northern Colorado, southern Wyoming were thick pools of their dark red blood.

Yakima peered toward the low sandstone shelf in the north, about sixty yards away, and stopped when a figure rose from behind it. The dry, high-altitude, sun-lit air was as clear as a lens. Yakima could see that the man was slender, dark-skinned, brown-clad, and he was holding a rifle in one hand, a black hat in the other. A green bandanna was knotted around his neck. As he stood atop the arroyo, he waved his hat broadly.

"All's clear!" came the man's deep, Southern-accented voice. "They're all dead." Then, a little lower as he looked into the distance: "All's that's still here, I'm sayin'."

Yakima kept his Yellowboy aimed straight out in front of him but eased the pressure on its trigger as he strode forward. He was a big, long-haired, green-eyed, rawboned man with cherry red skin, in a buckskin shirt under a heavy buckskin mackinaw, faded Levi's jeans, and high-topped moccasins. He wore a dirty gray scarf under his black hat, knotted over his left shoulder. The hands holding the rifle were clad in gloves; the right glove had its fingers cut off for easy shooting.

Such an imposing figure was the one that his and Lewis's savior saw as Yakima moved toward him, and the man seemed to hesitate a little, wisely, staring warily in the way every man greets a stranger in this harsh, merciless land. Especially a big green-eyed half-breed. The jade eyes set against the chiseled, granite-hard, red-brown face always evoked pause, sometimes trep-idation, often downright belligerence.

Yakima was about to throw up his own hand in affable greeting when a rifle barked. He jerked with a start and raised the Yellowboy again in both hands, raking the area around him carefully. Not seeing a shooter nearby, he flicked his gaze to the stranger, aiming the Yellowboy at the man atop the ridge. The so-called savior must have been setting a trap for him and Lewis.

Yakima frowned.

No.

The man stumbled forward, dropped the big rifle in his right hand, the hat in his left, and, clutching his belly, tumbled straight forward. He fell over the side of the ridge, turning a stiff somersault as he plunged behind a thick tangle of wild mahogany and piñons.

Yakima lurched forward. A man lay belly-down on the ground to his left, facing the ridge. Yakima saw the scarred face and long, tangled, greasy auburn hair of Wyoming Joe himself. Joe was turning toward Yakima and extending a carbine from the octagonal maw of which gray smoke curled. The gang leader, showing blood across his chest and shoulders, stretched his lips back from his teeth in a grimace as he brought the carbine to bear on Yakima.

The half-breed fired three quick rounds and watched all three puff dust from Joe's brown wool-lined vest and the checked shirt beneath it, causing a pendant hanging by a leather cord from his neck to jounce wildly. Wyoming Joe rolled onto his back with a sigh, as though he were merely going to sleep, and then jerked his arms and legs as he died.

Yakima ran ahead through the brush and rocks, bulled his way through a heavy stand of cedar and chokecherry. He stopped ten feet from the base of the sandstone ridge. The black man with the big rifle lay belly-down in a pool of blood oozing out beneath his brown wool coat.

The half-breed couldn't tell if he was breathing.

"Easy there," he said, setting his rifle down and kneeling to grab one of the man's shoulders gently and roll him onto his back. "Easy, partner."

The man didn't hear him. His broad jaws, lightly covered in a gray-flecked beard, hung slack. Full pink lips were stretched slightly back from thick, square white teeth. His chocolate brown eyes stared sightlessly up past Yakima at the cold blue sky yawning to accept him.

Chapter 2

"I'll be seein' y'all in hell soon, you yellow-livered sons o' bitches! You're killin' an innocent man here!"

Glendolene Mendenhour jerked her head up from a light doze at the man's intoned warning that vaulted above the thudding of the stage horses and the squawking of the Concord coach's thoroughbraces. She turned her head, elegantly adorned with a sleek marten-fur hat, toward the stage door on her right, and stared out past the drifting dust kicked up by the galloping team.

They were just now entering Wolfville, in the Wyoming Territory, and in the broad main street stood a tall wooden platform that she knew to be a gallows. A crowd of men as well as women—and, for heaven's sake, children!—was gathered around the death-dealing platform, as solemn as a church congregation. A few dogs milling with the crowd were the only ones making any noise, but suddenly above their barking sounded a wooden scrape and a man's agonized scream.

Close on the scream's heels, the crowd expelled a loud, victorious roar, several men pumping their fists in the air. The cacophony was so sudden and loud that one of the dogs gave a yelp and ran, tail between its legs, toward a gap between two of the main street's clapboard-sided business buildings. As the stage driver gave a bellow nearly equally as loud as the crowd's roar, the stage swerved toward the left side of the street and slowed until it came to a stop in front of the Andrews & Meechum Stage Line office, which shared the low, shake-shingled building with the Wells Fargo office.

Glendolene only glanced at the building out the stage's left door before looking out the right door window again, blinking against the dust that caught up to the stage in thick waves rife with the stench of ground horse manure.

She couldn't see much of the gallows because of the crowd milling around it, but as the shotgun messenger opened the door and she hiked her wool skirts up beneath her long brown wolf-fur coat to step down to the wooden platform he'd placed in the dusty street for her and the coach's three other passengers, the crowd parted slightly. She stepped to one side, squinting against the coppery late-afternoon sunshine that only partly warmed the chill December air, and found her stomach tightening.

She was unaware of the grimace twisting her face as she stared at the gallows, beneath the open trapdoor of which a man dangled at the end of a rope. No, not dangled. He appeared to be *dancing* there beneath the gallows, almost as though he were performing one of the old German dance steps Glendolene had frequently witnessed in a dance hall in her hometown of Belle Fourche, in the Dakota Territory—the old folk dances where the dancers lift their knees high, nearly to their chests, and thrust them down again while crossing their arms on their chests and nodding their heads.

Only this man who danced from the rope beneath the gallows did not have his arms crossed on his chest. They were tied behind his back. He wore no black hood, as Glendolene thought she'd heard that condemned men wore when they were executed in such a fashion. This man's long, stringy light brown hair danced about his head, the bangs sliding across his eyes. He stretched his lips back from his teeth, and they shone in a hard white line against the dark brown of his sunburned face as his head jerked and he continued to dance the bizarre old folk dance that Glendolene remembered from her childhood.

He danced with such vigor that one of his boots slipped down his right ankle; when he kicked that leg again the boot dropped into the street beneath him. The crowd had fallen nearly silent again as the men, women, and children stood in rapt attention as the man kicked and twisted at the end of the rope. Glendolene could hear the creaking of the straining hemp. A towheaded boy of maybe six or seven broke away from the crowd, ran toward the hanging man, and stooped to pluck the boot off the street. The boy turned, smiling broadly, and held the trophy proudly above his head.

A man whom Glendolene recognized as Sheriff Dave Neumiller dashed to the boy and, holding a sawed-off shotgun straight up in one hand, grabbed the boot from the boy with the other before tossing the boot back down beneath where the hanging man's kicks were losing their vigor, and brusquely shoved the boy back into the crowd.

Glendolene's knees had turned to warm mud. Now

as she swung around to walk around the stage to the Snowy Range Hotel just beyond it, a warm wave washed over her, and she dropped to her knees in the street. She heard her dress tear beneath the wolf-fur coat.

She'd seen men dead before. Dead men aplenty. Even a wagonload of dead Indian women and Indian children killed by the army back in Dakota, but somehow knowing that her husband was responsible not only for this death but for the celebration around it made her sick to her stomach.

"Oh, God, no," she heard herself rasp, both sickened by the spectacle and embarrassed by her reaction to it.

"Mrs. Mendenhour!" said the shotgun messenger, reaching down to wrap his hand around her arm. He was a stocky, ginger-bearded man dressed in a dusty brown vest and striped trousers, with a grimy cream duster sliding around his boot tops.

"I'm all right, Mr. Coble. I'm—"

"Glendolene!"

The familiar voice jerked her head up. Her husband, the prosecutor of Big Horn County, was striding toward her from the crowd still milling around the hanged man. Sheriff Neumiller was behind him, looking customarily smug and holding his shotgun and smoking a fat cigar, canting his head a little to one side to inspect the prosecutor's wife slouched in the dirt. Lee Mendenhour dropped to his knees beside her and placed his hand on her back. He, too, was smoking a cigar and held it now in his beringed left hand.

"Are you all right? Damn, you don't look good. The ride in from the ranch too rough for you?"

Glendolene looked at her husband—he was a cinnamon-bearded, handsome man in his late twenties, and his tailor-made suit beneath his long, natty elk-hide coat with a rabbit-fur collar fit his slender, well-proportioned frame perfectly. His beaver slouch hat was tipped at a rakish angle, opposite the wing of thick auburn hair slanting over his right brown eye.

"I'm fine, Lee," Glendolene said, letting him help her stand. "Just stumbled over my own clumsy feet, I guess." She glanced down at her elk-skin boots. "I haven't worn these boots yet this winter, and . . ."

"Sure?"

"Yes, of course I'm sure." Glendolene glanced past the administering eyes of her young, confident, accomplished husband on whose breath she detected a few fingers of celebratory brandy, to the hanged man who had now stopped dancing the macabre dance at the end of the rope. The man's body hung slack now, neck elongated, chin dipped toward his chest. He turned ever so gently this way and that, and his chin slid across his chest as he moved.

The crowd was slowly disbursing around him, and a low hum of conversation sounded along with the occasional screech of one of the painted ladies enjoying a midweek business boom over at the Silk Slipper Saloon & Sporting Parlor on the far side of the street, beyond the gallows.

Glendolene cleared her throat as she stared at the hanging body, one boot lying in the street beneath it. "Is that . . . ?"

"Preston Betajack, yes. You shouldn't have seen that, Glen. What a time for your stage to roll into town!" He thrust his dimpled, confident chin toward the jehu, Charlie Adlard, a middle-aged man standing nearby. "Adlard, couldn't you see what was happening here?

Good Lord, man, you might have stopped outside town and waited for this grisly affair to be finished!"

Part of Glendolene was glad she'd seen it. It gave her a better idea of who her husband was. Maybe it would help her make up her mind whether she wanted to stay married to him, a question that had been haunting her for several months now.

"It's all right. It's fine," she said as he took her carpetbag and steamer trunk from the shotgun messenger, Melvin Coble, who was unloading the coach's rear luggage boot. "I'd just like to go on into the hotel and have a hot bath. It was a chilly ride in from the ranch."

"Certainly, dear," the young prosecutor said. "He turned to a tall, broad-shouldered Indian standing nearby and who Glendolene knew worked for the hotel. He said, "Luther, would you please take my wife's bags on over to the hotel? Room twenty-two."

The Indian accepted the nickel proffered by young attorney Mendenhour and dropped the coin without looking at it in a pocket of his worn duck trousers. As he took both bags in his large red-brown hands, Glendolene could not help watching him, feeling a flush rise in her cheeks as she remembered a man with similar hands, with a similar build, and also with native blood running through his veins. She studied Luther's broad back clad in a black wool vest, remembering the grizzly claw necklace that dangled down the broad chest of this other man she'd known for a short time, as the full-blood turned toward the hotel beyond the stage station depot.

Glendolene looked away from the retreating Indian's back, the man's long blue-black hair braided with small gray feathers hanging down from beneath his bullet-crowned black hat to brush across his shoulders, but the memory of the caress of those other hands—large brick-red hands, rough but gentle—was slow to leave her.

Another flush rose in her cheeks when she saw the sheriff and several other men, including Lee's assistant, Mark Pettitbone, staring at her from where they stood near the stage. The men, business associates of Lee, had followed him over to the coach, and they studied her now with faint but obvious male interest, smiling as they puffed on their cigars. Glendolene was well aware, by the way she'd been turning men's heads since she was barely out of diapers, that she was a beautiful woman. But the men back home were able to conceal their goatish lust a little better than the breed of male out here. She supposed it was because that, outside of sporting parlors, even plain-faced young females with lush bodies and full sets of teeth were rare in these parts. The lascivious looks she attracted from even the most civilized males, like the ones she evoked now, caused a pang of revulsion to tighten her smile.

"Sheriff Neumiller," she said in greeting with a cordial nod, watching the lawman's lusty eyes flick furtively across her. "Mr. Pettitbone."

"Now, Glendolene," said Sheriff Neumiller, "I thought we agreed you'd call me Dave."

"Dave it is," she said with her winning smile, though wishing only to get off to her room to be by herself. "How've you been?"

"Very well, very well."

"Glendolene and I are catching tomorrow's stage for Belle Fourche," Lee told the two men, wrapping an arm around his young wife's slender shoulders. "We're heading there to spend Christmas with the aunt and uncle who raised her. And after what we accomplished here today, I do indeed feel it's time for a break."

"We did well here today, Mr. Mendenhour," said Pettitbone, brushing a tobacco speck from his thick red mustache set beneath a fine, pale nose. His round spectacles reflected the west-angling light beneath his crisp bowler hat. "Like the circuit judge said over drinks this morning, this execution will send a message to brigands throughout the county that no matter who they are or where they come from, they must toe the line along with everyone else!"

The law assistant smugly puffed on the cigar and grinned at Glendolene, showing off.

"Yes, but what about Floyd Betajack?" Glendolene said, glancing with concern at her husband. "Won't he . . . ?"

"Enough business talk," Lee said, straining slightly with his reassuring smile. "Fellas, my wife makes it to town so seldom, I'd hate for us to bore her ears off. I'm going to get her situated over at the hotel, and then I'll be down to finish up business for the day."

"Enjoy your trip, Glendolene," said Sheriff Neumiller, lifting his gray felt Montana-creased hat as Lee ushered her off toward the hotel.

"Thank you, Dave. Be well, gentlemen!"

She saw that several armed men with badges stood around in the street near the hotel's broad wooden veranda. They regarded her a little bashfully but also officiously, and they gave her husband cordial nods. She knew why they were there. And she also knew why Lee had decided to accompany her to Belle Fourche.

Because of Floyd Betajack, sometimes called Old Man Betajack and also—she'd overheard this from some of her husband's and father-in-law's ranch hands out at the Chain Link—known as Big-Bad Betajack, who had some of the most formidable, cold-blooded gunmen on the frontier riding for him.

One of the sheriff's deputies, cradling a shotgun in the crook of his right arm, pinched his hat brim to Glendolene, who nodded at the man before turning to glance once more at Preston Betajack hanging slack from the gallows, his lifeless body clad in a short, fringed elk-hide jacket turning in a chill, building wind.

Chapter 3

"Who you s'pose he is?" Lewis said as he and Yakima stared at the black man's unmoving body at the bottom of the ridge from which he'd fallen. The ends of his scarf blew gently in a building breeze.

"Don't know."

"Poor ole fella. Saved our bacon only to be killed by a dyin' desperado for his trouble."

Yakima stared down at the man.

They'd gone through the pockets of his shabby coat, wool vest, calico shirt, and twill trousers. They'd found nothing except a silver-chased watch and an old supply list scribbled in pencil. Yakima had removed the man's shell belt and holstered Russian .44 from around his waist. The shell belt was half-filled with .50-caliber rounds to feed the big Sharps rifle, commonly called a Big Fifty, and .44 cartridges for the pistol. The rusty six-shooter needed oil, and the walnut grips were loose and cracked, indicating the gun had probably mostly been used for grinding coffee beans and jerky, maybe pounding the occasional horseshoe nail.

Yakima looked at the blood soaking the man's vest

and calico shirt about midway between his breastbone and his belly button. Then he shook his head against his guilt at the man giving his life for him and Lewis, total strangers, and the senselessness of being killed by a desperado who likely would have died only a few minutes later from the slugs Yakima and Lewis had slung into him.

So damn senseless, like Faith three years ago in Colorado. . . .

The demons inside Yakima were limbering up, so he shook them back into the far reaches of his consciousness and looked around him and Lewis. "He must have a horse behind the ridge somewhere. You stay with him while I look."

Yakima rested his Yellowboy over his shoulder and walked over to where a fissure ran up the side of the ridge in a jagged line, offering a way to the top. Twenty minutes later, he walked around the ridge's far eastern side, leading a long-legged grullo with black legs from the knees down and with a black mane and tail. He also led a dark bay mule wearing a packsaddle. Lewis, sitting on a rock beside the dead man and holding a canteen, heard the hoof clomps of the two animals and stood.

"Prospector?" he said, frowning at the packhorse to which two shovels and a pick were strapped.

"Looks like."

While Yakima removed a pair of worn leather saddlebags from the grullo's back, the horse itself nickering as it lowered its neck to sniff its dead rider, Lewis went through the panniers strapped to the wooden packsaddle. Yakima sat on a rock and began going through the saddlebags. If they could find out who the man was and where he was from, they could take him home for burial, or at least send word back to his family, if he had one. They owed him that much.

"Nothin' much over here. Most of the panniers are empty. A little coffee and flour and pipe tobacco. Some rocks with a little gold color in 'em. Small bottle of busthead. He must've been headin' to Wolfville for supplies."

Yakima hadn't found much in the saddlebags, either. A few more small quartz rocks streaked with gold, a few old Confederate gold pieces in a small hide pouch, a bag of chopped pipe tobacco, and a pale envelope. All by itself in one bag was a burlap sack about the size and weight of a five-pound sack of sugar. He set the saddlebags and the envelope aside, then, balancing the sack on his knee, untied the whang string holding the neck closed, and peered inside.

He frowned. His heart beat faster.

He dipped a hand into the sack, poked his fingers into the sugary grain but knew right away it wasn't sugar. Why would a man be low on all other supplies and still carry five pounds of sugar around in his saddlebags?

Yakima carefully pulled out a handful and looked at the gold dust flashing beguilingly at him. "Holy Moses."

"Huh?" Lewis said, lowering the small liquor bottle he'd found in a packsaddle pouch.

"Somewhere he struck a vein."

"Let me see."

Lewis walked over in his bandy-legged way and stood over Yakima, extending the half-filled bottle of brandy to him. The half-breed shook it off and looked up at the small brown little man with a hawk nose and close-set gray-blue eyes that grew brighter by the second

as they stared down at the gold dust in Yakima's broad
red-brown palm.

"Holy shit," Lewis said, dipping a finger into the
small mound of dust in Yakima's hand, then touching
it to his tongue as though to prove to himself it wasn't
flour or sugar, though Yakima had never seen flour or
sugar that color. "How much you think he's got there?"

Yakima carefully poured the dust back into the
sack, then lifted the sack in both hands, hefting it. "I'd
say five, six, maybe seven pounds."

"Damn," Lewis said. "That man done found him a
fortune!" He paused, licked his lips. "You . . . uh . . .
you reckon it's ours?"

Yakima was about to set the gold on the ground, but
Lewis took it from him, hefting it in his hands, pale
eyes growing brighter, the older man's breath wheezing eagerly in and out of his lungs. Lewis was a wild-
horse hunter and breaker, and he was as wild as the
horses he trapped and sold to the army and area ranch-
ers, and sometimes as hard to figure and get along
with. His mother, Old Judith, was the same way, as
was his daughter, the scrappy but lovely Trudy.

"Go easy on that," Yakima said as he reached down
to pluck the envelope off the right saddlebag pouch.

"What—you think I'm gonna drink it?" Lewis chuckled. "Hell, I'm just gonna ogle it some's all. Why, this
bag here's prettier'n them teats on the beefy whore
over to the Silk Slipper in Wolfville!"

"I'm gonna tell Old Judith on you."

"Go ahead, and I'll tell Trudy about you cavortin'
with . . ." Seeing the flat, reprimanding cast to Yakima's gaze, Lewis let his voice trail off and looked away
like a chastised dog. His good mood returned only
moments later, however. He chuckled as he dipped a

long, gnarled hand into the gold bag and let the dust sift through his fingers.

Meanwhile, Yakima turned the envelope over in his hands and read the delivery address on the front. Mr. Delbert Clifton, Wolfville, Wyo. Terr. The return address was Mrs. Delbert Clifton, Belle Fourche, Dakota Terr.

Yakima used the pick and Lewis used the shovel to dig a neat grave about four feet deep. While they worked, hawks and buzzards circled over the dead marauders who'd attacked them, and they kept a close eye out for more.

It was late in the day, the shadows elongating from rocks and shrubs and surrounding bluffs, when the half-breed and Lewis Shackleford wrapped the man whom Yakima assumed to be the recipient of the letter he'd found in the saddlebags—Delbert Clifton, previously of Belle Fourche in the Dakota Territory—in the man's own soogan, and stared down at his face one last time. Guilt no longer pained Yakima. He knew it wouldn't bring the man back. Most men died ugly, needlessly out here.

The gold, however, burned in his brain. And the letter . . .

When he and Lewis had lowered the man into the grave and then covered it and mounded rocks over it to keep the predators away, Lewis leaned on his shovel, his wrinkled, sweaty forehead glistening like copper in the early evening sunlight angling under dark, flat cloud strips in the west. "What's it say?"

Yakima looked at him.

"The letter."

"I'll tell ya later. Best be gettin' back to the ranch."

Yakima walked over to where his black stallion, Wolf, stood tied to a piñon, near where Lewis's own blue roan mustang stood with Delbert Clifton's grullo and the bay mule. The black and the roan switched their tails eagerly, knowing it would soon be suppertime and they still had an hour's ride back to the ranch. The men had run the horses down before they'd dug the grave, keeping them close now that night was falling fast, as it did in December this far north.

Now as Yakima grabbed the grullo's reins and stepped into Wolf's saddle, he again looked around cautiously, making sure no more of Wyoming Joe's bunch was closing in on him and Lewis, and then reined Wolf around. He glanced at his left saddlebag pouch bulging around the gold. He'd stuck the letter in the pouch, as well.

"You know, Yakima," Lewis said, taking another pull from the black man's brandy bottle and then giving a sigh and smacking his lips, "that gold's ours now. Yours and mine. I say we split it like everything else—sixty-forty."

Yakima's belly tightened against the man's comments. He looked at the flat bottle that Lewis held low by his side as he stared up at Yakima. He sensed the fire that was starting to grow inside the old, horse-hunting Irishman, because tanglefoot often had the same effect on Yakima himself. That's why he kept a thumb on the vice, sticking mainly to beer and the occasional cigarette, though he knew that if a man smoked too much he lost his sniffer. And a man often on the run, as he was, couldn't afford to lose his sense of smell any more than a deer or an antelope could.

"We'll talk about it later, Lewis," Yakima said, apprehension stiffening his neck as he touched moccasin heels to the flanks of his black stallion, who gave an eager nicker at the prospect of a warm barn and a bucket of oats.

Yakima rode back through the canyon where they'd first seen Hendricks's men trailing them and had hightailed it to the dry wash. Lewis's roan clomped along behind, leading the black man's mule.

The half-breed didn't like Lewis riding back there. He'd gotten to know the man well enough over the past four months that they'd been working together, splitting their income from their mustanging sixty-forty, since Lewis had the ranch and the corrals they needed for breaking, but Yakima knew that you never really got to know a man as hardheaded as Lewis Shackleford. You never really got to know an alcoholic, especially one given to Lewis's dark moods that could often evoke the rough-hewn poetry in him but would often as not boil into a walleyed, unreasoning rage.

Those rages had not yet been directed at Yakima, but the half-breed knew they would be eventually. And the gold could be just the trigger. So he didn't like him riding behind him, because he wasn't entirely sure that Lewis wouldn't back-shoot him. Though not from anything specific Lewis had said, he knew that his partner considered him less of a man for his Indian blood, just as his mother, Old Judith, did. As he rode, keeping a sharp eye on the darkening land around him, he kept an ear skinned for the snick of Lewis sliding one of his old hog legs from its holster.

The only sound he heard besides some wailing wolves and coyotes, however, was the sudden screech of glass as Lewis, finished with the brandy, hurled the bottle against a rock along the trail. When Yakima

jerked with a start and looked back at the man, his
right hand instinctively closing over the horn grips of
his Colt, Lewis merely snickered.

When they rode into the ranch yard, it was good
dark, stars glistening across the sky. The high sandstone ridge looming up behind the two-story cabin
made the clearing even darker despite the glow in the
cabin's first-story windows, behind the flour-sack curtains that Old Judith and Trudy had dyed ochre with
Indian roots.

In the barn, Yakima and Lewis tended their mounts
in moody silence. They turned the horses and their
savior's mule into the rear paddock with seven half-
broken mustangs, then headed for the cabin.

Yakima had the black man's saddlebags slung over
his left shoulder. He didn't know what else to do with
them besides haul them into the cabin. He and Lewis
would have to have it out over the gold, so he'd best
keep it close. He already knew what he intended to do
with it. While Lewis wouldn't like it, he felt certain that
he'd made the right decision.

Trudy warmed some elk roast and potatoes for the
two men, who ate at the long half-log pine table while
Trudy washed supper dishes and the wizened Old
Judith sat in a rocking chair by the fire, knitting and
rocking. Neither woman said anything. They'd sensed
the tension between the two men who'd returned after
dark, and neither had even inquired about the saddlebags that Yakima had carried in with him and hung on
a peg by the door.

Lewis washed his food down with frequent sips
from his stone coffee mug in which Yakima had seen
him pour as much whiskey as coffee. The brown-
haired Trudy, who was eighteen but sported a full, ripe

body behind her gingham dress and soiled apron, had seen it, too, and she'd shot Yakima a tense, suspicious glance. When both men had finished, Lewis slid his plate forward and said to Trudy, "Get this plate out of here, girl. I'm done with it."

"Yes, Pa."

The girl gave Yakima another faintly accusatory glance as though to ask: "What did you do to rile him?"

When Trudy had taken both their plates and was working on them over at the scrub pail in the dry sink, Lewis said, "What'd the letter say? Read it to me."

Yakima stood and retrieved the letter from the saddlebags.

"Bring the gold over here, too."

Yakima looked at him and shrugged. Lewis wasn't going anywhere with the bounty tonight. The half-breed pulled the hefty sack out of the saddlebag pouch and set it on the table.

Trudy was looking over her shoulder at the sack, one brow arched, as she added hot water from the reservoir on the range to her bucket of dishwater. She held her head and lips so that Yakima could see the missing eyetooth, courtesy of a contentious, ewe-necked broodmare, on the left side of her mouth. Still, she was a pretty brown-eyed girl growing up too soon out here, on the backside of nowhere. Old Judith looked at the table over the half-glasses resting low on her age-spotted nose as she rocked and knitted.

"What you got there, Lewis?" She hadn't addressed Yakima directly since he'd thrown in with Lewis. She did her best to pretend the redskin heathen wasn't here, that it was still just her and Lewis and Trudy, though Lewis was getting too old and becoming too much of a drunk to do much horse trapping or hunting on his own anymore. Yakima knew the old Irish horse hunter had a good grubstake for himself and the women, however, for whenever he and Yakima had ridden to town for supplies, Lewis had paid from a large wad of cash he carried in a money belt.

"That there, Ma, is gold dust," Lewis said, throwing back another belt from his coffee mug. "Maybe ten pounds' worth."

The old woman stopped rocking. Trudy turned slowly from her bucket, holding her soapy hands straight down in front of her soiled apron and shabby gingham dress. The top of her dress drew taut against her swelling breasts. Her brown eyes were riveted on the gold.

"Go ahead and read the letter, since you can read so well, red man," Lewis said. The man's hard tone tied a half-hitch knot in the half-breed's gut.

The way the women were eyeing the gold made the knot even tauter.

Chapter 4

A gun blasted in the street outside the Snowy Range Hotel. A man screamed. Glendolene Mendenhour, dozing in her deep copper tub, awoke with a gasp. She pushed herself up out of the water, grabbed a towel, walked barefoot to the room's single window, and slid the rose red curtain aside with the back of her hand.

She squinted into the street below. The lit candles and oil lamp she'd lined up on the dresser were reflected in the dark glass, but then she saw beyond the reflections a man stumble out of the Longhorn Saloon on the street's far side, nearer the hotel than the Silk Slipper. This smaller, rougher saloon than the Slipper sat perpendicular to the hotel, its side facing the Snowy Range, so Glendolene could see only the man's profile as he staggered across the saloon's porch, clutching both hands to his belly.

There was a flash inside the saloon. A quarter second later, the gun's blast rattled the hotel window in front of Glendolene, and she gave another gasp as she took one step back but continued staring down at the street lit by oil pots and torches bracketed to porch posts. The wounded man jerked and then flopped forward down the porch steps to lie sprawled in the street. The five or six horses tied to the saloon's hitch rack whinnied and nickered and pulled against their reins.

Glendolene clutched the blanket tight around her dripping, wet body. "Good *Lord*!"

Two men in fur coats, one holding what appeared to be a gun in his right hand, walked out of the saloon to stare down at the man in the street, whom Glendolene could hear groaning and rolling from side to side in agony.

One of the two men on the porch holstered his pistol, said something to the man standing beside him. They laughed, then turned and walked back into the saloon. Behind them, the wounded man continued to thrash around, groaning. Glendolene stared, aghast, as the saloon's double front doors closed.

What were they going to do—just leave him there to die alone in the street?

It was a cold night, and no one else was out and about. Smoke wafted in ghostly gray tufts over the street. A single rider materialized from the east, to Glendolene's left, and the man dressed in a long hide coat and with a red scarf tied over his head beneath his hat merely glanced once at the wounded man and then crouched to casually light a cigarette before touching spurs to his horse's flanks. Horse and rider trotted on past the wounded man, disappearing to Glendolene's right.

Her heart thudded as she stood there before the window, clad in only a towel, her thick hair piled atop her head, and stared down at the thrashing figure of the man who was surely dying. Dying alone on a cold night in a Wolfville street, while a saloon full of men and parlor girls frolicked only a few yards behind him.

Wind gusted, blowing silhouettes of trash along the street. Something moved beyond the dying man, and Glendolene stretched her gaze toward the gallows beyond the saloon. Something long and dark swayed beneath the platform. More revulsion washed through Glendolene as she stared at the body of Preston Betajack still hanging there.

"What on earth . . . ?" she muttered.

But she knew why Betajack still hung from the gallows. He remained there as Lee's and Sheriff Neumiller's grisly example to any outlaws passing through town, and as a stern message to Betajack's outlaw father to clear out of the county. His brand of ranching, which mostly involved rustling cattle and horses from other men's ranches, and which had been a bane to Lee's own spread that he shared with his own father, Wild Bill Mendenhour, would no longer be tolerated in Big Horn County. It was also Lee's and Neumiller's message to Betajack that, despite the hired guns on his roll, they weren't afraid of him.

Sending such a message was all well and good, she supposed. It was the frontier's brand of justice. But word of the hanging likely would have spread by now. Why leave the body to the crows?

Glendolene returned her gaze to the wounded man thrashing now with less vigor in front of the Longhorn Saloon. "Help me," she heard him say, weakly, ramming the back of one fist into the ground beside him.

She backed away from the window. She turned away quickly, as though to rid the man from her mind as well as her eyes. She couldn't help him. She had no real desire to help. He'd probably deserved that bullet he'd been fed in the Longhorn, and it was none of her business, anyway. As Lee had told her over and over again, it was a harsh world out here. It begat harsh men who died badly at times. Such was the price of living at all.

"Help me. . . ."

Glendolene tensed her shoulders, trying to fight the image of the dying man, his weakening pleas, from her mind. She tried to think about the stage ride tomorrow, of spending Christmas with the couple who'd raised her—Uncle Walt and Aunt Evelyn Birdsong. They owned a harness shop and blacksmith business in Belle Fourche, and they'd raised her since she was seven years old, when her own parents had died in a plague. She even tried to think about Lee and their life together, and if she really wanted that life to continue on the ranch where she was treated like a child by Lee and his overbearing father, Wild Bill.

She couldn't even ride out alone on a horse, as she'd so enjoyed doing in Dakota, despite her being as capable in the saddle as nearly any of the men at Chain Link. If she did, she incurred a loud, castigating rebuke from Wild Bill himself, if one of the hands had seen her, and by Lee if he was around and not off riding around the county with Neumiller, laying down his hard, uncompromising brand of justice.

They thought that she might encounter a rattlesnake and her horse would throw her, or that she wouldn't be able to find her way back to the ranch. She knew how to avoid such dangers. They treated her like property, or worse—like a child incapable of fending for herself, though she had been raised to be no hothouse flower, and she was tired of it.

"Goddamn . . . sons o' bitches . . . !" came another deep-throated plea from outside. "Help . . . me . . . *bastards!*"

She turned back to the window. The wounded man was trying to sit up, fumbling to get a purchase on the Longhorn's porch steps. Still, no one appeared to be going to the man's aid.

What was Glendolene supposed to do—climb back into her bath and pretend she hadn't seen him and couldn't hear him while he bled his life out in the street?

Unable to stand by any longer while a man died before her—where was Neumiller, anyway?—Glendolene toweled herself dry, dressed quickly in a chemise and pantaloons, then threw on a heavy wool robe. She stepped into a pair of elk-skin slippers and left the room. She locked the door, pocketed the key, and padded downstairs.

There was no one at the hotel desk in the lobby. She glanced into the dining room, hoping she'd find the Indian who'd escorted her to her room earlier, but apparently the dining room had closed since she and Lee had dined together an hour ago, before Lee had left to play poker with several businessmen friends of his and his father's. The dining room chairs were stacked upside down on the tables from which the white cloths had been removed. Luther was probably out in his shack behind the hotel.

Spying no one else, Glendolene pushed through the double glass doors and looked around, shivering as a chill wind bit into her. She fought the doors closed against a strong gust and latched them. Reaching up, she removed the pins from her hair and let it fall in a messy tangle about her neck, somewhat keeping the wind from sliding its icy hands down her back, chilling her to the bone.

She looked across the street. The wounded man sat slumped on the bottom step of the Longhorn Saloon, elbows on his knees, head dipped toward his chest. In the windows of the saloon behind him, shadows slid this way and that.

She glanced at the dark, swinging figure of Preston Betajack, felt a shudder independent of the wind rattle through her, and then moved on down the porch steps. Halfway across the street, a newspaper blew against her legs, and she paused to kick it free, losing one of her slippers as she did.

She cursed, set the foot clad in a thin silk stocking down in the cold street, and hobbled forward until she'd regained the slipper. Continuing across, she stopped before the man slumped forward, legs extended before him, boot toes pointed out, spurs ringing as the wind raked them. He'd lost his hat, and thin strands of gray-brown hair blew back across his bony, nearly bald skull.

"Are you . . . alive . . . ?" she asked, feeling inadequate for the task, shivering, holding the robe closed across her breasts. The horses to her left all looked at her curiously, their tails blowing up over their backs.

The man lifted his head slightly. He was silhouetted against the saloon lights behind him, so she couldn't see his face clearly, but his eyes appeared slitted. He had a thin gray beard and a mole off the right corner of his thin-lipped mouth. The fur of his bear vest rippled in the wind.

"I'm hurt bad, lady," he said tightly, just loudly enough for Glendolene to hear. "Get me to a doc, will ya?" He smelled strongly of alcohol.

"Hold on."

Glendolene climbed the porch steps and pulled open one of the saloon doors. She stepped inside, drawing the door closed behind her, and looked around at the long, smoky, lantern-lit room.

There were a dozen or so scruffy-looking men milling about the place, some obscured by the thick tobacco smoke. Half were standing at the bar to her right. Glendolene nearly choked on the stench of the smoke, sweat, leather, strong drink, and women's sweet perfume. One of the three women in the room laughed raucously off to her right, pointing at a man crawling around on the floor on his hands and knees and swinging his head and whinnying like a horse.

"Jump on ole Charlie horse's back, Lil, an' I'll ride ya upstairs fer a tumble!" howled the drunkard.

Glendolene looked at several of the men staring back at her. Their eyes, opaque from drink, raked her up and down, lips stretching with vague lasciviousness.

"Hey," said the nearest man standing at the bar, blinking slowly beneath his broad hat brim.

Glendolene turned and went back out. She moved carefully down the steps and turned to the man slumped before her. "Do you know where the doctor's office is?"

The man lifted his head, looked at her, and pointed halfheartedly in the direction of the gallows. She looked that way to see several wooden buildings standing to the left of the Silk Slipper, before the brightly lit windows of which a dozen or so horses stood tied.

"All right," Glendolene said, crouching beside the man. "If I'm going to help you, you're going to have to help me. Can you stand?"

He nodded slowly.

Glendolene slid up against him and wrapped his left arm around her shoulders. "Help me now!"

He planted his boots in the dust of the street and used his legs to help Glendolene hoist him to a standing position. As he leaned into her, she stepped forward, grunting under the man's weight as she walked him across the street, keeping the gallows on her left, the Silk Slipper on her right. She felt the slick wetness of the blood oozing out of him, and she gave another inward shudder, hearing the painfully thin breaths wheezing in his lungs.

They were halfway to the other side of the street when a gurgle traveled up from deep in his throat and suddenly his knees buckled. He fell, dragging her down on top of him with a surprised scream.

"Glendolene?" said a familiar voice.

Sprawled over the top of the wounded man's body, she looked up to see two figures standing on the Silk Slipper's front stoop, above the fidgeting horses, staring toward her.

"Oh, God—help me, Lee!"

Both men ran down the porch steps and around the horses as Glendolene looked down at the wounded man, who lay now with his eyes open, his chest rising and falling shallowly. His mouth was open, and he was making a faint sucking sound.

"What in the name of Christ is going on, Glendolene?" Lee said as he dropped to a knee on the other side of the man she'd been trying to help. "What are you *doing* out here? Who *is* this man?"

"I don't know. I saw him—"

"Karl Luedtke," said Sheriff Neumiller, standing

over the man who now looked dead. "Wolfer. Comes in from time to time to cheat at cards over at the Longhorn."

"That's where he was shot," said Glendolene, sitting back on her heels. "No one was helping him. I saw him from the hotel window and came out to try to get him over to the doctor's."

"For cryin' out loud, Dave," her husband intoned, staring at Neumiller, "don't you have any deputies making the rounds this evening?"

"Sure I do. Warren's out delivering a subpoena, but Jim Harrison should be out here somewhere . . ." Neumiller let his voice, thick from drink, trail off as he looked around the nearly empty street. "Maybe he's warmin' up for a spell back at the office. Cold out here." He looked down at the wounded man and shook his head as he puffed on a fat, half-smoked stogie. "Luedtke's looked better—I'll give him that."

Glendolene slid her exasperated gaze from her husband to Neumiller and back again. Both men reeked of tobacco smoke, alcohol, and—this was no surprise and it troubled her only slightly—women's perfume. "He has little chance of looking any better until we get him to the doctor, gentlemen!"

"Of course!" Lee leaped to his feet, glancing down at the bloody man distastefully, then turning to Neumiller. "Can you . . . ?"

The Silk Slipper's front doors opened, and Lee called to the men walking, slightly staggering, onto the stoop. When the men were moving between the horses and heading toward the wounded Mr. Luedtke, Glendolene climbed to her feet and brushed the dirt,

gravel, and flecks of horse manure from her robe. As
she did, she glanced toward the gallows to her left.

Something there flashed in the light from several oil
pots and the lamplight emanating from the Silk Slipper. She stared at the darkness beneath the gallows. As
Lee and Sheriff Neumiller guided the other men, who
bore Mr. Luedtke between them, toward an outside
stairs that climbed to the doctor's office, Glendolene
wandered slowly, cautiously over to the gallows, feeling a deep revulsion growing in her belly.

She scowled up at the silhouetted form of the man
hanging from the rope, twisting this way and that in
the chilly winter wind. Again, something flashed on
Preston Betajack's dead body. Up near his right shoulder.

Something compelled Glendolene to get a closer
look.

She took several more steps, staring up at Betajack,
hearing the rope above his head creak and groan.
Only, the man hanging from the gallows was not the
man she'd seen hanged earlier. It was not Betajack.
Betajack was no longer here.

The man here now was a stocky blond gent with
a thick blond handlebar mustache. He wore a brown
suit, and on the right lapel of his brown tweed suit
coat, a deputy sheriff's badge flashed as the body
turned, catching the light from the Silk Slipper.

Glendolene stumbled backward, fell. "Lee!" The
shout got tangled up in her throat and came out as a
hoarse whisper. "Sheriff Neumiller!" she said again, a
little louder this time, but the words were still lost in
the wind.

The man hanging before her stared down at her

through half-open eyes, his swollen tongue poking out one corner of his slack-jawed mouth. He seemed to be leering at her.

Glendolene cleared her throat, tried again: "I think . . . I found Deputy Harrison. . . ."

Chapter 5

"Pshaw—he can't read!" intoned Old Judith.

Ignoring the woman, Yakima smoothed the letter onto the table. He positioned the flickering oil lamp so that the shadows slid aside, and the buttery light bathed the large, rounded, flowing, female script before him. Yakima cleared his throat and, using the year of schooling in a Denver boardinghouse for Indian boys and then his own self-schooling afterward, haltingly but relatively smoothly, he read:

> *Dearest Husband,*
>
> *The children and I feel so blessed that you will be home for Christmas this year, and that you are bringing a very special present. It was so wonderful to receive your last letter and to read in it your most welcome news! I am relieved that you will be staying home from now on, and that you have managed to find a way to buy the hotel. We will all work together, the four of us side by side, and be happy that we are all together at last. Jimmy's become a strapping lad in*

this past year. He can haul two buckets of water from
the well at once, with Mr. Whiskers on his shoulders!
Caroletta is a beautiful young lady, Del, and she is
Mrs. Overholser's best student in both reading and
math. Just like her pa. Ha!

Travel safely home to us, Del. Today, we are
cutting a tree in the hills and will have it decorated by
the time you arrive! This will be a most special
Christmas!

Bless you, my husband. I and the children will be
eagerly awaiting your return.

Your loving wife,
Annabelle-Day Clifton

"Who's that letter for?" asked Old Judith, staring over her glasses at her son, unmoved by the missive's sentiment. The fire popped behind her.

Yakima refolded the letter and slipped it back into its envelope. "The man who saved our hides."

"I wasn't talkin' to you!" Old Judith cawed like an angry blackbird, pinching up her wizened face behind her reading glasses that had slipped lower on her nose. It was, in fact, the first time she'd addressed Yakima directly.

"Well, that's just too damn bad," said Lewis, ignoring his mother. "So the Negro was goin' home for Christmas. Hell, I am home for Christmas." He fumbled beneath the table and brought up his old Colt conversion revolver. As he slid his chair back and stood awkwardly, placing one hand on the table to steady himself, he ratcheted back the pistol's hammer. "And I'll be keepin' my cut of the gold. You can do with your share of it whatever the hell you wish."

"There you go, boy!" said Old Judith, adjusting the wolf skin draped around her spindly shoulders. "I don't care who that money belonged to." She balled up her tiny red fists. "It's here now, and here it will stay less'n someone wants to come fightin' for it!"

"Grandma," Trudy said, eyes aghast, "it's Christmas!"

"It ain't Christmas yet."

"Yeah, but those poor people."

"They're black people," Lewis said. "And they're used to doin' without. Just like this red nigger standin' here before me." He wagged the pistol at Yakima. "You leave the gold there. Go on. Pull your picket pin. You done wore out your welcome here, dog-eater." This last he bellowed, red-faced: "Saddle up and fog the damn sage!"

Yakima looked up from the dark maw of the old Colt shaking in Lewis's fist, to the man's beet red face, the nostrils of his long hawk's nose flaring, upper teeth showing through his snarl. Calmly, Yakima reached for the gold sack, untied the rawhide strings from the neck, and emptied his coffee cup onto the floor.

He stared hard at his former partner, not sure whether the man would shoot him or not, or, if he did squeeze the trigger, if the slug would land anywhere near him. With the way the half-breed's luck was holding, it would likely punch out his heart, but his hands remained steady as he poured the gold dust into his tin cup until the cup was filled to the brim. The granular flakes glistened in the lamplight.

He retied the neck of the sack. "That there is more than you deserve. Call it a Christmas present from Mrs. Clifton."

"Don't you dare, goddamn you," Lewis bit out as Yakima rose from the table and, feeling the muscles writhing like snakes beneath the skin of his back, turned to drop the gold into the saddlebags. He buckled the flap over the pouch, then donned his flat-brimmed, low-crowned black hat and his buckskin mackinaw. He draped the saddlebags over his shoulder, went to the door, and opened it.

"I'm warnin' you, goddamn your red hide!"

"Pa!" Trudy screamed.

The gun cracked, its explosion filling the room. Old Judith gave an exasperated bellow. Yakima looked over his shoulder at Trudy wrestling the smoking gun out of Lewis's gnarled hand. There was a hole in the middle of the table. Trudy gave another scream as she pulled the pistol out of the old man's hand, and Lewis cursed sharply as he fell over his chair. The chair slid out from beneath him, and he hit the floor with a loud thud and an angry wail.

"You're drunk, Pa!" Trudy stepped back away from her father, whom Yakima could no longer see from his vantage at the door. Voice shaking, Lewis's angry bellows dying gradually, she said, "You'll thank me in the mornin'." She glanced at Yakima, her eyes cold and hard.

Yakima went out and drew the door closed behind him, standing there on the stoop for a moment, feeling a cold rock in the pit of his stomach.

Yakima saddled Wolf and rode out to an old, seldom-used line shack in the hills above the Shackleford ranch-stead. He wanted to ride farther, but it was a dark night. Wolf was tired from the earlier ride, and Yakima didn't want to risk injuring his prized stallion in the dark. Lewis wasn't worth it.

He wasn't worth the gold Yakima had given him, either, but it made him feel better to leave that filled cup behind as he lit out for Belle Fourche. At least, in the direction of Belle Fourche. He wasn't sure how long it would take him to reach the little town up northwest of Deadwood in the Dakota Territory. With winter coming on fast, which could mean snow at any time, the trip could take anywhere from several days to a week.

What the hell? He didn't exactly have anything else lined up, as he'd figured—foolishly, he realized now—on spending the winter on the Shackleford Ranch, breaking horses and trapping more as the weather permitted.

The small brush-roofed log line shack sat against the shoulder of a broad, low hill, with an escarpment rising off its eastern side. There was a dilapidated corral in front of it and a small stable and a corral in better condition attached to its west side. The half-breed was glad to see no lights in the windows, no smoke issuing from the rock chimney. There were no actual trails except wild-horse trails through this remote country, so he didn't doubt that he'd been the last visitor here.

He and the woman.

He tried to press her image to the back of his mind, still unsure she hadn't been a ghost that his own lonely, lusty imagination hadn't conjured, because she'd told him so little about herself, wanting to know nothing about him. They'd met by accident out here at the line shack, and one thing had led to another. Then they'd met here a few times before she'd said she wouldn't be back and simply ridden away. Toward a near ranch, he'd assumed.

Yakima rode up to the cabin and looked around, always cautious, always wary. Occasionally, he had men hunting him—bounty hunters paid by those who'd felt they had been wronged by him in one way or another, on his many wanderings throughout the frontier as he'd searched for something he hadn't yet found and doubted he ever would.

It was his old Shaolin monk friend, whom he'd called George because he hadn't been able to pronounce his Chinese name, who'd once told him while teaching him Eastern fighting techniques that we all searched in vain, because we'd long ago found what we were looking for—the secret was in knowing what that thing was.

"So, what is it, George?" he'd asked, incredulous.

"Oh, you are the only one who could answer that, my friend!" George had said, chuckling, drawing on his perpetual, crudely rolled cigarette and then taking a pull from his ever-present whiskey bottle.

Odd man, George. Yakima had understood only about one-quarter of the man's riddles, though he'd appreciated the way he'd taught him to fight and hone his senses to a razor's edge. He brought those senses into play now as he looked around and felt a prickling between his shoulders. Whatever he'd sensed, Wolf had sensed it, too. The stallion raised his head and nickered softly, pricking his ears.

Yakima curveted the horse to stare along his back trail, a faint, pale path dropping down the hill and disappearing in a crease between black granite dikes. A sickle moon had risen, limning the tops of the dikes with silver but also casting velvet shadows.

"What is it, boy?" Yakima said softly, holding the black's reins taut.

A wolf gave a mournful howl from one of those dikes. The horse jerked with a start at the sound of its ancient blood enemy. Yakima continued to sit the horse quietly, watching and listening, and when the horse's muscles relaxed beneath him, he assumed that what they'd both heard behind them was the prowling wolf and swung down from the leather.

He led the horse into the stable, went into the cabin to make sure he was alone, and lit a hurricane lamp. He tossed his gear on a bunk and went out, rubbed Wolf down carefully with a scrap of burlap to cool him down, then watered him from a rain barrel and draped a feed sack with a scoop of oats over his head. As the horse ate, Yakima went into the cabin. He had gotten a fire going with the kindling and split pine logs he'd left piled in a crate near the fireplace, and was leaning down over the small stone hearth to blow on the fledgling flames when a gun cracked in the distance.

The shot echoed and reechoed over the hills. In the stable, Wolf stomped and nickered.

Yakima blew out the lamp, grabbed his Yellowboy off the table, and went into the stable to calm the horse, who stared bright-eyed over the corral toward his and Yakima's back trail. Yakima stared in the same direction, cooing to the horse softly while patting Wolf's left front wither and gently racking a shell into the Winchester's breech with one hand.

"Easy, now, boy. Easy."

He stepped away from the horse, knowing the well-trained mount would heed his admonition. As he ducked through the corral and into the yard in front of the cabin, another shot reverberated shrilly. There was no thud of a slug landing anywhere near the cabin. Yakima wasn't surprised. The shooter was too far away to be shooting at him.

But if not him, who?

He moved slowly out away from the cabin and

sidestepped over to the escarpment rising just east of it. He followed the scarp down the gradual slope, heading in the direction from which he'd come, toward a dark gap between the slab-sided dikes.

When he came to the end of the gap, he ran on down the hill, crouching, holding the Yellowboy low so that the moonlight wouldn't reflect off its brass receiver. He paralleled the horse trail he'd followed here, staying wide of it, until he gained the bottom of the hill. The crease was tight here, and he had no choice but to follow the trail between the large, granite boulders pressing close on each side, spewed here eons ago by some volcano blowing its lid here between the Mummy and Snowy ranges.

Yakima had run several yards down the trail when another shot rocketed around him, much closer now, and a girl screamed.

Chapter 6

"Get her outta there, Colby," a man said in the brush somewhere ahead of Yakima. "Get her the hell out of there!"

"I'm tryin'!" yelled another man.

The same voice shouted, "Get out here, you little bitch, or I'll shoot your damn ass off. And this time it'll be for real!"

Yakima had walked into a notch in the escarpment on the trail's north side, and now he hunkered down behind a fallen tree to see several shadows thrashing around in the brush before him. They were obviously searching for someone beyond them. Off to the left, several horses milled, nickering nervously.

"We just wanna know where the half-breed went, little girl," one of the men said. "That's all we wanna know. You tell us that, and we'll let you go!"

"I don't know where he went!" came Trudy's high, angry-fearful scream. "I don't know where he went, I done told you. I'm just out here on the run from my drunken pa!"

"Bullshit!" retorted one of the men moving about

thirty yards ahead of Yakima. "You left not ten minutes after the breed lit out, so we know you're after him. What we're thinkin' is, you see, is you and him got the gold!"

Yakima wished he could get a better fix on the three or four, possibly five men before him. It was too dark in this notch in the rocks and brush, and all he could see were the occasional flashes of moonlight off gun steel. Trudy must be holed up in a particularly thick snag, because it seemed her stalker had only a general idea about where she was.

"Got the gold and were plannin' on meetin' up someplace," said another man off to Yakima's right.

A gun blasted, flames stabbing skyward. Yakima heard the screech of the ricochet off a rock somewhere high on the scarp. Trudy screamed again, and shouted, "Stop shootin' at me, goddamn your eyes. You got no right to be stalkin' a girl alone out here when she's tryin' to get away from her drunken old man!"

One of the men chuckled and said as though to one of the others: "She's got a point, boys. Maybe we oughta let her go."

"*You* let her go, if you've a mind," said another man. "The way I see it, it's too damn dark to track the breed, but I know this little Injun-lovin' whore knows where he's headed and that they planned to take all the gold fer themselves and meet up somewheres."

"I got her!" one of the men shouted amidst a loud thrashing and crackling of brush.

Trudy cursed shrilly, and then all the shadows appeared to converge on a spot somewhere ahead and right of Yakima. The half-breed had waited long enough. He stepped forward, dropped to a knee beside an aspen, and said loudly, "Let her go. The jake you're after is right behind you." He'd spoken softly but loudly enough to be heard above the thrashing in the brush ahead of him.

The thrashing stopped.

"Yakima!" Trudy cried.

Suddenly, the darkness in front of Yakima lit up like Saturday night in Sonora. He pulled his head back behind the tree, shouting above the thunder of what sounded like four pistols, "Trudy, get down flat and stay there!"

The slugs chewed bark from the far side of the tree. The flashes gave him a pretty good idea where each man was shooting from, so as soon as there was a lull in the fire, he stepped out from behind the tree and, hoping like hell that Trudy was following his orders, cut loose with the Yellowboy. He aimed as high as he could while still hoping to hit his targets. From the grunts and groans and clipped squeals as well the crackling of brush beneath falling bodies, he was doing all right.

He kept shooting until the Yellowboy's hammer pinged on an empty chamber. He ejected the last spent cartridge, heard it clatter into the brush behind him, then lowered the rifle and palmed his Colt, ratcheting the hammer back. One of the men was groaning. He heard another give a wheeze, and then there were the thuds of someone running off, stumbling through the brush to Yakima's left.

He dropped to a knee, aiming the pistol straight out in front of him, half expecting one of the shooters to fire another round at him. He had no way of knowing just how well his ploy had worked, though he suspected he'd given them all at least one pill they couldn't digest.

"Trudy?" he said.

"Uh-huh," came the girl's thin reply.

"Follow my voice. Come to me, get around me fast. Don't dally."

He heard her give a grunt and a groan and there was more crackling of brush as she gained her feet. A slender shadow moved before him, and then he saw her in her man's felt hat and torn, knee-length buckskin coat stumble toward him, breathing hard. She stopped beside him, turning toward her fallen stalkers, and then Yakima shoved her back behind him and opened up with the Colt until he'd fired four more shots. He heard Trudy leap back away from him with a gasp.

The echoes died. If the men he'd brought down had had any intention of getting up or of firing at him from cover of darkness, they didn't now.

As the pale powder smoke wafted in front of Yakima, a horse whinnied to his left. Running foot thuds rose. A man cursed, and the horse nickered. Yakima ran toward the man and the frightened horse, leaping deadfalls. He bulled through low branches and brush and when he came out the other side, horse and rider were bounding away from him, toward a charcoal gray escarpment wall.

Yakima raised the Colt and triggered the two remaining shots as horse and rider bolted around the wall and out of sight, one of Yakima's slugs slamming the wall with a shrill whine. Hearing the dwindling hoof thuds, Yakima turned and walked back to where Trudy stood in the darkness. He walked past her to stare down at the dark shapes of four fallen men, blood glistening in the starlight. None was moving.

"You know these bastards?" he asked Trudy, keeping his voice low in case any more stalkers lurked in the darkness.

"Never seen 'em before in my life," she said, staying where she was. "They musta known about the gold. Seen you leavin' the ranch."

"And figured I had it," he said, half to himself, prodding a boot of one of the dead men with the toe of his moccasin.

The boot he prodded was a low-heeled cavalry boot with worn spurs. The man's pants were dark blue army-issue, though his coat was a brown-striped, cream-colored blanket coat, and his hat was a dirty Stetson. Yakima looked at the other men, finding nothing about them he recognized or that stood out.

Quickly, staring down at the dark shapes before him, he reloaded his Colt, wondering who these men were and how they'd known about the gold. Likely claim jumpers who had had their sights on Delbert Clifton for some time. They must have been trailing the man, intending to jump him for the gold before he reached Wolfville. Yakima and Lewis had spoiled their plans. He wished he could have taken one of them alive, but he hadn't wanted to risk getting Trudy shot.

He turned to her now as he clicked the Colt's loading gate closed and spun the cylinder before dropping the pistol into its holster and snapping the keeper thong over the hammer. "What're you doing out here?" he asked gruffly, walking toward her.

"Pa's goin' crazy," she said, her voice quaking slightly as she continued staring toward the dead men. "You saw how he can get. When he gets like that, only Old Judith can handle him. I usually light out for the line shack. Figured on spending a couple nights there and ridin' back to the ranch after he had a chance to sober up and sweat it out."

"Those fellas jumped you?"

She nodded. "They musta been trailin' you, and then I came along, and they got around me. Scared the pure hell out of me, too!"

"Yeah, well, it's that kind of night."

"I didn't even know you were out here. You headin' for the line shack?"

Yakima picked up his rifle and began reloading it. "I reckon we had similar ideas." When he'd loaded the Yellowboy, he set it on his shoulder, then turned and started walking back toward Wolf. "Come on, let's go find your horse. Gettin' cold."

As he walked back through the brush, Trudy gave a groan behind him. He turned to her. She stood where she'd been standing, favoring one foot and wincing.

"I think . . . I think I twisted my ankle when I fell off my horse," she said. "Would you mind giving me a hand?"

He walked to her and looked down at her right foot that she wasn't putting much weight on. "How bad is it?"

"Just twisted. It'll be all right in the mornin', I'm sure. I have thin ankles, and they twist easy. I've done it before."

Yakima gave a sigh and handed her his rifle. "Take that."

When she'd taken the Yellowboy, he leaned down and picked her up in his arms and carried her through the brush and back to the trail. His Winchester lay between them, the barrel angling up past her shoulder. "Sorry to be so much trouble," she said as he began following the trail up through the crease toward the cabin.

"I reckon it's the gold that's the trouble. That much in one place is bound to be, and I'll be happy to be rid of it."

"Are you really going to take it to Belle Fourche and give it to Mr. Clifton's family?"

"Look," he said, breathing hard with the climb, "I ain't no angel, in case you haven't noticed the lack of wings and a halo. It's just that I've done enough bad things in my life that I reckon it's time to start makin' up for a few before I visit my maker. I can't stand the smell of butane."

"And you think that's the right thing to do?"

"Don't you?"

"I reckon." Trudy's breath came hard as she jounced in his arms, her own arms encircling his neck. He felt her sort of squirm against him as she said, "Seems like a lot to go through, though. For people you don't even know."

"He went through a lot for me. And—"

"I know, I know. You got some makin' up to do." Trudy paused. "I reckon we all do."

"What would you have to make up for—a girl of your few years?"

"They ain't all that few. I'm almost nineteen, you know. When I dress up, Pa says I'm goin' on thirty." She smiled.

"Yeah, well, still."

"You can set me down and take a breather, if you want."

"Don't need one."

"Impressive."

Yakima walked across the clearing and kicked the cabin door open. He paused just inside to let his eyes adjust to the darkness, then set her down in one of the two ladder-back chairs at the table.

"Foot feelin' any better?" he asked her.

"It's my ankle and no, not really," she said, leaning

back in the chair and lifting her right boot off the floor. "I think it's swelling a little."

He set his rifle on the table. "I'll get the fire built back up and take a look at it."

"You can look at pretty much anything I got," she said.

Yakima looked back at her, startled. "Huh?"

She was looking at him with a lusty grin, cheeks dimpled. "You heard me."

Yakima gave a wry chuff and then rebuilt the fire until the flames were leaping and dancing. "What would Old Judith say about that?"

"Old Judith ain't here." She narrowed an eye at him as he knelt in front of her and set her right foot on his knee. "And you wouldn't be my first," she added.

Yakima sighed, not liking the direction the conversation had taken. He was a red-blooded man, susceptible to the weaknesses of his ilk, and he didn't want the temptation. It was a cold, dark night, and they were alone here in the cabin in which he thought he could still hear the sighs and laughter of another woman he'd met here. In such a situation, a man could easily make the wrong decision.

"That hurt?" he said, gently moving her boot around.

She sucked a sharp breath through her teeth, scowling. "Yess!"

"Sorry."

"You're gonna pay for that, mister!"

Yakima looked up at her. She was smiling down at him, her eyes sparking in the firelight.

Yakima dropped his bare feet to the floor. Trudy groaned and reached for him, but her fingers only lightly raked the back of his thick upper right arm as he rose from the cot and walked naked to the fireplace.

The fire had nearly gone out again while he'd allowed himself to be seduced—what the hell was he supposed to have done, when she'd practically thrown herself at him like that?—and now he built it back up with several split logs from the crate.

She stirred on the cot behind him. "Was I all right?"

On his knees in front of the fire, he peeled some damp bark off another log and glanced over his shoulder at her. She lay on her side, head propped on an elbow, the blanket pulled down to reveal her pale breasts sloping toward the cot.

"You were fine," he said, irritated at himself now for indulging himself against his better judgment. Trouble was, he was used to taking comforts when and where he found them. While they were not necessarily few, they were sometimes far between.

She gave a caustic snort. "You sure know how to make a girl feel special, Yakima Henry."

"Don't let it go to your head." He used the last log to arrange the others so they'd burn long and hot, then went over to the table and dug his makings sack out of his saddlebags. He had only his own saddlebags now, and the gold was in the same pouch as the makings. He'd left Clifton's bags in the Shackleford barn. The bulge in the pouch was reassuring, but he'd be glad to be rid of it.

He stood at the table, the girl watching him, and rolled a rare smoke. He went back to the fire and used the burning end of a twig to light the quirley, then, puffing smoke, walked back over to the bed. He stood over Trudy, who quirked her mouth corners as she reached up and touched him.

"Take me with you."

He glanced over his shoulder at the bulge in his saddlebag pouch, then shook his head. She wrapped her hand around him. His loins burned. He swatted her arm away, crawled under the covers, and leaned back against the wall at the head of the cot. She rested her head against his chest, left her warm hand on his thigh, and didn't say anything for a time before she said forlornly, "Come on. Let's get hitched. What the hell?"

"I did that once. Don't intend to do it again."

"What happened?"

"Nothin' good." He meant the end hadn't been good. In fact, it had been hell. But everything before that had been as close to bliss as any man ever had.

"Wouldn't have to be like that with us, Yakima."

"No, I suppose it wouldn't. Not if we took the gold and headed—where? San Francisco?"

She moved her hand again. "Anywhere but here."

"An eighteen-year-old white girl and a half-breed." He chuckled wryly as he blew smoke over her head toward the snapping flames. "We might be a little conspicuous."

"With the gold, we could buy us a nice big ranch. That's what we both know. Horses. We could build it somewhere no one would ever find us."

"I did that before, too."

"The horse ranch?"

"Yep."

"Where?"

"Arizona. Take your hand away."

She smiled and looked up at him. "You like my hand."

Yakima held her gaze. "He wasn't really going crazy, was he? And you weren't really running away from him. You're just running away. Figured you'd find me and the gold here."

She took her hand away, scowling. "Was I that bad?"

"No, you were a hell of a lot better than I expected. But that gold is going to Belle Fourche, and that's all there is to it." He flicked the quirley stub into the fire, where it bounced off a log and dropped in front of it with a dull thump. It quickly became a burning worm.

"You go to hell." With a haughty chuff, she turned away from him, curling into a ball.

"Been there." Yakima paused, staring at the ceiling. "And that pistol you got ain't loaded."

Her voice was muffled. "What pistol?"

"The Colt you took out of my holster when I banked the fire. I unloaded it in case you weren't happy with how things went tonight."

She didn't say anything. Then she rolled toward him, bounded up quickly, and swung the Colt at him butt first. Yakima threw up his right hand, grabbed her fist. He pulled her across him. She snarled like a wild-cat, kicking, until he jerked the gun out of her fist and returned it to its holster hanging from the near bed-post.

"*Bastard!*" she squealed.

Then she flopped back down, gave him her back, and sobbed herself to sleep.

Chapter 7

Lee Mendenhour rolled off his wife.

Glendolene closed her legs, pushed her nightgown down around her thighs, drew her knees toward her belly, and turned onto her side. Lee dropped his long legs over the side of the bed, ran his hands through his thick, wavy auburn hair, and glanced over his shoulder at her.

"You might have at least feigned a little pleasure from that."

"I could say the same thing to you." She drew a ragged breath. "Maybe you got all the pleasure you needed over at the Silk Slipper last night."

He scowled though the nubs of his handsomely sculpted cheeks flushed slightly beneath his brown eyes. "Don't be ridiculous. I don't partake of what the females are selling. I play cards and I drink. I socialize with my friends. That's all."

She wondered if he was telling the truth. Funny how she'd never wondered about that before. They were drifting apart, so that neither could really tell what the other was thinking. At least, she couldn't tell what he was thinking. Maybe it was because she didn't care anymore.

After only three years of marriage?

Guilt was a bone in the pit of her stomach. He'd given her so much—wealth, a sprawling Victorian-style house, several servants who helped her tend the place and the large irrigated garden behind it. Her aunt and uncle had a story-and-a-half shack a couple of miles outside Belle Fourche, and they'd been married—happily, as far as she could tell—for over fifty years.

She'd fallen in love with the Lee Mendenhour she'd met in Council Bluffs four years ago—the precocious, somewhat freewheeling, and romantic young man reading for the law in Iowa, where she'd been attending a teacher's college. They'd met at church, and he'd visited her at her boardinghouse bearing flowers he'd picked along the river; they'd picnicked on weekend afternoons in the country, sharing their life's stories, their dreams.

He'd wanted to be a lawyer—a prosecuting attorney—and eventually a judge. He'd wanted to bring law and order to the lawless land he'd grown up in. The land in which his mother had been killed by a stray bullet fired by rustlers stealing horses from the Chain Link corral.

Glendolene had wanted to be a teacher, but she'd fallen in love with the dashing young Westerner, and his dream had seemed more important than hers. So she'd come to Wyoming with him, where they'd been married in the house Lee had grown up in as an only child. Those first few weeks, his father, Wild Bill, had openly scrutinized her as though she were a mare bought for one of his Morgan steeds.

She'd never measured up for Wild Bill. She'd once heard the gruff, bandy-legged old man telling his son that she was too pretty, her hips not stout enough. She didn't have the sand it took to raise tough sons out here.

"Oh, well," he'd muttered. "The first flu of next winter will likely take her."

She stared at her husband's bare back now as he walked over to the window and, crouching, slid the curtain aside with the back of his hand. Gray morning light washed into the room, silhouetting Lee against it. She watched his profile as he stared across the street. She'd once known him to smile more, but he was smiling less and less these days, and his sense of humor had all but vanished. That had been replaced by a steely, self-satisfied, often overbearing determination coupled with an acerbic glint in his brown eyes. Which was why she was taken aback by the expression she now saw in his eyes—or thought she saw:

Fear?

"What is it?" she said, sitting up in bed. "Don't tell me they've hanged another of Neumiller's deputies!"

He glanced at her sharply, embarrassed. He let the curtain drop back into place and reached for the pitcher on the marble-topped washstand. "Of course not," he said with what she perceived to be a feigned casual air. "And who do you mean by 'they'?"

He poured water into the washbasin and reached for a washcloth and soap cake.

So he is afraid. . . . The revelation startled her. She'd never seen that before in him. It would have been endearing, had he not tried to hide it so well, had he allowed it to become a bridge between them.

Glendolene sank back against her pillows, crossing

her arms on her breasts over the sheet and quilt. "Who else would have done such a thing?"

"Oh, you think Floyd Betajack slipped into town, cut his son down, and hanged Harrison?" Lee chuckled as he scrubbed his face with the soapy cloth.

"Don't you?"

"Betajack doesn't have that much imagination. Or, forgive my language, balls."

"Who does have that much balls?"

Lee gave her a quick look of reprimand. He hated when her language verged on risqué, as though he thought she might carry it over into dinner parties with his respectable associates. "My guess is some man or men around town had a bone to pick with Harrison and took advantage of this whole affair with Betajack to shoot him and hang him. Neumiller is probably right now going over the list of men he's had in jail over the past couple of months."

He lifted his head to scrub his long neck. "Former prisoners or friends of former prisoners, most likely. Maybe friends or kin of one of the other rustlers we've hanged in recent weeks. I'm not worried about it."

"Don't you think you should be? You would have had a hand in those killings."

"Killings?" Lee turned to her, scowling again with his particular brand of haughty disapproval that made her recoil like a sensitive child. "Good Lord, Glen. That isn't what you think I'm doing, is it? *Killing men?* Dear, I am *executing* convicted stock thieves and killers."

She drew another ragged breath, not wanting to get into an argument, because she knew she couldn't win but only be made to feel smaller in his eyes than she already was. Still, she couldn't help saying, softly,

"I guess it depends on what you'd like to call it, doesn't it?"

"Of course it doesn't!"

"All right, Lee."

He walked over to the bed and sat down on the edge of it, half turned toward her. "Bringing law and order to this chunk of Wyoming is what I intended to do, Glen. And that means hanging killers and stock thieves. I'm sorry if it seems savage to you, but sometimes savagery is the sword that is needed to bring savagery to ground."

"You don't think savagery begets savagery?"

"No, I don't." Lee shook his head vehemently, drilling her with those assured, wide, dark eyes, his brown, carefully trimmed mustache and beard set against the ruddiness of his otherwise long, narrow, young-looking face. "Crime is down in Wolfville, as well in the country surrounding it. True, Claw Hendricks is still running wild south of here, with his ragtag band of renegade Utes and Arapahos, but he's mostly wreaking his havoc on the mining camps in Colorado. He rarely ventures into Wyoming," Lee added with a shrewd, self-satisfied smile, "because he knows if he does, I'll bring hell down on him. Neumiller doesn't have enough men to bring the gang in, but after Christmas I intend to bring in U.S. marshals and the military to run a dragnet through the Mummies."

Lee rose and walked back to the washstand, where he resumed his sponge bath. "By Easter, we will be hearing no more of Claw Hendricks and his wild savages."

As it usually did after one of their discussions, confusion rippled over her, and she found herself once again feeling as though she didn't understand life's harsh realities. And that she'd been spoiled by the life this ambitious young man had given her.

"I do apologize, Lee," she said with a weary sigh as, finished washing, he was now methodically dressing. "I shouldn't be talking about things that I don't really understand."

He looked at her as he sat down in a chair to pull on his black wool socks over his wool long handles, and offered a charitable smile. "You never need apologize to me, Glen. It's your provincial innocence that has always drawn me to you."

"Perhaps, Lee," she said, pausing to choose her words more carefully. "Perhaps . . . I should go on alone to Belle Fourche." Before he could object again, as he did the first time she'd mentioned it, she said, "I do hate to take you away from your duties here in Wolfville, and I just know how absolutely bored you're going to be at my aunt and uncle's place. It's a very small farm, Lee—it's not a ranch. I don't think there's a horse on the place. Just a few cows and plow mules!"

Guilt for her disingenuousness added to the flux of emotions within her. The truth was, she wanted some time away from the man. To think about their future. To decide if there *would be* a future. She glanced down at the sheet and quilt covering her belly.

She needed time, as well, to consider the child she was carrying inside her. She'd been convinced that she was barren but after three years was finally pregnant. . . .

"Nonsense, Glen," he said, standing up and pulling on his shirt. "I'd have to be half savage myself to let you board that stage alone. The country north of here is still riddled with outlaws and Indians of the same caliber as Betajack and Hendricks. The travel will be good for me. I need some time away. I've brought plenty of papers to keep me busy, and I have those letters to the army and the U.S. marshal's office to draft. Besides"—he smiled at her as he stepped into his steel gray wool trousers—"it's Christmas."

She formed a smile as manufactured as his own. She wasn't thinking about Christmas, or about him, but about another man—a red-skinned man with a tangle of long night black hair, large gentle hands, and jade eyes—the memory of whom she hoped to sort through and resolve, along with all her other problems, on her trip to Belle Fourche.

Someone rapped loudly on the door. Glen gasped. Lee jerked with a start, fumbled a pearl-gripped derringer off the dresser, and aimed it awkwardly at the door.

"Mr. Mendenhour?" It was Luther Morning Lake's deep, flat voice.

Lee relaxed, flushed with embarrassment, as he glanced at the derringer in his hand. "Yes, what is it, Luther?"

"The stage for Belle Fourche'll be pullin' out in forty-five minutes."

"Thank you, Luther."

Lee sighed and set the derringer on the dresser. He glanced at Glendolene, who studied him curiously, feeling all the other feelings she'd felt that morning giving ground to a rising apprehension.

"Well, you heard the man, dear," Lee said, turning away as he knotted his four-in-hand tie around his neck. "The stage will be leaving soon. You'd best get dressed, don't you think?"

Chapter 8

If he wasn't being followed, he wasn't a half-breed son of a bitch.

Yakima stopped Wolf at the top of a low rise between two rimrocks, and, staring along his back trail from beneath the brim of his flat-crowned hat, he reached into his saddlebags and pulled out his brass-chased spyglass. He raised the glass and telescoped and adjusted it, bringing up the trail he'd been following along the meandering bed of Snake Creek, dry this time of the year.

A fine snow falling out of a high gray sky dusted its rocky banks. Despite the weather, Yakima could see fairly clearly for almost a mile down the canyon the stream had cut, and if someone was shadowing him, they'd slipped behind cover.

Maybe he was wrong. But he'd been on the run often enough—hell, half his life—to have developed a sixth sense, an instinct for knowing when someone was tracking him. It was really little more than a tightening of the muscles between his shoulders, but that tightening had saved his life enough times that he'd come to abide by it.

"You're out there, aren't you?" he said to himself, lowering the glass and ramming it against his open palm to close it. "But who are you?"

He had a pretty good idea. The hombre he'd left alive last night after that man and his three fellow brush riders had jumped Trudy. Again, he considered whether they were part of Claw Hendricks's bunch, and nixed the idea. They hadn't been well enough armed, and if Hendricks's men had wanted revenge for what Yakima, Lewis, and Delbert Clifton had done—leaving a good eight or nine in bloody piles at the base of the ridge from which Clifton had fired his Big Fifty—they'd have found a more efficient way of doing it.

The men who'd jumped Trudy were part of another group. Or maybe they were their own group. A motley crew of common mine thieves, most likely, who'd been tracking Clifton with the intention of jumping him and taking his gold. The man behind him now was likely the survivor, too stubborn to leave the gold well enough alone.

Yakima would have to expend a bullet on him.

That was all right. He intended to lay in some more—along with other trail supplies—in Wolfville. It would be a long pull to Belle Fourche, northeast of Wolfville in the Dakota Territory, and he'd need plenty of everything including oats for Wolf.

He dropped the spyglass back into the saddlebag, swung up into the leather, and put the black stallion up and over the ridge, heading northeast through low dun hills stippled with piñons. Lines of wolf willows followed slender watercourses. When the clouds parted and the sun shone, the Snowy Range loomed straight ahead of him, west of Wolfville—lime green and brown mounds with ragged crests mantled in white.

He'd ridden another mile when Wolf's right front knee buckled slightly, and Yakima saw one of the stallion's shoes roll out away from the mount and clank against a rock. With a curse, he swung down from the saddle and replaced the shoe temporarily with a couple of nails he found in his saddlebags, hammering them back into the hoof with his pistol butt. The remedy wouldn't last, however. He'd have to have a new shoe forged in Wolfville, before lighting out on the trail to Belle Fourche.

He looked around. The sky was lightening in both the east and the west. It looked as if the good weather was holding. He hoped it held for a few more days. He wanted to get to Belle Fourche as fast as possible and then head back south before true winter set in. Since he no longer had a reason to stay north, he'd get as far south as possible. He'd winter in New Mexico, maybe Texas. It was a hard time of the year to find ranch work, but he'd have to find work of some kind to feed himself and his horse, then maybe head north again come spring.

Almost as bad as the northern cold and snow was the southwestern summer heat and sun.

Keeping a sharp eye on his back trail, he walked Wolf ahead and entered Wolfville an hour later. It was midmorning, and the sun bathed the motley-looking town and the smoke issuing from stone chimneys and stovepipes. He was just pulling over toward the Bart English Livery & Feed Barn, knowing that Bart English was also a blacksmith, when a red-and-gold Concord coach pulled away from the Wells Fargo office on the street's opposite side. A face appeared in one of the stage windows.

Yakima glanced at it once, turned away, then looked at it again, frowning. It was a pretty face beneath a woman's black fur hat. The woman's brown hair spilled over her shoulders. He was too far away to see her clearly, for him to be sure of who she was, and then she abruptly turned away from him and jerked back in her seat, facing forward, as the six-hitch team lunged into a thundering gallop, the middle-aged, bearded jehu in a long muskrat coat whom Yakima recognized as Charlie Adlard standing up in the driver's box and yelling and cracking his blacksnake over the horses' backs.

Yakima stared after the coach, jade eyes riveted on the rear luggage boot until the coach turned onto a left fork in the main street, which became a trail at the edge of town, and disappeared, the creaking and clattering of the stage wheels and the thunder of the team's hooves dwindling quickly.

Dust sifted. A collie dog sniffed the recently gouged furrows in the well-churned dust of the street and then got distracted by a cat poking its head out of an alley mouth and gave chase.

"Bad damn luck." This from Bart English himself, who stood with his big fists on his hips as he stared after the coach. He was a large man—taller than Yakima by a good three inches—with long, frizzy gray hair tumbling down from his shabby bowler hat, and wearing a long leather apron.

"What's bad damn luck?"

"Startin' out with a cracked felloe," English said, still staring after the coach. "That's bad damn luck, startin' a run that way. They had to limp back so's I could fix it. That means two more bad things is gonna happen before they make their destination."

Yakima continued staring northeast, as did the blacksmith. He'd only half heard what the man had said. He was thinking about the face he'd seen in the window, wondering if it had been her, whoever the hell she was. She'd insisted they not exchange names, though they'd exchanged everything else a man and a woman possibly could in the line shack he'd shared last night with Trudy.

"Ah, hell!"

Yakima looked at Bart English. The man was scowling at him, big fists still on his hips.

"What?" Yakima said.

"Not *you*!"

"Why the hell *not* me?"

"Yakima, goddamn it, I was in the Longhorn the night Neumiller and his deputies threw you out. They rode you of town and told you not to come back or they'd throw your half-breed ass in the hoosegow and mail the key to God!"

Yakima raised his hands palm out. "That was a simple misunderstanding. Your Mr. Andrews said I was cheatin' because he didn't want to pay up the money I'd won that night playin' cards. Well, I was drinking the devil's nectar that night—and of course that part is *my* fault. I know better than to do that, especially when there's pretty women and dishonest mucky-mucks hovering around—and I took offense at the man's demeanor, not to mention him callin' me a cheater. And then when he started wagging that little popper around in my face . . . Say, did they ever get that derringer dug out of his nose?"

"They did, but it took some doin'," the blacksmith said, unable to choke back a delighted chuckle. "Took the doc and his wife and a Chinese assistant to dig his nose out of his cheek and sew it back together. The whole town heard Andrews's howls till pret' near dawn, and the doc says that nose will always be about the size of a wheel hub."

"At least they got the gun out of it. Nice little popper."

The blacksmith wiped the grin off his broad, bearded face and scowled up at the half-breed. "Damn it, Yakima, Andrews runs the Big Horn County Bank, and he's got more friends than the whores over at the Silk Slipper. Sheriff Neumiller is one of 'em. Now, you'd best head back out to Shackleford's ranch an' stay there."

"Me and Shackleford ain't friends no more."

"Oh, boy."

Yakima swung down from his saddle, tossed his reins to the blacksmith, and grabbed his saddlebags. "Wolf here needs a new front shoe. Forge me one, will you, Bart, while I head over to the general store and lay in some trail supplies?"

"Yakima, if Neumiller sees you—!"

"Check the other shoes, too, Bart." Yakima hitched his shell belt higher on his lean hips as he strode toward the mercantile. "Got a few days' travel ahead."

The blacksmith grunted his disapproval as Yakima continued across the side street. He mounted the wooden steps rising to the mercantile's porch and paused to glance once more toward the northeast, where the stage was just now climbing the shoulder of a bluff. White smoke drifting from a near chimney slightly obscured it. It was about the size of his thumbnail from this distance, the brown team pulling the red-and-gold stage that shone in the weak morning sunlight. Distantly, Yakima heard the snaps of the blacksnake poppers as the jehu flicked the whip over the team's back.

He felt the urge to inquire about her, to at least find out her name. But he wouldn't. A half-breed—especially one who'd been shepherded out of town by the local law—could only cause folks to question her reputation. The only ranch within twenty miles of the line shack, however, was the Chain Link owned by Wild Bill Mendenhour and his son, whose name Yakima couldn't remember. She was likely from there.

No point in thinking about her anymore. The reason they'd had such a good time together was that they hadn't known anything about each other, and that's the way it would stay. He'd likely never see her again, but he'd keep her memory in a quiet corner of his mind for revisiting on lonely nights stitched with distant wolf howls and the crackling of his coffee fire.

He mounted the porch and walked into the mercantile, causing the bell over the door to rattle. "Shit, what the hell are you doin' back here, Yakima?" said the mercantiler, Curt Findlay. "I done thought—"

"Yeah, I know, you thought I was run out of town on a rail. But I'm back for trail supplies. I'm hopin' I can sneak in and out without Neumiller gettin' his back up, so the faster you can fill this order for me . . ." Yakima walked to the back of the shop, where Findlay was arranging canned goods on a high shelf with a long pole that bore a hook and a steel hand on the end of it, and set his order on the counter, beside a large glass pickle jar filled with rock candy. Beside the list scribbled on lined note paper, he set his saddlebags.

"Neumiller's gonna boil over like an old black pot if

he sees me doin' business with you," Findlay said, scowling over the counter as he set down his pole. He was stocky, with a big gut pushing out his apron, and his face was as pockmarked as a coffee can used for target practice.

"Come on," Yakima said. "Where the hell am I supposed to get supplies? I just rode in to do a little business. I'll be ridin' out again in twenty minutes."

"Where you headin'?"

"North."

"Why?"

"Why the hell are you askin'?"

"Because I'm curious—that's why," the mercantiler said, picking up the grocery list and smoothing it against his bulbous, rock-hard gut. "And because I don't have to do business with you, Henry!"

"Belle Fourche."

"No shit?" said Findlay, studying the list. "That's where the stage is headed. Damn near the end of the line. It'll return once more, and then that's the end of stage travel in these parts for the season."

As he started shuffling around the store, filling the order, Yakima almost asked him about the woman but caught himself. He spent the next ten minutes, while Findlay stuffed the possibles into his saddlebag pouches, sucking on a chunk of rock candy and otherwise keeping his mouth shut. When the order was filled, he paid the man, draped the saddlebags over his shoulder, pinched his hat brim, and walked out.

He was halfway across the side street, heading for the blacksmith shop from which the clangs of English's hammer rose sharply, when he spied movement across the main street on his right and ahead about forty yards. A wiry little man with a long, hawkish nose under a floppy canvas hat brim was hurrying along the boardwalk toward Yakima, who cursed. Lewis! Behind his former partner was none other than Sheriff Neumiller in his brown suit and bowler hat and with his sheriff's badge pinned to his left lapel, twin Colts tied low on his thighs.

"There he is!" Lewis shouted, pointing. "There he is right now. I told you I followed him to town! Arrest the half-breed son of a bitch, Sheriff!"

Lewis hung back as Neumiller left the boardwalk and walked toward Yakima, canting his head to one side, his handlebar mustaches blowing in the chill morning breeze. Both hands were touching the walnut grips of his Colts.

"*Arrest* me?" Yakima said. "On what charge?"

Neumiller stopped a few feet away from Yakima, the sheriff's brown eyes hard, his pale, freckled face set in a scowl. He jerked a thumb toward Lewis remaining safely behind a hitch rack near the boardwalk on the far side of the street. "This man says you stole a cache of gold from him and raped his daughter."

Chapter 9

"He does, does he?" Yakima glared at Lewis standing behind the hitch rack, grinning.

Sheriff Neumiller said tautly, "You'd best ease those saddlebags to the ground, Henry. And I'll be taking the six-shooter." Keeping one hand on one of his own Colts, he extended his hand toward Yakima, palm up. "Nice an' slow."

"I didn't rape his daughter, Neumiller. In fact, it was closer to the other way around."

"That's a damn lie an' he knows it!" Lewis yelled, pointing a long, crooked finger. "My Trudy wouldn't lie with no Injun!"

Yakima kept his narrowed eye on the sheriff. "And the gold in these saddlebags doesn't belong to either one of us—Lewis *or* me. And I'll be damned if I'm gonna turn it over to you to give to *him*."

"I'll be damned if you're *not*." Neumiller glanced over Yakima's shoulder. There was the quick, loud, metallic rasp of a cartridge being levered into a rifle breech.

Yakima glanced behind him. One of Neumiller's

four deputies stood crouched behind a hitch rack off the near front corner of the mercantile, aiming down the Winchester he had propped over the rack's crossbar.

Yakima turned forward and saw two more deputies taking up positions on either side of the street, the one on the left with a rifle, the one on the right holding a double-barreled shotgun in his crossed arms and grinning. The one on the left, standing in front of the Wolfville Drug Emporium, loudly cocked his rifle and aimed with squint-eyed menace from behind the rear wheel of a parked stylish black buggy.

A young woman wearing a cream rabbit hat, from which blond sausage curls dangled toward her slender shoulders, stood in the drugstore's open door behind the deputy, staring wide-eyed. An older woman drew the young one back inside the drugstore and slammed the door. A CLOSED sign jounced in the door's curtained windowpane.

The deputy standing behind the buggy wheel grinned, his sandy mustache pushing up hard against his broad, sunburned nose. "Let me drop the hammer on him, Sheriff. We got no time for muckin' around with this half-breed."

Behind Yakima, the second deputy piped up with "We escorted him out of town once, Sheriff. I see no reason to do it a second time. 'Specially if he soiled a white girl."

"Shut up—all of you," Neumiller drawled. "The judge'll decide the half-breed's fate. I hate to spend the money feedin' you, Henry, but I'm gonna have to jail you till the circuit judge rides through again in two, three weeks. Now, with two slow fingers, slide that

pistol out of your holster and set it gently in my hand."
He gave a foxy smile.

Yakima glanced once more at Lewis smiling jeer-
ingly behind the hitch rack, then let the saddlebags
drop to the ground. Dust blew up around them. He
unsnapped the keeper thong from over his Colt's hammer and, using two fingers, pulled it out of the holster
and dropped it into the sheriff's hand.

The sheriff stepped back, and, aiming Yakima's
own gun at him, canted his head toward the sheriff's
stone office building standing a half block up the street
on the right. "Move."

As Yakima started walking up the street, Lewis
ducked under the hitch rack and ran toward the saddlebags. Neumiller placed an open hand on Lewis's
chest. "Leave it, Shackleford. Judge Vining will decide
what happened to your daughter, and he'll decide the
fate of the gold, as well."

As Lewis scowled his disappointment, Neumiller
looked at the deputy now walking up from the mercantile. "Larry, bring the bags to my office."

"You got it, Sheriff."

As Neumiller fell into step behind Yakima, Lewis
ran hop-skipping up to the sheriff and said, "That
gold's mine, Sheriff. I think I oughta be able to take it
back to my ranch with me right now. Why, it's my word
against a damn dog-eater's!"

"Forget it," Neumiller said.

"Nice try, Lewis," Yakima said. "You lyin' son of a
bitch." To the sheriff, he said, "There's a letter in them
bags along with the gold that'll help prove who that
gold belongs to, Neumiller."

"That's *Sheriff* Neumiller to you, breed!" the man

said, stepping in front of Yakima to open the door of his office. "And I'll give the judge both the gold and the letter, and he'll decide. Now get in there and shut up." He slanted a cautious eye around the street. "I've got bigger fish to fry than you and Shackleford's fallin'-out."

The man's wariness made Yakima wonder what that was. As he stepped through the open door, he cast his own cautious glance toward the other side of the street.

"Move!" Neumiller said, ramming a fist against his back and sending the half-breed stumbling into the small office lit by a potbellied stove in the middle of the room. Yakima ground his teeth against his rage. It took a powerful act of will to keep from swinging around and smashing his right heel against the man's face. He knew he could do it. And he could likely take the three deputies just now moving toward the office, too, before they even knew what had happened to their boss.

On the other hand, the one carrying the gut shredder looked as though he enjoyed using it. . . .

His name was Hannibal Howe, and he stood filling up the doorway with that shotgun in the crook of his arm. Neumiller grabbed a ring of keys off a roof support post near the smoking woodstove and opened the middle of the three cells lined up along the building's rear wall. He stepped aside, waved Yakima in, then closed the door and turned the key in the lock.

Yakima glanced behind him to see Lewis standing outside on the rotted boardwalk fronting the place, staring through the window over the sheriff's cluttered rolltop desk. Another deputy was walking toward the office behind Lewis, holding his Winchester on one shoulder and puffing a long cheroot while flicking lint or maybe tobacco flecks off the front of his black frock coat.

As Neumiller glared through the bars at Yakima, he said, "Make yourself at home, Henry. You'll be here awhile, I 'spect."

Yakima looked behind him once more in time to see the deputy walking toward Lewis stumble forward. At least, Yakima thought the man had stumbled forward. But he didn't catch himself, and at the same time that his knees hit the ground, there was a loud *crack* from the far side of the street.

Yakima lifted his gaze to see a man with a rifle hunkered atop the harness shop, smoke wafting around his Winchester's barrel as he pumped another shell into the chamber. Lewis turned around quickly, as did Neumiller, yelling, *"What . . . ?"*

There was a *plink* as a bullet hammered the window. Neumiller screamed and flew back against Yakima's cell. He caromed off the doors and dropped to the floor a few feet in front of it, grunting and groaning and clutching his upper right chest from which blood oozed thickly. Outside, several rifles were popping and men were shouting and screaming.

Another deputy ran toward the jailhouse's open door, twisting around to trigger his rifle. He was only six feet from the door when one slug punched through his chest at the same time another hammered the side of his head.

Blood flew as he rose off his feet and, dropping his rifle, piled up, quivering, on the boardwalk fronting the open door with a heavy thud of breaking bones and cracking wood. Hannibal Howe had turned around with his gut shredder, facing the street and shouting, *"Where are they, goddamn it. Where—?"*

More rifles thundered.

Howe was blown into the office near Neumiller with two gushing holes in his chest. He tried to sit up, but another shot blew off the top of his head. He tossed the shotgun to his left and it piled up against the wall in front of the door.

There were several more shots as Yakima, crouching and gripping the bars of the locked door in front of him, stared in disbelief out the open door and the broken window, unable to see much more now than wafting powder smoke. He looked down at Neumiller, who lay flat on his back about three feet in front of Yakima's cell.

The man was pale, breathing hard, lifting his hatless head to stare out the door. Yakima's pistol lay around the man's boots, near the ring of keys.

Hearing foot thuds and men's voices growing louder outside, Yakima dropped to his knees and stuck his arm through the cell door, trying to stretch his hand out for the key ring. No good. He was several feet short.

"Neumiller," Yakima said. "Toss me them keys."

The man merely grunted as blood continued to pump out of his chest. He laid his head back against the floor and stared up at the ceiling.

"Neumiller," Yakima said again, more insistently, "hand me the damn keys!"

Neumiller shook his head slightly, though Yakima couldn't tell if it was in response to his demand or a death spasm. His chest continued to rise and fall sharply.

Yakima looked out the door, glimpsed a man walking toward the jailhouse holding a Winchester on his hip, a tan duster buffeting about his buckskin-clad legs. Meanwhile, a girl was screaming shrilly on the other side of the street. A couple of men in dusters were hauling a kicking and screaming girl into the drugstore while another woman screamed inside the place. There were hoof thuds as horses approached the jailhouse, and through the broken window, from his kneeling position, the half-breed saw several bouncing, hatted heads of oncoming riders.

A cold stone was growing colder in the pit of his gut. This wasn't how he wanted to die—unarmed in a cage.

He reached for the pistol protruding from Neumiller's right holster, but he could get his hand to within only three inches of the walnut grips, and that was with nearly ripping his shoulder from its socket. Outside, horses blew and stomped. Spurs *chinged*.

A figure appeared in the doorway—a big man in a black opera hat and rose-colored glasses. He had a thick cinnamon beard, and he wore a long hair-on-horsehide coat over soiled fringed buckskins. A fat stogie poked out one corner of his mouth. Around his neck he wore a pouch—either a medicine pouch or a tobacco sack. As he stared at Yakima, the half-breed pulled his hand back into the bars and straightened slowly, holding the man's gaze—or what he thought was his gaze, because he couldn't see the man's eyes through the rose-colored spectacles.

From descriptions he'd heard, however, he knew he was looking at Claw Hendricks. The recognition was like an additional cold stone dropping into place in his belly beside the first one.

What in hell was Claw Hendricks, an outlaw leader as notorious as Wyoming Joe Two Wolves, doing this far east?

He'd thought the man restricted his gang to regions farther west and north, in the no-man's-land around the Wind River Mountains, where he hid out from the army and the U.S. marshals.

As Hendricks stepped inside slowly, dipping his chin to look at Neumiller grunting and groaning and breathing hard on the jailhouse floor, another man walked in behind Hendricks. This was an older, gray-haired man with a paunch pushing out a gray wool vest. He wore striped wool trousers and a quilted elk-hide mackinaw over the vest and work shirt, the heavy coat unbuttoned. A red scarf encircled his neck. He had two pistols positioned for the cross draw on his hips, behind the flaps of his open coat. Two bowie knives rode in leather sheaths across his chest.

When he looked at Yakima, his eyes were flat and colorless. His broad face was pasty pale and framed by roached gray muttonchops. He filled the room with a sickly sweet body odor.

Hendricks said nothing as he stepped over Neumiller's feet. He removed his opera hat to brush broken glass off Neumiller's swivel chair, and then he donned the hat again, positioning it carefully, and sagged into the chair, which squawked and groaned beneath his weight. He turned to face the room.

The second, older gent walked into the room and stared down at Neumiller while a third person stepped into the doorway behind him. This was a young, coyote-faced blond man wearing a long wolf-fur coat, the hem of which dangled around his high-topped black boots. There was a wildness about the kid—in his tangled blond hair, in his quick blue eyes and the way he cocked one foot forward and, glancing at

Yakima, drew the wolf coat back behind a Schofield pistol positioned for the cross draw on his left hip, behind a sheathed ivory-gripped Green River knife.

Between his thin pink lips, a corn-husk cigarette jutted, and he squinted his blue eyes as he took in the room through the smoke wafting around his head.

"There he is," the kid said, looking around the older man at Neumiller. "Look at him—looks like a landed fish!" He laughed, showing small brown teeth between his lips from which the quirley bobbed and smoldered. He drew on it, showing a missing eyetooth, and let the smoke dribble out his nostrils.

"Where's the county's fearless prosecutor, Neumiller?" he asked, hardening his voice and scowling down at the sheriff.

The old man said, "Shut up, Sonny!" Then he stared down at Neumiller writhing before him, and said, "Where's Mendenhour? We done checked the hotel, and he ain't in his room there and we couldn't get nothin' out of Humphries. When he seen us walk in, he pissed down his leg and passed out behind his desk."

The old man's nostrils flared disdainfully.

The old man dropped to one knee and grabbed Neumiller by his coat lapels and raised his head brusquely up off the floor. "Where is he, Sheriff? Where's Mendenhour? I wanna see the man who convinced the judge to hang my boy! Now, where is he, goddamn your mangy, rotten hide?"

Yakima stared down in shock at the old man. He let his eyes flick across the almost feminine-looking young man, feral as a wolf pup, then over to Claw Hendricks sitting back in the sheriff's chair and grinning maliciously behind those rose-colored glasses.

Yakima vaguely wondered, as he felt the sand quickly pouring through his hourglass—certainly they wouldn't leave a witness alive—how Neumiller and Mendenhour had gotten themselves in such a whipsaw.

And how was it that Yakima had gotten himself situated right at the top of the blade?

Chapter 10

"Go to hell, Betajack!" Neumiller raked out, then spat in the old man's face. He added just loudly enough for Yakima to hear, "Your boy's waitin' for you. . . ."

Claw Hendricks threw his head back and laughed, rose-colored spectacles flashing in the light from the broken window over the sheriff's rolltop desk. The old man smashed the back of his hand against the sheriff's face, then hauled one of his knives out and poked the upturned tip into the wound oozing blood from Neumiller's chest.

Neumiller scrunched his face up and howled. A girl had been screaming on the far side of the street while an older woman wailed, and the sheriff's agonized cry drowned the girl's screams for a good ten seconds. Old Betajack scowled down at Neumiller as he turned the knife handle this way and that, screwing the tip into the wound. He pulled out the dripping knife tip and held the blade up in front of Neumiller's face.

"Tell me where the prosecutor is. I know he didn't go back to his ranch, 'cause we was watchin' the road. Where'd he go, Neumiller? You tell me, we'll let you

live. You don't tell me in the next ten seconds, you're
gonna go out howlin' like a gut-shot lobo!"

The coyote-like kid called Sonny hooted and laughed
as he puffed his cigarette.

Neumiller grunted and panted, squeezing his eyes
shut as though to clear them. Blood dribbled down
over his right arm to puddle thickly on the floor beneath his writhing frame. "Go to hell, you old—!"

He screamed as Betajack shoved the tip into the
wound again, scrunching his own face up, eyes flashing wolfishly as he ground the knife a good couple of
inches into the tender open wound. Again, Neumiller's howls drowned out the girl's squeals sounding
from the far side of the street.

Yakima stood behind the closed door of his cell,
staring at the grisly happenings, though his green-
eyed face betrayed no emotion whatever. He'd seen too
much in his thirty-some years for this post-bloodbath
torture to bother him overmuch. His only concern was
for himself and the gold that caused one of his saddlebag pouches to bulge on the floor not five feet beyond
Neumiller's kicking legs but which none of the killers
had apparently seen yet.

He wasn't sure why he was thinking about the gold,
because he'd already decided quite calmly that he'd
come to the end of his trail. All he could really hope for
was a faster end than the one Neumiller was currently
experiencing.

"Stage!" the sheriff screamed so shrilly that Yakima
didn't understand him at first. "He's . . . he's on the
stage!" The man was panting, sweat glistening on his
face, sopping his mustache.

The coyote-like boy with a strangely feminine face
laughed in the office's open door, one hip cocked as he

leaned against the doorframe, arms crossed on his chest, smoking. He seemed to enjoy the grisly display to no end.

"What stage?" he called.

"Shut up, Sonny!" the old man said without looking at him. Staring down at Neumiller, keeping his knifepoint ground into the man's bullet wound, he said, "What stage, Neumiller?"

Out the window behind Claw Hendricks, Yakima could see several men with rifles milling around. A couple were looking in the windows.

Neumiller screamed, panted, kicking his boots loudly against the floor, and said through a long, harrowing squeal, "Belle *Fooooooooosh*, you son . . . son . . . son of a *bitchhhhhh!*"

"Belle Fooooosh!" mocked Claw Hendricks, lifting his chin and howling the town's name. "Belle Foosh! Belle Foosh! You got it, Floyd!"

Sonny clapped his gloved hands in the doorway. "Good goin', Pa! Must be the stage we seen pull out just a few minutes ago!"

"Yep." Betajack wiped the blood off his bowie knife on Neumiller's wool coat, sheathed the knife under his left arm, and planted both his hands on a knee to hoist himself to his feet. "Must be the one, sure 'nough."

Yakima was not surprised when the man pulled out one of his pistols and shot Neumiller in the head. The half-breed didn't even blink. He merely stepped back away from the door and sat down on the creaky wooden cot to calmly await his fate. He looked at the saddlebags. He felt no particular emotion at the prospect of Betajack and his wild boy, Sonny, and Claw Hendricks running off with the gold. Maybe a touch of disappointment at his not being able to accomplish what he'd set out to do. But there was no emotion involved other than having to leave Wolf behind.

He'd die now, and that would be the end of it.

"Come on, Pa!" Sonny said, beckoning to the old man who stared down in satisfaction at Neumiller as he holstered his hog leg. "Looks like the boys is headed on over to the Silk Slipper. I'll race ya there!"

Yakima could see a vague family resemblance in Betajack and the boy. They both looked hard and wild, as if they lived in a den and only came out to hunt.

Betajack turned around without so much as another glance at Yakima and followed his fidgety blond son out of the sheriff's office and into the street. Claw Hendricks stared at Yakima, who sat on his cot with his elbows on his knees, stoic-faced.

"Well, well, mister." Hendricks pushed himself out of the chair and hooked his thumbs behind his cartridge belt. "What you in for?"

Yakima said, "I'm told I stole from my ranching partner and raped a white girl."

"You don't say!"

Hendricks moved to stand only a few inches from the cell door. "Good on ya, old son!" He laughed. And then, to Yakima's jaw-dropping surprise, the outlaw leader stepped over the still, bloody form of Dave Neumiller and went out. The half-breed thought the big killer had glanced down at the saddlebags, but he hadn't done any more than that before he'd walked on out of the sheriff's office and into the street, where it appeared that his and Betajack's men were drifting off toward the whorehouse, in no hurry to get after the stage, it appeared.

The stage and the prosecutor, apparently, could wait.

They could enjoy themselves for an hour or two and still have no problem running the Concord down.

Yakima straightened, slow to comprehend that he was still alive. Damn, it felt good!

He glanced down at the sheriff staring at the ceiling through half-closed lids. "Sorry, Neumiller." He half meant it.

Quickly, he went to work stripping the single, moth-eaten army blanket off the cot and using it to snag the key ring and drag it over to the door. A few seconds later, he holstered his Colt, draped his saddlebags over his shoulder, and walked out of the jailhouse, drawing a deep draft of steely-cool air into his lungs and not minding the stench of horse shit and privies. All three deputies lay around him.

So did Lewis, who must have taken a bullet soon after the first deputy had gone down.

Lewis was still alive, piled up in front of the board-walk fronting the jailhouse, clutching his wounded upper right leg and breathing hard, wheezing. He was facing away from Yakima as he said, "Help . . . help me, gall blast it . . . will you, buddy?" Then he turned his head toward Yakima, and a stricken look fell over his wizened, hawkish features, angular jaws clad in a few scattered, dirt-colored bristles.

Yakima walked over to him, stared down. Lewis sort of cowered, like a dog about to be whipped, but then Yakima continued on past him and walked up the street to Bart English's Livery & Feed Barn. Bart stood behind one of his thrown-open doors, staring around it and down the main street in the direction the cutthroats had disappeared.

"You got my horse shod?" Yakima asked him.

English shuttled his stricken eyes to the half-breed. His big face was nearly as pale as Lewis's. "They gone?"

"Took their business over to the Silk Slipper."

Yakima looked up and down the street once more. Closed signs hung in most of the doors, and curtains were drawn across windows. The good citizens of Wolfville were staying indoors until the cutthroat storm had passed. He couldn't blame them. They were a bad lot.

He looked again at English. "Well?"

The big liveryman/blacksmith scowled. "Well what?"

"What about the black?"

"What about him? In case you didn't notice, this town was just raided, a girl raped over yonder at the Drug Emporium, and every star packer shot to shit!"

"I noticed."

"And now who knows what kinda trouble they're causin' over to the Silk Slipper?"

"I got an idea."

"And you're worried about your *horse*?"

"I'm burnin' daylight here."

"Well, ain't that convenient!"

"You got that part right."

Yakima brushed past English as he walked into the blacksmith part of his shop, the forge and anvil and corrugated tin water barrel occupying a lean-to side shed. He dropped his saddlebags against the wall near the water barrel. "Now get to it, Bart. I got a trail to fog."

Yakima removed his buckskin mackinaw and his hat and rolled up his shirtsleeves. He dunked his head in the water barrel, the water smelling like hot iron but refreshing and cleansing just the same. When he pulled his head up, shaking the water from his long coal black hair, English was still looking warily around his open barn door, his bulky body tense, as though he expected the gang to head this way and do to him what they'd done to the star packers.

Yakima sighed.

He donned his hat, then went over and used a tongs to pull down a raw horseshoe from a nail hanging from a ceiling beam and commenced to shaping his own shoe, pumping the bellows methodically as he did. The work was no problem. He'd forged many of Wolf's shoes himself using far less than English's shop had to offer.

When he'd finished hammering the glowing shoe on the anvil—he knew the shape of Wolf's hooves as well as he knew his own hands—he dunked the iron in the water barrel, making it hiss, then took it and a hammer and four nails over to where Wolf stood in the barn's shadows, tied to the wheel of a parked buggy.

"What the hell are you doin'?" English said, just now looking at him, his lower jaw hanging.

"What's it look like?"

Yakima led Wolf out into the light near where English still stood, looking dazed, and commenced hammering the shoe to the black's right front hoof. "Since when did Claw Hendricks start ridin' this far east?" he asked English.

"Since today, I reckon."

"Why's he ridin' with old Betajack?"

"Who the hell knows? Maybe they both had the same beef with Neumiller." English turned to direct his gaze down the street again as Yakima continued hammering nails through the shoe. "The sheriff hanged

Preston Betajack just yesterday. Last night, somebody—
Betajack, I figure—hanged one of Neumiller's deputies.
The prosecutor's wife was the one who found him."

Yakima looked up from his work. "Prosecutor's
wife?"

"Yeah, Mrs. Mendenhour."

Yakima considered that a moment while holding
Wolf's hoof between his knees. Then he looked at English's broad back once more. "She the woman I saw in
the stage earlier, when they was just pullin' out?"

"If she was just about the purtiest creature you ever
laid eyes on," English said, "then it was her, all right."

"And they're after her husband," Yakima said, half
to himself.

"I'm sure they are." English shook his head darkly.
"What those men do when they run down that stage is
anyone's guess." He looked at Yakima, narrowing one
bushy-browed eye. "But I don't have to guess what
they'll do to the man's purty wife."

Yakima felt that stone drop in his belly again.
Inwardly, he cursed. He cursed the killers and the
sheriff and the prosecutor and even the prosecutor's
wife. He cursed them all for the fix they were in. Most
of all he cursed himself for being here in the middle
of it.

And for not mounting up and taking the gold and
riding south to Texas. Maybe Mexico. All the gold he
was carrying would take him a long ways, for many
years, in Old Mexico.

The good feeling he'd felt only a few minutes ago
was gone.

When he'd finished hammering the shoe onto Wolf's
hoof, he tossed the hammer to English, slung the saddlebags over Wolf's back, and stepped into the leather.

He stiffened when he saw Lewis still writhing on the ground in front of the sheriff's office. The double-crossing rancher was the only living person on the street. All the rest of the town appeared to still be cowering behind closed doors and shuttered windows.

Yakima looked at English and said tightly, "Find Shackleford's horse. Get him on it and slap him home!"

Then he rammed his moccasin heels against Wolf's flanks and loped along the street, taking the left tine at the edge of town and following after the stage toward the northeast.

Chapter 11

She'd ridden her sleek palomino, Taos, through the notch in the rocky bluffs and come up through the aspens to see him working in the corral of the old line shack.

He was repairing the corral, with several slender logs lying around him and the white-socked, coal black stallion standing nearby, always close at hand. The two seemed part of each other. He'd taken his shirt off because of the heat; it hung over a corral slat. One log rested across two sawhorses on the corral's left side, away from the cabin. A tendril of white smoke rose from the cabin's chimney, unspooling amongst the pines jutting around the scarp to the right of the shack.

The sun made a shimmering gold line along the stallion's broad back.

Even as he sawed the slender log stretched across the sawhorses, he was looking toward her, for he'd obviously heard her and Taos riding toward him. He had a shell belt and a holstered revolver slung over the corral, near his buckskin shirt, and a rifle with a brass receiver leaned against a post, below the pistol.

His black, sweat-damp hair dangled to his broad, muscular

shoulders, his skin the color of varnished cherry. Sweat glistened on his bulging arms and on the heavy slabs of his thick chest that formed a mantle beneath his stout brown neck. He'd been quite a vision working and sweating there in the midafternoon, high-country sunshine. He paused in his sawing to watch her and then, as she came on, feeling apprehensive but also curious, he resumed sawing the log, causing the ridged muscles of his shoulders, arms, and chest to ripple like sun-gilded waves, until the cut log tumbled off the sawhorse to lie at his moccasin-clad feet.

She stopped Taos a ways from the corral and canted her head to one side, studying him, feeling miffed at first to find someone here, for she'd considered the cabin her own sacred refuge. But her annoyance disappeared beneath her fascination for the man, obviously a mixed breed, whom she was surprised to find here at work on the dilapidated corral.

"Have you moved in?" she called.

He'd picked up the cut log and was placing it between two corral posts, sliding it into two notches he'd made in the posts. He shook his head. "Buildin' up the corral so we can corral some horses here next week." His voice was deep, but it had the light ring of a white man, not the harsh tones of an Indian speaking English.

He hammered one end of the new rail into the old post with the heel of his hand.

"I usually stop here for water," she said.

The black stallion, turned sideways to her, was watching her and Taos obliquely, its ears twitching, its shaggy tail arched.

"Help yourself," the black-haired man said. "But you'd best let that palo cool off first."

"I know to do that," she said defensively, stepping down from her saddle.

She walked Taos in several broad circles in front of the

cabin, watching as the big red black-haired man continued working, placing the one rail and then cutting another slender pine pole to replace another one that had rotted out. He didn't look at her as she walked and he continued working. His black hair danced about his broad shoulders, and the banded muscles in his stomach expanded and contracted as he bent and stretched and squatted and sawed another length of log—a man at home in his own fine body, a man both accustomed to and adept at hard labor.

Finally, when Taos had warmed down, she led the gelding into the corral. The two horses nickered curiously, a little warningly, and then Taos took his eyes off the arch-tailed black and dipped his snout in the rain barrel abutting the side of the cabin, in the swatch of purple shade there, and drew water.

The man glanced at her, and she noted the sunlight glinting off his eyes like chips of jade embedded in a dark granite mountain wall. The stallion whinnied and came prancing aggressively over to the palomino. The palo lifted its snout from the water with a start, sidestepping and ramming Glendolene back against the corner of the cabin. She gave a groan as something cut into her arm, and she pushed the palo's hindquarters back away from her with an angry grunt.

"Easy, easy, boy!" the man said.

The black shuffled around, bobbing its head half playfully, half territorially, and the palo lifted its own head and backed away, eyes nervous, fearful. The man stepped between them, rammed his left shoulder against the black, and turned the stallion away to go prancing, mane buffeting, around the corral, swinging and bobbing his fine head.

"Don't mind him—he's just showing off." The man moved to her, grabbed her arm. "Are you hurt?"

She looked down at the large red-brown hand wrapped around her forearm as he canted his head to look at where a

*nail had scraped against her upper arm, tearing her white
cotton blouse above her elbow.*

"Are you all right, Glendolene?"

Her husband's voice nudged her from the reverie
and she found herself staring at the man sitting across
from her in the lurching coach—a bearded prospector
in a scruffy watch cap and muffler heading back to his
home in Dakota for Christmas. The miner slept with
his head tipped forward, snoring. Glendolene realized
she was sort of half smiling, and an embarrassed flush
rose in her cheeks.

She glanced at Lee riding to her right, another married couple riding to her left, the four of them facing
forward while four other travelers, including the prospector, faced them.

"I'm fine," she said, vaguely wondering why a smile
would have Lee so concerned.

Did she smile so seldom?

She remembered that what had spawned the reverie
was seeing the man who'd taken center stage in it as
the coach had pulled out of Wolfville—the man whose
name she'd never learned, and had never wanted to
learn—and now a hollow feeling swept over her. The
hollowness became a lonely ache, and suddenly she
felt as though she was about to cry.

She tried to suppress the feeling, but then it was ag-
gravated by a feeling she'd woken up to several morn-
ings in a row, terrifying her. It terrified her now.

She squeezed her hands around the small leather
traveling purse she held on her lap, fighting it, staring
out the window. It wouldn't leave her. In fact, she felt
sweat breaking out on her forehead, and then her
upper lip trembled until she felt as though she was
about to convulse with a sob.

She turned to Lee and tried hard to pitch her voice evenly as she said, "In fact, I do feel a little under the weather. Do you think you could have the driver stop so I could get some air?"

The other passengers looked at her concernedly— all except the still-dozing prospector—as Lee said, "Certainly."

Lee removed his bowler hat and tilted his head out the window to yell up at the driver, "Mr. Adlard, can you halt the team? Mrs. Mendenhour is needing a break."

He had to yell several times before he could make the jehu understand him. When the stage had lurched to a stop, dust rising outside the windows, Lee opened the door and stepped out quickly, his eyes concerned. He took Glendolene's arm as she rose a little unsteadily from the hide-covered seat and ducked through the door. She waved him off and did not look at the shotgun messenger, who said, "Everything all right, ma'am?" but merely nodded her head and hurried off through the boulders and shrubs lining the trail.

Glendolene felt foolish, but she also felt genuinely sick. When the stage was out of sight behind her, she dropped to her knees, felt the nausea rise out of her belly, and retched in the rocks and gravel before her. When she finished, she opened her leather traveling purse, extracted a handkerchief, and wiped her lips with it.

A woman's voice said behind her, "Does he know?"

Glendolene jerked her head around, saw one of the other two women from the stage standing behind her— a plain-faced, red-haired woman with expressive blue eyes and a long, thin mouth that smiled understandingly. A mole adorned her chin, a little off center. She wore a man's striped blanket coat over a brown wool dress and short fur boots. She wore a green knitted scarp over her head, covering her ears against the wintry cold that had finally descended on the northern Rockies.

"Does who know what?"

"Does your husband know about your condition?" the woman said. She stepped forward and continued to smile kindly down at Glendolene. "Believe me, miss, I know the symptoms of pregnancy. You couldn't have been regular sick, because it all happened so fast, and I'd say the morning sickness was brought on by a mood as much as all the bouncing around."

She hitched her skirts up her thighs, beneath the heavy coat, and dropped to a knee beside Glendolene. "I'm from Whitfield, over yonder. I helped Doc O'Reilly out for years with his female patients. Had a few babes myself, though they all died."

Glendolene looked at her, feeling stricken. She'd figured she was pregnant, but this woman seemed to validate her fears, caused her now to stare at the cold, hard fact of her condition.

"Oh," the woman said understandingly. "It's not as happy a time as it might be, is it?"

Glendolene looked away as she dabbed at her lips, felt tears dribble down her cheeks. She felt lonely and hollow, and the breadth and starkness of the country around her—the rolling, sage-covered hills with occasional rust-colored rimrocks rising here and there seemed to intensify the emotion. Guilt racked her, as well, because the realization that she was undeniably pregnant also made her realize how much she didn't want the child.

Her unexpected confidante said, "I'm sure, once you tell him, he'll be thrilled. All the men are!"

"Yes," Glendolene said, feigning an optimistic smile. "Yes, I suppose he will. . . ." And he would be, she knew, and that also made her feel guilty, because she herself was not.

"Where are my manners?" the blond woman said. "I'm Lori. Lori O'Reilly. Dr. O'Reilly's wife. His widow. Heart attack took him last spring, and I'm moving up to Montana now. One of my nephews is up there, offered to take me in. And you're . . . ?"

"Glendolene Mendenhour."

Lori O'Reilly frowned curiously.

"Prosecutor Mendenhour is my husband."

"Oh . . . ," Lori said, obviously impressed. "You live out at the . . . ?"

"The Chain Link, yes."

"Nice place, I hear."

"It's not bad," Glendolene said, unable not to add, "A little isolated."

"I suppose it is. Especially for one in your condition." Mrs. O'Reilly pulled a small flask out of her coat pocket and popped the cork. "Here, take some of this. Don't worry. It's just water, though it probably has a brandy taste to it. It's the doc's." She smiled, and her smile contributed to Glendolene's sadness because it told her how much the woman missed the doctor, whom she'd never see again.

"Thank you." She accepted the flask and took a sip. The water was still cold. It refreshed her, took some of the heat out of the uncomfortable flush she still felt in her face, and some of the pain from the dull ache in her head.

She handed the flask back to Mrs. O'Reilly, who corked it and slipped it back into her coat. "I'm better now." Mrs. O'Reilly took her arm and helped her rise from her knees. "I'm ready to ride, though the thought of it still makes me a little queasy, I'm afraid."

"We'll be stopping again soon, Mrs. Mendenhour. The Eagle Butte Station is just a few more miles up the trail. They'll have food there. That'll put some color back into your cheeks."

Glendolene liked the woman's open, almost salty demeanor. She didn't seem like many doctors' wives she'd known. Most of them were persnickety.

"Please call me Glendolene."

"Only if you call me Lori."

The two women walked back through the rocks to the stage. Of the passengers, only Lee and the bearded prospector had destaged. The young married couple and two men who appeared to be traveling drummers were still on board, conversing in a desultory way. The driver and the shotgun messenger were standing up in front of the team, glancing down at one of the lead horses' hooves and conversing, while the prospector stood near the stage's front wheel, smoking a loosely rolled quirley and staring obliquely at Glendolene and Mrs. O'Reilly.

"Feeling better, Glen?" Lee said, stepping forward.

"Much better," Glendolene said. She had turned to Mrs. O'Reilly to thank the woman for the water and the encouragement when a strained look crumpled the woman's face and she lurched straight back with a scream. A quarter second later, before Glendolene had time to react, a rifle cracked hollowly.

"*Injuns!*" the old prospector screamed, pointing along their back trail. "Oh, Lordy, it's *Injuns!*"

Chapter 12

Yakima jerked sharply back on Wolf's reins. As the horse ground its front hooves into the turf with an indignant whinny, the half-breed shucked his Winchester from his saddle boot and leaped out of the leather.

Ahead of him, rifles cracked and pistols popped as a pack of Floyd Betajack's and Claw Hendricks's killers whooped and hollered, galloping toward the stage. The coach was stopped along the trail ahead and left of Yakima, about thirty yards away. The killers were on his right, galloping toward him and the stage. Both parties were below his perch on the shoulder of a steep bluff.

Half an hour before, he'd been surprised to see the gang ahead instead of behind him. Apparently, they'd done fast work at the whorehouse and then taken a shortcut through rough country to work ahead of Yakima, getting between him and the stage. Soon after he'd seen them, he'd done his own working around. Now he dropped behind a boulder along the side of the bluff and planted a bead on one of the three riders racing toward the stage, expertly firing their rifles while at the same time steering their horses.

Yakima squeezed the Yellowboy's trigger. The rifle leaped and roared. The middle rider released his reins and his rifle at the same time and rolled off the back of his striding cream stallion.

Again, Yakima fired and watched in satisfaction as the second of the three lead riders lurched sharply sideways, losing his own rifle as he reached for his saddle horn. His gloved right hand slid off the horn, and he gave a scream as he careened down his right stirrup and bounced along the trail behind his swerving roan.

The third rider had only just glanced over his shoulder at his still-bouncing and rolling companions when Yakima unseated him, too, and turned his attention to two more riders galloping behind the first three, with the rest of the dozen-man pack feathered out behind them for nearly a hundred yards.

Yakima had just planted a bead on a fourth killer when the man's horse rammed a knee against the head of one of the first three riders Yakima had downed. The horse gave a shrill whinny as the knee buckled and it turned a somersault over the downed man while launching its own rider high in the hair to be battered by the horse's flailing, scissoring hooves.

Yakima drew another bead, but a bullet crashed into the boulder a few inches to his right, and his next shot sailed wide of the rider who'd shot at him—the next rider in the pack. Yakima cocked the Yellowboy once more and shot true this time, his bullet hammering through the rider's face and snapping his head back sharply.

The man's arms fell slack. His hat blew off behind him. He sat suspended in the saddle for several seconds before he turned slowly to his left, then fell down that side of his horse, his left boot getting hung up in the stirrup. The rider's horse dragged its dead rider along past Yakima's position and then off the trail beyond him, swinging east.

Yakima racked another cartridge into the Yellowboy's chamber but held fire. The other riders were turning back, shouting and waving their arms at those behind them, apparently believing they'd been caught in a trap—one likely set by more than just one man.

Since he was only one man against an entire pack, Yakima was glad they'd made the mistake. He doubted, however, they'd make many more.

He turned to the stage sitting fifty yards away, two passengers crouched over a fallen one. The fallen one appeared to be a woman. A redhead, not a chestnut-haired beauty, as he knew the county prosecutor's wife to be. Two men whom Yakima assumed were the driver and the shotgun messenger were each hunkered behind separate rear wheels, aiming rifles toward the pack that had attacked them, but also turning their heads slightly to frown curiously at Yakima.

The half-breed glanced once more at the retreating killers, hearing their hoof thuds dwindling quickly, dust sifting, then turned back to the stage and waved his rifle in the air above his head.

"Haul ass!" he shouted.

The driver and the shotgun rider looked at each other. Then the jehu, Charlie Adlard, shouted, "Who the hell *are* you?"

Yakima cursed and then shouted louder, "Haul your asses the hell out of here *now*!"

Shoving fresh cartridges through the Yellowboy's receiver, Yakima walked back to where Wolf cropped at patches of still-green grass amongst the dried-up yellow buck brush, on the far side of the bluff, and mounted up. He slid the Yellowboy back into its boot and sat staring in the direction the riders had gone.

They'd disappeared into a low area between him and a rise of dun hogbacks shrouded with leafless aspens. He thought a thin tendril of smoke lifted from around the base of the hill, but he couldn't be sure.

What the hell are you doing? he thought. You got out of one mess in Wolfville to put yourself into another one out here. You should aim Wolf at the Dakota territorial line and powder some sage, get the gold to Belle Fourche before you get caught out here in one storm or another, likely a lead storm.

He knew from experience that those were even worse than snow.

Yeah, I should.

"But I'm not," he grumbled aloud.

Not only because of the woman he'd thrown down a few times with in the line shack. But because he couldn't just ride on and let the killers do what they intended, because other innocent people besides her were likely to die. He owed Mendenhour nothing. But Betajack and Hendricks would likely make everyone else on the stage suffer for what they saw as the prosecutor's transgressions. They'd leave no witnesses.

Yakima would follow the stage as far as Jawbone simply because, with the lawmen in Wolfville dead, there was no one else to help. The jehu would find a lawman in Jawbone, another day up the line, and the law could take over the guiding duties, or hire a posse to see the coach safely to Belle Fourche.

Yakima glanced at the sky. There were some broad masses of thin pewter clouds high above him, but around that benign mass was blue sky. Maybe he'd still get south to warmer weather before the snow boxed him in.

He touched heels to Wolf's flanks and put the stallion up and over the hill and down the other side, heading for the stage trail. He wasn't thinking about the woman—about how she'd smelled and how she'd smiled and how the light from the line shack fire had glowed in her chestnut hair.

He wasn't thinking about her at all.

"Here they come," said Claw Hendricks, looking across the dry wash as he held a steaming coffee cup between his large gloved hands. He wore a ring on his right middle finger, over the glove. It was a symbol of success and prosperity, and after the meagerness he'd come from, he saw no reason why he shouldn't show off a little.

Floyd Betajack thought it looked prissy, but he'd said nothing about it and he said nothing now as he looked over the flames of their coffee fire to the rise of land beyond the wash. Sure enough, the gang composed of his own six men and six of Hendricks's men from his hideout in the Mummy Range was galloping toward him.

"Uh-oh," said his younger and sole remaining son, Sonny, rising. "I don't see Mendenhour amongst 'em, unless that's him ridin' with Albert, but that don't look like the man I seen in Wolfville that time." He glanced at Hendricks and threw his shoulders back, trying to look tough. "Him an' Neumiller braced me, tried to run me out of town, but I told 'em to eat rat shit and I was a citizen with rights, and I was no dog to poke with a stick." He snickered, chew dribbling down his thin lower lip. "They let the matter lie."

"They did, did they?" said Hendricks.

"Sure enough, Claw," Sonny said, flaring his nostrils. "Don't you believe me?"

"Oh, I'm sure they took one look at you and knew they had the tiger by the tail," Hendricks said.

Sonny glowered at him, fair cheeks flushing with anger.

"That's enough," Betajack said, feeling the burn of his customary anger as he tossed the dregs of his coffee on the fire and grabbed his Henry repeater. "I told you to lay off Sonny. He can't help it he's full of shit."

Hendricks snorted. Sonny turned his wrathful gaze on his father but held his tongue. He knew better than to respond to his father's bile, and the old man was full of bile now in the wake of Pres's murder.

Betajack moved around the fire to get a better look at the dozen riders riding toward the temporary bivouac. They were fanned out left to right for fifty yards.

"What'd you bring him along for, then?"

"Because I go wherever Pa goes!" Sonny said defiantly, his voice acquiring a harsh rake, yellow javelins firing from his girlish eyes. His fierce temper had an almost feminine haughtiness to it. "I ain't no wet-behind-the-ears shaver who stays home to tend the chickens while Pa an' Pres go off raisin' hell! Hell, I'm a *killer*!"

Hendricks just stared at the bizarre man-child, not saying anything to rile Betajack further.

Betajack himself said distractedly, "That's enough, boy."

He shouldered his rifle and walked across the dry wash —a big man with cold gray-blue eyes and a clean-shaven face set harshly between thick tufts of roached muttonchop whiskers. He was middle-aged now and gone to tallow, though with a muscular strength beneath the fat. But he'd been a demon for the Confederates during the War of Northern Aggression. Men who knew his reputation for Rebel savagery, and that included most of Claw Hendricks's men, sort of saw Betajack as a hero. Hendricks saw him as a mentor. If anything in the years since the war, Betajack had gotten meaner and more rebellious against authority.

Especially Yankee authority, which meant government authority. Which meant any kind of *civilization*, truth be known.

That's why he and his boys and his outlaw gang had thrown in with Claw Hendricks when Hendricks had started branching out from Boulder and Jamestown in the Colorado Territory, and moving their sundry nefarious doings up into Wyoming, where new mines were opening up in the Wind River and Big Horn ranges, and in the Buckskin Buttes. The riders reined to a halt in a long line in front of Betajack, Sonny, and Claw Hendricks, who was walking up behind the old rebel cutthroat and his strange, girlish son.

"I see you're missing a few men," Betajack said, his disapproval rumbling up from deep in his chest.

"What the hell happened?" asked Hendricks.

"You ain't gonna believe it, Mr. Betajack," said Albert Delmonte, Betajack's first lieutenant, who sat his paint horse in front of the old Rebel outlaw, an injured rider astraddle the same horse behind him. "There was someone else there. Looked Injun. We didn't see him till we'd started firing on the stage and he started firing on us behind cover."

"One man?" asked Sonny, incredulous.

"At first we thought there was more, 'cause he was shootin' so damn fast. But . . ."

One of Hendricks's men, a half-breed Ute named Lyle Two Moons, said in his deep, guttural voice, "A green-eyed warrior I'd seen before, hunting horses in the Mummy Mountains."

Hendricks shoved his rose-colored glasses up his nose with his beringed middle finger, then cocked his shaggy head as though to hear better. "You mean you let this green-eyed redskin get the better of you? *One man?*"

Lyle Two Moons wore a heavy, short buffalo coat, a bullet-crowned black hat, and black-checked orange twill trousers with hide-patched knees. He held a Winchester carbine across his saddlebow, thumb rubbing nervously against the uncocked hammer. His chocolate eyes held Hendricks's wry, indignant gaze.

"He fights like five men," Lyle said quietly.

"Ah, hogswill!" Betajack steered the conversation back to the task at hand. "You didn't get Mendenhour like you was supposed to. A simple job for twelve men. And you didn't get him. Instead, you let one man deplete your numbers by . . . how many?" He lifted a finger, counting the number of riders before him. "Four?"

"Four, boss," said the rider crouched behind Albert Delmonte. "I'm still kickin'." He hardened his jaw as he said over Albert's left shoulder, his wavy, dirt-crusted brown hair hanging over his forehead, "My horse only kicked me, but I'm still game for a fight."

Sonny planted his small fists on his hips and ran his wild eyes from one end of the chagrined pack to the other. "Let me get this straight," he said, wanting very much to be part of the conversation. "A whole passel of our men and Claw's men were turned back by *one* man?"

"Wait a minute," Hendricks said, fingering the spade beard hanging six inches below his chin. "Did you say a green-eyed half-breed?"

"That's right," Albert said, who looked a little Indian himself, though, being a nephew of Betajack, he owned the Scotch-Irish blood—and emotional disposition—of his uncle and cousin. "Green-eyed half-breed in buckskin pants and mackinaw. Black hat with a flat brim. You know him?"

Hendricks's broad face paled a little. He furrowed his brows above his rose-colored spectacles.

Betajack turned to him. "The fella in the jailhouse with Neumiller fit that description."

Still, Hendricks said nothing. He turned to Betajack blandly, sucking his cheek pensively.

"I figured you'd kill the son of a bitch," Betajack said. "But come to think on it, I never did hear a pistol shot."

Hendricks said, a tad defensively, "I asked what he was in for, and he said he was a thief and a rapist of uppity white women. So I figured why kill him? Hell, I would have given him a cigar if I'd had one."

"A real upstandin' citizen," said Sonny snidely.

"You're one to talk," Hendricks said, pitching his voice low with menace.

"What's that mean?"

"I seen you over at the Silk Slipper." Hendricks gave a foxy grin.

Sonny wrapped his hand around one of his six-shooters and opened his mouth and squinted his eyes for a typically blasphemous retort, but his father closed his own hand around the firebrand's wrist, shoving the pistol back down in the leather. "That's enough! Let it go. Remember, boy, we threw in with this man because we didn't have enough of our own." He looked at Hendricks. "I reckon we gotta allow a few missteps . . . since we got Pres to think of."

"We'll get him," Hendricks said, turning away to cover his embarrassment. "Don't worry. The half-breed's as good as dead. His ears and his scalp will be dangling from my neck by sundown tomorrow. I'll do it myself this time"—he glanced over his shoulder at his seven surviving riders, Betajack having five—"since I obviously ain't got the breed of men I *thought* I had! Only the kind that's a goddamn embarrassment."

His pack of tough-jawed, bewhiskered white men, half-breeds, and one black man, whose name was Soot Early, merely looked off, too proud to show any more than the most subtle signs of incredulity.

Hendricks angrily kicked dirt on the coffee fire, giving the coffeepot a good kick as he did.

Betajack turned to the man, Delvin Torrance, riding behind Sonny. "Torrance, how bad you hurt?"

"Horse kicked me in the head." Torrance grinned. "Woulda hurt me worse if he'd stepped on my foot."

"Since you don't have a horse, I should shoot you now." Betajack narrowed his pewter eyes at the man who sat behind Albert Delmonte without a hat, blood dribbling from the large, blue lump rising on his right temple. "Under most circumstances, that's exactly what I'd do. Because that's the price of bein' a damn fool."

Sonny snickered.

Betajack ignored him, continuing with "But since

we obviously need all the guns we can get, you'll have to switch off ridin' double until we can find you another horse."

"Yessir, Mr. Betajack," Torrance said, holding the old Rebel's gaze with a determined one of his own. "Yes, sir, that's not a problem. I'll secure one at the next stage relay station. Not a problem."

"All right, we're done mucking around here chewin' leather," Betajack said, walking back to where his steel-dust stallion milled with Hendricks's and Sonny's mounts, on the other side of the wash. "Let's get a move on. I got a county prosecutor to kill, goddamn it!"

He mounted up and galloped off, whipping his horse savagely with his rein ends. Glancing back over his shoulder and grinning wolfishly, he said, "After Claw cuts off that half-breed's ears, that is!"

He laughed as he rode away.

Sonny shrugged and shook his head as he swung up onto the back of his coyote dun. "Preston was a sad price to pay for it, but I do believe the old coot's feelin' pecker-high in yellow clover again!"

Chapter 13

Yakima saw the stage climbing a hill ahead of him. He galloped Wolf on up to it and passed it on the driver's side. The driver and shotgun messenger had spied him a ways back, and they eyed him suspiciously, the old driver narrowing one eye beneath a grizzled gray brow.

"Who the hell *are* you, man?"

Yakima knew who the driver and messenger were, because he kept his eyes and ears open, but they wouldn't know him. Being a half-breed, he was invisible to most whites—and that wasn't always a bad thing.

"It ain't me you need to worry about, Adlard," Yakima said as he put Wolf on past the stage and the team leaning hard into their collars as they continued up the hill. "It's them boys who hoorawed you."

"Who were *they*?" called the shotgun messenger, who was a good fifteen, twenty years younger than the driver. His name, if Yakima remembered, was Mel Coble.

Yakima was beyond the team now. "Best talk to the prosecutor about that, Coble!"

Then he continued up and over the hill. Another mile farther on, he rode into the yard of the Eagle Butte Relay Station. An old man in a black wool coat, deerskin mittens, and earmuffs was leaning against a corral post, smoking a cigarette. He squinted at Yakima as the half-breed rode past him and turned his horse toward the corral's gate, where a tall young man in woolly chaps stood with a pitchfork, eyeing the big half-breed with the same suspicion the older gent had.

Yakima dismounted the black and tossed the boy the reins. "Tend him for me, will you? I'll be pullin' out with the stage."

The kid's lips barely moved as he said, "Who're you?"

"Me?" He shrugged. "I'm Yakima Henry."

The half-breed strode over to the low-slung, brush-roofed cabin and went on inside. He was sitting at a table in the rear shadows, eating beans, eggs, and ham from a large wooden bowl, when the stage came jouncing into the yard behind the weary team. The driver brought the coach right up to the cabin, and Yakima watched out the window right of the door, the thinly scraped deer hide stretched over the window frame giving a distorted view of the yard, as the driver and the shotgun messenger guided a redheaded, middle-aged woman in a blanket coat out of the coach. She was slumped forward, the front of her coat bloody. One on each side, they led her up the steps and then through the screen door and the winter door.

The woman who ran the place, a stocky, dark woman in a shapeless wool skirt over which she wore a ragged bobcat-skin cape, her salt-and-pepper hair in a tight bun atop her head, came out from around the bar. Her black eyes danced. "Good Lord—were you *robbed*?" She had a slight accent that Yakima thought was French.

"Nope, we wasn't robbed," said the old driver. "Mrs. O'Reilly took a bullet, though, Yvette. She thinks it went all the way through. Can you sew her up?"

"Bring her on back!" called Yvette, hurrying on ahead of the two men and the woman, who was wincing and breathing hard but otherwise holding up well.

Yakima lowered his eyes when the man he took to be the prosecutor, Mendenhour, wearing a beaver hat and a long, elegant-looking coat of elk hide trimmed with rabbit fur and black leather gloves, followed his wife into the cabin. It was relatively dark in the cabin, and neither saw Yakima right away.

He looked them both over carefully, and then his eyes held on hers, which had found him back in the shadows. They stared at each other for several seconds, her expression for the most part indecipherable, as he assumed his was, before he lowered his eyes to his bowl once more and continued eating hungrily.

"Lee," he heard her say, noting the familiarity of her voice—the voice of a woman he'd never expected to see again after that third and final meeting in the line shack. "I'm going to go back and help with Lori."

"All right, Glen," the woman's husband said, "but stay close."

She removed her gloves and took them in one hand as she strode around the tables, passing Yakima without looking at him, and continued to the rear of the room and through a blanketed doorway in the back wall, beneath an impressive set of deer antlers. He couldn't help turning his head to watch her, noting the familiar smell of her on the breeze she'd made when she'd passed him.

As the other stage passengers—another couple, an old man in a watch hat and with a gray bib beard, and two middle-aged men who looked like drummers in felt bowler hats, cheap suits, and age-worn wool coats—came into the station and gravitated toward the pot-bellied stove, the prosecutor continued standing in front of the door. He stared at Yakima almost suspiciously. For a moment, the half-breed considered whether she'd confessed her sins to him. The man slowly removed his gloves and then his heavy scarf as he walked slowly, arrogantly toward Yakima's table, and for a few seconds Yakima wondered if he'd have to shoot the man himself.

Mendenhour stopped a few feet away, staring down as Yakima continued forking food into his mouth, the half-breed's sun-bleached black hat on the table beyond his plate and coffee cup. His rifle lay there, as well. His saddlebags were slung over the back of the chair to Yakima's right.

"Who are you?" the prosecutor asked, an officious tone in his voice.

Yakima stared up at him. He was tall and handsome. A moneyed man. Yakima wasn't surprised that she would have chosen one like the young attorney, though he couldn't help wondering now why she'd also chosen *him*, Yakima—at least for a little nasty fun in the line shack. He'd never thought of it before, but maybe she was a harlot. She hadn't looked or acted like a harlot, but he'd seen enough in his life to know he hadn't seen it all.

He knew the assessment wasn't fair, and that it

was evoked by natural male, petty jealousy, but there it was.

"I asked you a question," Mendenhour said, lightly wrapping the knuckles of his pale white hand on Yakima's table.

Yakima swallowed a bite of food and followed the man's slender arm up to his handsome face. "I was in the jail in Wolfville when Betajack's men rode in and shot hell out of your lawmen."

The prosecutor's thin auburn blows furrowed slightly as he continued staring at Yakima, his brown eyes dubious.

"Betajack's and Claw Hendricks's men," Yakima added. "After that, I didn't see a good reason to hang around. 'Specially since I got business up north." He forked another bite of food into his mouth and continued to hold the glowering stare of the prosecutor, who was resting the tips of his knuckles on Yakima's table.

"Good . . . God . . . ," Mendenhour said finally, when Yakima thought he was incapable of saying anything more at all. "Betajack and . . . ?"

"Hendricks, yep. Got her right. You poked your snoot in the wrong henhouse, amigo."

"That isn't for you to judge," the man said tightly.

Yakima shrugged.

"They're all . . . dead?"

Yakima nodded. "Bushwhacked."

Looking stricken, the prosecutor slumped into a chair across from Yakima. As Yvette came out of the back room, she said, "I'll bring you all some food and coffee, folks. Looks like you'll be here an hour or so . . . on account of Mrs. O'Reilly. She'll be okay, though. The bullet just creased her!"

She got to work at the cupboard and chugging range behind the plank-board bar. The young couple who appeared to be married sat at their own table, talking in hushed tones. They were dressed like a young farm couple in mismatched, heavy clothes. The old prospector sat at the same table as the two middle-aged men who looked like drummers. He was smoking a quirley and not taking part in the heated conversation the drummers were having. He was staring oddly at Yakima, almost as though he had a secret he was thinking about sharing with the half-breed. Or maybe he'd just been in similar situations, and he wasn't surprised by any of this at all.

Mendenhour continued to sit sideways at the table, one elbow propped on it as he stared anxiously at the floor, ankles crossed beneath his chair. "I thought for sure Neumiller knew what he was doing. Thought for sure . . . he could hold Betajack off."

"I reckon he didn't figure on Betajack throwin' in with Claw Hendricks."

"No," Mendenhour said, shaking his head, trying to puzzle it through as he continued staring at the floor, "I never would have figured on that, either." He looked at Yakima, his eyes sharp, fervent. "How many . . . ?"

"I counted a dozen. Managed to whittle 'em down by four, maybe five."

"Well, maybe you've discouraged them."

"I wouldn't count on it."

"I wouldn't count on it, neither," said the driver, who'd just pushed through the blanketed doorway at the back of the room.

The bearded jehu, in a long wool-lined sheepskin coat and with a thin salt-and-pepper beard carpeting jaws so sun-seared that they looked like beef charred on a hot spit, came over to Yakima's table. He was trailed by the younger shotgun messenger, who held a Winchester repeater on his shoulder and had a snide, peeved look on his rugged face.

The driver looked at Yakima. "I heard you mention the names Betajack and Hendricks. That who's behind us?"

"That's who."

The driver and the shotgun messenger both looked down at Mendenhour with concern. They didn't say anything. Their looks said it all. The prosecutor raked his gaze across both anxious men, then looked uncomfortably over his shoulder and through the thin scraped-hide window to the front yard lit by weak, gold-hued winter light.

There was a rustling behind Yakima. In the periphery of his vision he saw the prosecutor's wife step through the blanketed doorway. She stopped just inside the main room. Yakima glanced at her. She did not look at him but held her gaze on her husband.

"I reckon you fellas best think through your options," Yakima said, scraping his chair back, rising, and picking up his Yellowboy. He donned his hat. He set the rifle on his right shoulder and slung his saddlebags containing the gold over his left shoulder, pinched his hat brim to Mrs. Mendenhour, and sauntered past the others, who'd stopped talking to watch him gravely, curiously.

He moved on outside and down the porch steps, past the kid he'd seen earlier and two other ones of different ages—all under eighteen—leading the fresh team of six horses toward the stage.

The young men looked at him with wary suspicion.

Yakima ignored them. He walked over to where Wolf stood in the corral with the blown stage horses, facing Yakima and flicking his ears curiously. His bridle was slipped and his latigo hung loose beneath his belly.

Yakima draped the saddlebags over the top of the corral, then reached over and ran his hand absently down the black's long snout that wore a white blaze in the shape of Florida. The horse stared at Yakima, as though eager to light a shuck.

"Yeah, I'd like to," the half-breed grumbled, staring past the black and the other horses that were still cooling down, steam rising from their backs, and waiting for the young hostlers' tending.

No sign of Betajack and Claw Hendricks. They were back there, though. They might even be nearer than they appeared. He could imagine them breaking up and circling the relay station. That's how he'd do it, if he wanted to kill Mendenhour badly enough. He'd circle around and maybe take a shot at him from one of those brushy knolls.

Would they settle for only the prosecutor? Or did they want his wife, too? Did they want her dead or did they just want her? They were men, after all, and they likely knew what the prosecutor's wife—was her name Glendolene?—looked like. How much woman she was.

Most likely, the killers intended to shoot everyone who saw them, eliminating all the witnesses.

Yakima drew a long, ragged breath and looked at the black still watching him with his tobacco brown eyes. The horse was wondering what they were doing here when they had a mission to bring the gold back to Delbert Clifton's family and then, as they did or tried to do most years, head south to warmer weather.

Or, hell, maybe Yakima just imagined that was what

Wolf was thinking, because he was thinking the same thing himself.

Behind him, the cabin door scraped open, hinges squawking softly. Men's voices sounded. Boots thumped on the porch. Yakima turned to see Mendenhour and the driver and shotgun messenger stepping down off the porch steps and, looking around cautiously, walking across the yard toward Yakima.

"Any sign of them?" the prosecutor asked as he approached.

"Not yet."

"Damn," said the driver, Adlard, tugging worriedly at his beard. "Floyd Betajack and Claw Hendricks? You sure that's who's trailin' us, Mr. Mendenhour?"

"That's who this man said he saw in Wolfville." The attorney scowled at Yakima. "You never told me who you were."

"Said his name was Henry," the shotgun messenger said, the brim of his weathered cream Stetson bending in the chill breeze. Coble's eyes were faintly jeering. "What was it—Yakima Henry? Injun name, I'd say."

Adlard raked his eyes up and down Yakima with faint distaste, then said, "His pa musta been a white man."

"My family history is the least of your worries, you mossy-balled son of a bitch." Yakima smiled to cover the angry burn that had so suddenly wrapped itself around his heart.

"Say," said the stocky shotgun messenger, swaggering forward, "you got no call to talk to Charlie like—"

"That's enough, Coble," intervened the prosecutor, giving the man a commanding look, then turning back to Yakima. "What's your piece of this, Henry?"

The burn stayed with Yakima, and tightly he said,

"You mean—why did I save your bacon back there? Well, now, I don't rightly—"

He was cut off by the scrape of the cabin door again. Looking past the three men standing before him, he watched her move on out of the cabin to stand over the porch steps. She placed a hand on the roof support post beside her, staring toward him.

Chapter 14

She wore an ankle-length black bear coat over her purple velvet traveling dress and a marten fur hat that complemented the rich chestnut of her hair, which was gathered into a ponytail by a wide gold clip. The clipped queue hung forward across her left shoulder. It glistened in the coppery sunlight angling through the high, thin clouds.

Yakima had a memory flash of the ponytail curling down over the alabaster skin of her bare back. . . .

The prosecutor and the other men glanced at her, as well, and then they turned to Yakima once more. "My wife," Mendenhour said with a proprietary air. He was obviously well aware of her attractiveness, her desirableness.

"That's what I understand."

"I hate that she's a part of all this."

"I reckon she's just one of several," Yakima said, sliding his eyes away from her to the driver. "I reckon your responsibility is to all your passengers. How are you going to handle this?"

"Don't try to tell me my business, half-breed!"

"Will you help?" This from Mendenhour. His eyes were no longer as haughty as before. They were faintly beseeching, in fact.

Yakima disliked the man instinctively. He didn't know how much that was the result of his experience with other privileged men like him, and how much his wife.

"I'll pay you," the prosecutor said. "Five hundred dollars if you get us through to Belle Fourche in the Dakota Territory."

"The other passengers want to continue?"

"I've told them how it is," Mendenhour said. "About who those men are out there and what they did to the lawmen in Wolfville. What they want with me. I told them they could stay here, but then they'd of course have to find another way to their destinations. And the stage won't be making its last return trip for the season until after New Year's, so they'll be stuck here for at least three weeks."

"What about you, Mendenhour?" Yakima asked the man. "Did you consider staying here?"

"That's *Mister* Mendenhour," snapped Coble.

Ignoring the shotgun messenger, Yakima held his implacable gaze on the prosecutor.

Mendenhour studied him, tensing his jaw. The nubs of his cheeks flushed. "Why not turn myself over to them?"

"Somethin' like that."

"That would be suicide, Mr. Henry."

The shotgun messenger gritted his teeth as he stared pugnaciously at Yakima. "No need to call this half-breed 'mister,' Mr. Mendenhour. We don't need him. We can get you through to Belle Fourche just fine."

The old driver glanced at his younger partner uncertainly.

"Maybe so," Mendenhour said, "but *Mister* Henry is obviously good with that Winchester. He's already killed four, possibly five of them. I'm right handy with a long gun myself. I have one in the rear luggage boot, and I'm certainly not afraid to use it. I was born and raised out here, and I've fought all manner of hard cases. The four of us aboard a fast stage might just have a chance to save ourselves and keep all innocent bystanders from harm, as well."

Yakima looked at the prosecutor's wife, who had descended the porch steps and was walking toward them. The others turned to watch her, as well. She was like a queen to whom everyone administered and deferred, protected. A beautiful queen who put all the men on edge.

As she approached, Mendenhour said, "Glendolene, you'd best wait in the station house where it's warm."

"I'm sorry to interrupt," she said, glancing only fleetingly, with vague shyness, at Yakima. "But what's this about?"

Mendenhour spoke to Yakima. "I've offered Mr. Henry here the job of escorting us to Belle Fourche. There are few lawmen between here and there, and the only real town we'll be passing through is Jawbone. The sheriff there is no good. A drunkard. We won't be able to depend on him for help."

Glendolene lifted her eyes to Yakima. "What do you say . . . uh . . . Mr. Henry, was it?"

"I say keep your money. Just so happens I'm headin' the same direction." Yakima turned to Glendolene. "How is Mrs. O'Reilly?"

"We've seared the wound closed and bandaged her

arm. She says she's ready for travel. She's very strong. I think she is ready."

"Well," Mendenhour said eagerly, "let's go, then!"

He and the driver and shotgun messenger started walking toward the coach. The hostlers were finished hitching the team to the doubletree and were checking the snaps and buckles.

Glendolene stared at Yakima for another second. then lowered her eyes, turned, and walked back toward the station house.

Yakima rode out ahead of the stage and scouted his back trail from the top of a haystack butte. When the stage had passed safely along the trail that angled around the butte's base, he followed from a distance of about a hundred yards.

He saw no sign that the cutthroats had circled around them and gotten ahead, so he paid close attention to the country flanking him, spying nothing but deer grazing sunny slopes carpeted in grass the same color as their winter coats, and a couple of coyotes meandering along a shallow wash.

It was nearly thirty miles to the next station, and by the time they reached it three and a half hours later, the sky had cleared but the temperature had dropped below freezing. He did not venture into the yard of the station that sat in a hollow amongst rocky escarpments, but kept watch on a high stone shelf on the yard's southern edge.

While Wolf cropped grass behind and below him, he sat in the shelf in the rocks, perusing the country to the southwest through his spyglass. It was all rolling sage- and cedar-stippled hogbacks, dusty green in the winter light. The Snowy and Wind River ranges beyond them formed broad, dark lumps in the south and west. Low hills, box-shaped bluffs, and small mesas swelled against the eastern horizon. The Big Horns loomed like near storm clouds in the north, though they were still about seventy miles away. Yakima knew that the stage trail skirted their southeastern-most slopes around the town of Jawbone.

He glanced at the cabin. The passengers were emerging after a fifteen-minute layover, Glendolene walking beside Mrs. O'Reilly, whose right arm was hooked through a makeshift sling. The air was so quiet he could hear Glendolene's voice tinkling like chimes.

After their first day together, coupling on the big cot in the line shack, they'd dressed together slowly in the sunlight pushing through the two front windows from which he'd thrown back the shutters. They were lethargic from exertion and slumber, and they dressed without speaking, though they exchanged long, admiring glances.

When they'd gone out and saddled their horses, he lifted her up onto her palo's back and said, "You don't want to know my name?"

She shook her head. Her slightly tangled hair danced about her smooth ivory cheeks and shoulders. "Nope!" She laughed and reined the palo away.

"You could tell me yours!" he called after her.

She glanced back, smiling, over her shoulder. "Same time, next week?"

He shrugged.

She turned her head forward and galloped down the long hill and swung right to disappear amongst the stone escarpments. He stood there, still feeling the texture of her ripe body in his hands.

Now he waited until the stage had lurched away

from the relay station behind the lunging team, then mounted Wolf and rode down to the trail. He skirted the yard and the two hostlers—a couple of Indians and a black man—tending the sweaty team in the corral—and headed out after the stage. He kept it just within sight as he rode, casting frequent looks behind.

Still, the cutthroats were staying out of sight. They'd wait and try to catch him and the others off guard. Maybe attack them tonight when they were overnighting at the Hamburg Station on Seven-Mile Creek.

Ten minutes later, he topped a hill to see the stage stopped between two piles of glacial rubble at the hill's bottom. The passengers had climbed out to stand in a semicircle around the driver and the shotgun messenger, the driver on his knees to inspect the right rear wheel.

"What happened?" Yakima said as he rode up.

Charlie Adlard looked up at him, scowling. "Broke the felloe again." He glanced at a rock leaning out from the side of the trail. "The horses swerved to miss that rock there and swung the back end right into it. It wasn't there last week—I'll damn sure tell you that."

He glanced at the three women in the bunch and added sheepishly, "Pardon my tongue, ladies."

Yakima dismounted and led Wolf up along the opposite side of the coach from the group gathered around the driver. A few yards ahead of the team, he found the imprints of one shod horse that had entered the trail from the west. He stared in that direction, saw a jostling brown speck climbing a distant hill.

He cursed under his breath. One man had gotten around him and kicked the rock into the trail.

Yakima tied Wolf to a cedar and walked back up to

where Adlard was talking to Coble and Mendenhour. "One got around me."

"One what?" said Mendenhour.

"Who do you think?"

The men looked at each other. The three women looked at Yakima, fear in their eyes. Then the third woman, the wife of the young, roughly clad young man, turned to Mendenhour. Tears streamed down her flushed cheeks beneath the frayed wool scarf she wore over her head. "It's because of you, isn't it? They're going to kill us all because of you!" She sobbed and turned to her gangling, rawboned husband standing beside her.

"Now, Sally!" the young man said.

"We should have stayed at the last relay station, Percy! But he made it sound like we'd seen the last of those killers!"

"I didn't say that," Mendenhour said defensively.

Mrs. O'Reilly took Sally's arm and led her away from the group and the coach. The young woman—round-faced, snub-nosed, with curly blond hair frizzing out around the scarf—glanced back worriedly at the young man, who stood with the other men, though he looked nearly as frightened as his young wife.

Yakima turned to the driver. "Can you fix the wheel?"

"No, we was just talkin' about that," Adlard said, looking down at the cracked wheel, the iron rim half off, several spokes hanging toward the ground with splintered ends. "I'll have to ride on to the next station and bring one back. Hamburg'll have a spare."

"Too late to go now," Yakima said, staring west. "The sun'll be down long before you get back."

"What do you suggest, Mr. Half-Breed Know-It-All?" said the beefy shotgun messenger, fire in his small light brown eyes set too close to his wedge-shaped nose. "You think we oughta just camp out here with them cutthroats on the prod? One of which, I might add, slipped around your eagle eyes and wrecked the wheel!"

"I say we take the horses and ride to the next station." This from one of the two drummers sitting off away from the larger crowd of drivers and passengers and Yakima.

They were standing together, smoking and holding their own council, regarding the others soberly. The man who'd spoken wore a spruce green bowler with a frayed brim, and a pair of cheap metal spectacles sat atop his nose. His eyes were rheumy, his voice slightly slurred. Yakima had seen him and his friend passing a small, hide-covered traveling flask.

Yakima's back stiffened as raw fury bit him. He held his ground, however. Glendolene stood nearby, watching him uncertainly, flicking her anxious gaze from him to the shotgun rider and back again.

Suddenly, she turned away with a disgusted chuff and walked back into the rocks to stand with Mrs. O'Reilly and the young Sally. Before Yakima could say anything to Coble, Adlard said, "We can't expect the women to ride bareback to the station."

"Maybe not," said the other drummer—short and fat, slightly older than the first, and wearing a cheap brown suit under a long rat-hair coat—"but we two can." He gestured at his younger, bespectacled buddy. "How 'bout if we ride to the next station on two of the stage horses? We'll bring a wheel back in a wagon tomorrow morning."

Yakima looked around at the others. They were staring at the two drummers.

Coble said, "How do we know you'll come back?"

"We'd have to come back," said the younger drummer, taking a pull from the flask. "How else we gonna get off this backside of the devil's ass? No other coaches. No trains that I can see."

"You might take saddle hosses," said Adlard. "And leave us high and dry."

"We stay together," Mendenhour ordered. "There's safety in numbers."

"Frankly, Mr. Mendenhour . . . ," said the older drummer, stopping when Yakima, having had enough, swung around and walked away from the group with a subtle, frustrated air. Let the cows chew their cud. He retrieved his horse and led him off the east side of the rocks and down a hill at the bottom of which stood ponderosa pines and aspens.

"Where you goin'?" the driver called, looking insulted.

Yakima stopped. They were all looking at him peevishly.

"I'm makin' camp down there at the bottom of the hill. If any of you has any brains, that's what you'll do, too, and wait for tomorrow to fetch another wheel."

He didn't trust the two drummers farther than he could throw them together from one end of a large barn to the other. He didn't trust any of the men from the stage, and he didn't trust the women, either. Throw Glendolene Mendenhour into that category. He figured she'd married well. Any woman who looked like her could have about any man she wanted. But finally meeting the man she *had* married was a big disappointment.

She'd been right about one thing—the less they knew about each other, the better. He'd liked her better when he hadn't known her name or who she was or anything else about her aside from the fact that she was beautiful and was even more beautiful naked and writhing on a crude cot in the summer sunshine. He trusted Trudy Shackleford more than he trusted Glendolene Mendenhour.

To hell with all of them.

What the hell was he doing here?

Why didn't he just ride on? His only real obligation was to the man who'd saved his life.

He continued down the hill and into the trees.

Chapter 15

When he got to the bottom of the hill, he scanned the hill rising beyond it. It was a steep slope carpeted in forest duff and bristling with sparse pines, firs, and upthrust chunks of pitted dark gray granite. He saw an opening about halfway up the slope and led Wolf to it, slipping a couple of times on the slick needles and fallen pinecones.

He inspected the spot. Judging it relatively level and well sheltered by both trees and humps of granite and sandstone of various sizes, he decided he'd throw down here, build a small fire. He'd camp alone. He had no desire to be anywhere near the others.

Funny how at times when he was alone he felt a prickling need for human companionship. Only, when he found that companionship it was, more often than not, far from companionable. Humans were the rottenest of creatures. He had no delusions that he himself was any different, but he had no choice but to tolerate himself. Amongst others, he found himself yearning to be back alone in some remote stretch of mountain range or saguaro-studded desert plain—just himself, Wolf, and the wind.

He let the black graze on the slope beneath his own niche in the rocks and took his rifle and climbed to a high, rocky perch, where he had a good view to the south and east. Since the one cutthroat had come from the west, it was likely that more would come from a different direction, and he didn't want to get caught with his pants down.

As he sat there, cleaning the rifle with an oily handkerchief, voices and the snapping of pine needles rose on his left. The others from the stage were moving down the hill through the pines, the men hauling and dragging luggage. Yakima kept a sharp eye on the larger area around them, knowing they could be attacked at any time, but he glanced occasionally at the other passengers—the driver and the shotgun messenger must have been caring for the horses—setting up a camp in the crease between the hills.

Mendenhour chose a sheltered area abutted on Yakima's side by the steep, rocky hill and on the other side by the shallower slope and the trees. There was a thin stream farther south along the crease, and he saw Glendolene and the other young woman, Sally, walk toward it. Yakima watched the women closely, because the men seemed too careless about the women separating themselves from the group. The men themselves—the grumbling drummers, the young honyocker, and the prosecutor—conversed tonelessly while they set up a rudimentary camp, rummaging through luggage for whatever camping gear they had amongst them, and gathered firewood.

It was after three, and this time of year the sun sank fast. Soon it was down behind the Wind River Range in the west, and the crease was in shadow. Adlard and Coble led the horses down to the water and picketed them on a long rope strung between trees in the tall, saffron-colored brush.

The others sat moodily around their fire, Glendolene near her husband, the redheaded Mrs. O'Reilly near Glendolene, reclining against a steamer trunk, several blankets covering her. The wounded woman almost seemed to be enjoying the campout, for she stared dreamily into the fire, one arm hooked behind her head. The other arm was suspended by a cotton sling.

Yakima cursed under his breath, then climbed down out of the rocks and walked down to where Wolf stood ground-tied. He pulled the sack of gold out of the saddlebag pouch, hid it amongst the rocks, then mounted up and rode down into the passengers' camp. He stopped at the edge of the firelight, reached back for his saddlebags, and dropped them on the ground near where the young honyocker couple sat together in moody silence, sipping water from a single tin cup.

"Coffee and other supplies in there," he said. "A couple pounds of jerky, salt pork, some beans." He looked at Mendenhour. "If you're gonna have a fire, keep in mind them killers will see it, and you'd best keep a close watch."

With that, he swung Wolf around and rode on up the hill through the trees. Passing the stage, he continued into the open country west of it.

"I don't know about him," said Melvin Coble. He was staring suspiciously up the dark slope in the direction the half-breed had disappeared half an hour ago.

"What do you mean—you don't know about him?" Glendolene asked as she forked salt pork around in the half-breed's cast-iron skillet.

She and the young woman, whose name she'd learned was Sally Rand, had built up the fire for cooking, and they were throwing a meal together with Yakima Henry's generously proffered supplies. Glendolene looked again at the shotgun messenger crouched on the other side of the fire from her. Coble was still staring broodingly up the slope while absently poking a stick in the crackling flames.

"What do I mean?" the man said in his customarily snide, angry tone. "What I mean is, who is he really? And how do we really know about all that went on back in Wolfville?"

Lee was standing a ways off, smoking a cigar while he stared southward along the dark crease between the hills, his back to the fire. He glanced over his shoulder, gray smoke billowing around his head. "You mean, you think he's lying?"

The others were looking at Coble now with interest. "How would I know? But if he was in jail in Wolfville, how do we know he didn't escape and kill them lawmen himself? How do we know he wasn't in with Betajack and Hendricks? Maybe he got crossways with them over somethin'."

"Over what?" asked Charlie Adlard.

"Have you seen how one of his saddlebags pouches?" Coble shrugged and grinned at his partner, showing a chipped front tooth glowing in the firelight. "Maybe he stole loot off of 'em. In fact, maybe them killers ain't after Mr. Mendenhour at all. Maybe they're after the breed." He arched a wolfish brow at the prosecutor.

"So, what's he doing here?" Mendenhour asked,

turning around to face the fire, holding his stogie down low by his side, turning it thoughtfully between his thumb and index finger.

"You said it yourself, sir," said the older of the two drummers, whose name was Kearny. "There's safety in numbers."

"That's ridiculous!" Glendolene said, unable to keep from laughing in exasperation. "Why would he throw in with us when he's obviously much more capable of taking care of himself than any of us are!"

She shot a quick, vaguely accusatory look at her husband, who scowled as though he'd been slapped.

"Hold your tongue, Glen," he said with a mild threat in his voice. "He might have gotten the drop on those cutthroats earlier today, but any one of us could probably have dropped as many as he did. I'm right handy with that Winchester over there."

"For heaven's sake, Lee," she said, wishing she could stop herself from continuing, "he gave us the food we're about to eat! And he's the only one out there in the darkness, probably keeping an eye on the camp!"

"How do we know he's keeping an eye on the camp?" asked the younger drummer, Kimble Sook, who was carefully filling his traveling flask from a whiskey bottle. "Maybe he just dumped this gear to lighten his load."

Adlard looked down at the saddlebags. "Yeah, and look there—he took whatever was bulging his saddle-bag pouch right along with him! That's it! I got a feelin' Melvin's right. I got a feelin' it's the breed *himself* that Betajack and Hendricks is after. Not Mendenhour at all!"

"What about Preston Betajack?" Glendolene said. "You think his father has forgotten about him?"

"No," Lee said, "but how would he know I was aboard the stage?"

"I don't believe it," she said, shaking her head. "He wouldn't do that."

All eyes turned to her. She felt the heat of them, hotter than the fire. She glanced at Lee, who stood frowning at her curiously. Glendolene turned away from him, silently castigating herself for having taken part in the conversation as she resumed forking the side pork around in the pan. She hadn't eaten all day, but she wasn't hungry; in fact, the food was making her feel queasy again.

Sally Rand huddled down in her old, patched wool coat and gave a shiver against the intensifying chill. "Injuns scare me. What're we gonna do about him? If he's not gone, I mean?"

"Don't you worry, honey," her husband, Percy Rand, said, hardening his eyes and fumbling an old cap-and-ball pistol out of his coat pocket. "He comes near you, I'll put a bullet in him."

"You ask me, I think you're all crazier'n bedbugs!" Lori O'Reilly hadn't said anything all night, and all eyes turned to her now, incredulous. "And we should think about nice things, not bad things—like what we want to do to Mr. Henry just because his skin is a little darker than ours. After all, as Mrs. Mendenhour said, we will be eating his food tonight. Good Lord, folks!"

"Ah, shut up, Lori," intoned the driver. "We all know where the doc found you. You probably preferred men like him!"

Glendolene gasped in shock, staring from the driver to Lori O'Reilly, who seemed to take umbrage with neither the man's harsh tone nor what he'd implied. In fact, she seemed quite amused by it, laughing heartily, throwing her head back against her steamer trunk.

"That ain't no way for you to talk to Mrs. O'Reilly," scolded the old prospector, Elijah Weatherford, sitting on a rock at the far end of the firelight from Glendolene. He heaved himself to his feet, crouching and pointing at the jehu. "You apologize, Charlie, or by God I'll drag out my bowie knife and cut your *guts* out!"

His eyes flicked down to the bone handle of the knife jutting from the top of his stovepipe boot.

"Stop it!" squealed Sally Rand, closing her mittened hands over her ears and squeezing her eyes closed. "Please, stop! I can't take any more of this!"

Her eyes snapped wide as a rifle spoke twice in the distance.

Fifteen minutes before, Yakima had ridden Wolf into a dry wash half a mile west of the passengers' camp. He slipped out of the saddle, tied the reins to an upthrust branch of a log that had been deposited here by a previous spring flood, one end buried in the sand and gravel, then very quietly pumped a cartridge into the rifle's breech.

He stood staring up a low hill on the far side of the wash. Stars were out and a thumbnail moon rose in the southeast, showing a strip of solid gray rock topping the rise. From the other side of the rise, smoke rose. He couldn't see it, but whenever the slight breeze gusted like an exhaled breath, he could smell it.

A wood fire. Rabbit roasting on it. Coffee cooking, too.

Wolf turned to him but did not nicker or even

jangle his bit chains. The horse knew from experience something was about to happen, though he didn't know what, and his own blood was up.

Yakima ran a reassuring hand down the black's long snoot, over the white blaze, staring toward the gray rock topping the rise, then stole slowly forward and up the far side of the wash. Just as slowly, striding assuredly, avoiding all obstacles, he climbed the rise at an angle toward the western end.

It was a cold night, the sky so clear that he imagined he could hear the stars crackling. Far to the west a pair of wolves howled. As he continued climbing, the sound of voices came to him.

His heartbeat quickened. That the voices belonged to members of Floyd Betajack's and Claw Hendricks's crew he had little doubt. How many were holed up on the other side of the ridge? If it was the entire crew, he'd have his work cut out for him.

He climbed to where the caprock protruded from the top of the rise's west end, and crouched down, looking around the stone spine and into the hollow down the other side.

Three men hunkered around a low fire, the flames dancing and twisting like several separate devils, smoke and sparks rising from their jagged tips. Two big, skinned rabbits roasted on sharpened willow branches far enough back from the flames that they wouldn't burn. Yakima could see the grease glistening against the cooking meat, dribbling down the sides, sputtering in the fire, and his mouth watered.

The meal at the relay station hadn't held him.

He looked at the three men, saw the furs and leather they were dressed in. One was a black man. Many guns and knives flashed about them in the fire's flickering light.

One had a rifle across his knees as he sat looking at the other two lounging against their saddles. This man wore wool mittens with the fingers cut out. They were all holding smoking tin cups.

Three unsaddled horses milled down the slope beyond them, maybe fifty yards away. Two of the mounts stood head to head, still as dark statues, while the third grazed a little farther off. The wind was from the south, so they shouldn't detect Yakima until he no longer cared.

Soundlessly, weaving between small boulders, the half-breed stole straight down the slope on his moccasin-clad feet and then swung toward the fire, moving in.

Chapter 16

"What was that?" one of the three men around the fire said.

"What was what?"

Yakima rose from behind the boulder he'd stolen up to, and snapped the Henry to his shoulder, raking the hammer back. "I think he means this."

They all jerked at once, reaching for near rifles or sliding hands toward pistols on their hips.

"Uh-uh," he said. "Now, why would you wanna go and kick up a racket on such a peaceful night . . . and get yourselves killed?"

They all froze at once, dark eyes finding him now in the darkness about fifteen yards southwest of their camp. The one in the middle wore buckskins and a long sheepskin coat with a wool collar on the outside of which three guns and two knives were holstered. His dark face was decorated in black and white war paint. He had one hand wrapped around a knife handle, the other around pistol grips.

"Raise those hands above your head," Yakima said.

When they all hesitated, he said it again, more softly:

"You got one second before I kick up a helluva racket myself."

They raised their hands shoulder high.

"Get 'em higher."

They did. The one on the far right—a black man in a gray wolf coat and black, round-brimmed hat with a red scarf underneath—began to rise. "Uh-uh," Yakima said. "I prefer you sittin'."

The black man relaxed, the silver trimmings on his brown leather leggings flashing in the firelight. Yakima stepped out from around the boulder, keeping the Yellowboy aimed straight out from his right shoulder, narrowing that eye as he aimed down the barrel, his jaw hard, lips a dark red knife slash.

"What're you doin' out here?"

He had a good idea, but he wanted to be sure. He'd thought there'd been a slender chance they weren't part of Betajack and Hendricks's crew, but with all the weaponry around them, that chance was getting as fine as a cat's whisker.

They slid their eyes to each other, and then the man on the left, a beefy white man with a cream felt sombrero shoved back off his broad forehead, said haltingly, "We . . . we're just—"

No point in letting him waste time making up a lie.

"Forget it. Where's Betajack and Hendricks, the rest of your bunch?"

They slid eyes around again before the Indian said, "Who, mister?" His voice was low, toneless.

"I want a straight answer from one of you in three seconds, or that racket I just mentioned is going to occur in half a pull of a whore's bell."

The beefy man said, "West, fer chrissakes! You wanna go over and say hi?"

"How far west?"

"Half mile. Hell, I don't know. Maybe a mile."

"We didn't measure it," said the black man, holding his gloved hands about around his black hat brim.

"All right, good," Yakima said, sliding the rifle barrel from the black man to the beefy one, then slowly back again. "Here's what I want you to do. . . ."

The Indian's eyes widened as he dropped a hand toward the big bowie knife he wore in a beaded sheath against his belly.

The Yellowboy roared.

The Indian jerked backward, grunting as he continued to slap at the knife handle.

Yakima levered another shell and fired again, watching dust puff from the dead center of the man's sheepskin. The slug blew him off his heels before he twisted around and fell on his belly, grunting and jerking.

The other two had just closed hands around gun handles when Yakima's second spent cartridge clinked off the rock behind him, and he aimed down the barrel of the freshly cocked rifle, planting a bead on the center of the beefy gent's ruddy forehead.

That stopped them both. They stared wide-eyed and tight-lipped at Yakima.

The half-breed looked at the Indian, who lay belly-down on the fire's far side, quivering as though he'd fallen on a nest of rattlesnakes. "Nope," he said, "that wasn't what I had in mind."

He planted the Winchester's sights on the black man's wrinkled forehead. The black man raised his arms higher above his head, as did the beefy gent. "Now, see all the racket that made?"

"Shore did," said the black man solemnly.

The beefy white man shifted his weight from one knee to the other, fidgeting.

"I know why you three are here," Yakima said. "Because it's easier for three to move in on a camp on a night this quiet. Which means you know where me an' the others are camped."

"What's your piece of this, breed?" asked the black man with frustration, spreading the fingers of his hands thrust high above his head. "What's your stake in it? We're just after Mendenhour. What the hell you care what happens to him?"

The beefy gent said, "Mendenhour hanged the wrong Betajack, see? We ride for Betajack, and we know for certain sure that young Pres did not rustle them hosses, like the prosecutor said he did. The man Pres bought them horses from done lied and Neumiller and Mendenhour believed him because they been wantin' to make an example of Betajack ever since he got elected."

Yakima stared at him. He didn't really care what was true or not true. At this point, it didn't make any difference. He'd bought chips in this game, so he had to play it out.

Yakima cursed as he walked over to the black man. Keeping the gun leveled on his belly, he reached down and pulled the man's saddle blanket out from beneath his saddle. He tossed it down in front of the fire, kicked the corners wide so it lay flat. He ordered the two men before him to disarm themselves as well as the dead Indian, and to toss the Indian's and their own pistols and knives onto the blanket.

They did so reluctantly.

Just as reluctantly, they tossed over their and the Indian's carbines.

"Now your boots."

"Now our what?" said the black man.

Yakima just stared at him.

When both men had kicked out of their boots and stood there glaring from across the dwindling flames at Yakima, who stood behind the blanket heaped with guns, knives, and boots, the half-breed said, "When you see 'em again, tell your bosses I aim to kill 'em."

The two men glanced at each other, incredulous. The beefy man squinted one eye and arched the brow over the other eye at Yakima. "Tell them what?"

"Tell 'em I'm gonna kill 'em if they keep comin'. Tell 'em Yakima Henry sent you. I'm the man who beefed about six of Claw Hendricks's men the other day, and I intend to finish off the whole damn bunch of his men and Betajack's men . . . if you keep movin'."

The beefy white man laughed. "That's what they said about you. They aim to cut your ears off, breed. And I think they got a better chance because, hell, you're only one man!" He laughed again.

"You'll see how many men I fight like if your bosses keep comin'." Yakima narrowed a hard green eye. "You tell 'em that . . . when you see 'em again."

Quickly, keeping his rifle aimed on the two cut-throats, he folded the blanket into three points and then tied the points together with a strip of rawhide he found among the cutthroats' gear. Rifle barrels and rear stocks stuck out of the pack as he tossed it over his shoulder, gave a parting glance at the two men before him, then backed over to where their horses grazed from picket pins.

He cut the ropes tying the horses to the pins and

fired two shots over the horses' heads. The mounts whinnied and galloped off into the night.

Yakima strode toward the west end of the ridge. He looked back toward the fire several times. The two bootless cutthroats hadn't moved. They continued staring at him in hushed awe until he'd disappeared along with their horses in the night.

Yakima stopped Wolf west of the stage trail. Ahead, the stagecoach sat silhouetted in the darkness, moonlight glistening on the brass rail that ran around the roof. He'd heard something—the slightest squawk of a thoroughbrace in the coach's undercarriage.

A figure squatted atop the roof. A gun flashed against the figure, and Yakima threw himself off Wolf's back to hit the ground on his shoulder. He came up firing his Colt, purposely missing his target, watching the man give a terrified scream and drop to the stage's roof, squealing.

Wolf gave a shrill whinny, turned sharply, and, trailing his reins, galloped wildly off to the north. His hammering front hooves missed Yakima by mere inches. "Hold your fire! Hold your fire!" shouted another man crouched behind the stagecoach's slanting tongue. "Goddamn it, that's Coble!"

"I figured." Yakima heaved himself to his feet, pistol smoking. He glanced to his left. Wolf was still galloping, though beginning to slow, snorting angrily.

Fury was an exploding keg of dynamite in the halfbreed's chest. He stared through his pistol smoke wafting around him toward the stage, where the shotgun messenger was rising to his knees. "Who's *that*?" he asked.

Charlie Adlard said angrily, "The breed, goddamn it!"

"Well, hell," Coble said, "how was I supposed to know that?"

"You weren't," Yakima said, his calm tone belying his fury. He was walking toward the stage, shaking the spent shells from his Colt's wheel and replacing them with fresh from his cartridge belt. "You were just supposed to start shootin'."

As he stopped in front of the stage, the shotgun messenger stared down at him, holding his pistol down low but aimed cautiously at Yakima. His voice was slow, defensive, as he said, "Figured you'd pulled out."

Yakima reached up quickly, grabbed the man's left ankle, and jerked it out from beneath him. "Hey!"

Thump!

"Ah, you son of a bitch!" Coble yelled, writhing around supine on the coach's roof. His pistol bounced off the roof, as well, and dropped over the edge to land at Yakima's feet.

"What the hell is going on over here?" It was Mendenhour, stepping out around the far side of the stage to stand beside the driver. "Don't we have enough trouble without you men shooting at each other?"

His wife walked up behind him, though Yakima could only see her silhouette in the darkness. Because of the shooting, she was sticking close to her husband. That was wise. Yakima didn't like it in some vaguely primitive way, but there it was. He didn't like anything about this night. Or the past three days . . .

"I think he broke my back!" complained Coble, leaning forward on his knees and hooking an arm behind him.

Yakima looked from Mendenhour's wife to the prosecutor to the driver. "You'll find a blanket full of guns and knives out there where my horse left it. I suggest you haul it in and do something useful with them."

"Such as?" Mendenhour asked.

"Make sure everyone's armed. And I'd move your camp. The horses, too. They know where we are. No more fires."

Yakima walked away to the northwest.

"Where're you going?" the driver said.

"To fetch my horse," Yakima said, staring forward. "Where the hell you think I'm goin'?"

When Yakima had walked down Wolf, he rode back to his niche in the rocks on the far side of the crease between the hills. He watched as the others doused their fire and moved their camp farther north along the crease, their jostling shadows disappearing behind him.

He sat there atop the scarp, his legs hanging over the edge, his Yellowboy across his knees. The cool air kept him awake. That and the knowledge that Betajack and Hendricks could be stealing up on him and the others from any direction.

He knew that his message to the cutthroat leaders could very well be taken as a challenge, and it likely would be. But it would also give them something to chew on, too. Some men knew his name, as he'd had to kill quite a few men in his thirty-odd years. Some of the living might think twice—or at least one and a half times, anyway—about taking him on.

It might make Betajack and Hendricks hesitate. Men

who hesitated were easier to take down than men who didn't. He'd become one of those who didn't. Not when the chips were down and all players were showing their cards. Word had gotten around.

It was a quiet night.

The morning was a little louder.

"Hey, breed," Melvin Coble said, yelling up from the bottom of the scarp. "Come down here. Wanna have a little chat with your half-breed ass this mornin'."

Chapter 17

"Someone's comin'," said a man squatting atop the cut-bank, across from where Floyd Betajack, Claw Hendricks, and their near-dozen men were lounging around two small cook fires.

It was sometime in the very early morning.

Some of the men were snoring under animal skins and hats; others were playing cards. One—Miguel "Wolf" Calabasas—slowly strummed a mandolin with surprising sonorousness for a man who'd killed enough men to make him wanted in nearly every territory west of the Mississippi and in several Mexican provinces.

He was the best of Betajack's men—one of about seven he still had on his roll. An old gun hand from Santa Cruz, he was even a better killer than Albert Delmonte. Betajack was getting too old to do much bank, train, or payroll robbing or rustling anymore, so he'd been legitimizing his ranch business, actually bringing some seed bulls over from Missouri, until Dave Neumiller had arrested Betajack's oldest son, Pres, for stealing horses after the sheriff had killed two of Pres's partners. A trumped-up charge, that. Cold-blooded murder.

Now the veteran of the War of Northern Aggression needed every good gun he had left on his roll, and on Claw Hendricks's roll, too, though Betajack had grudgingly partnered up with the man. Betajack saw Hendricks as a wild grizzly, mostly rogue—one of the younger breed of outlaw with few principles. Claw hired men like himself—dull-witted, cold-steel artists—who were better at murder and rape than stealing. Send the pistoleros to Buffalo Bill's Wild West show, was how Betajack saw such nonsense.

You didn't need men who were randy as hogs and fast with a gun. You needed men who could shoot straight without hesitating when the chips were down.

The old war veteran and train robber scoffed at the whole affair, and grunted as he heaved his old, creaking bones up out of his deerskins, cursing his age. It was cold out here, and his fifty-three-year-old marrow felt frozen solid. He hitched his double-gun rig around his ever-broadening waist, under his long buffalo coat, slid his knives into the sheaths strapped to his chest, and walked over to the base of the bank.

"Who is it?" he asked the man squatting there, beside a gnarled cedar.

They had only one man on scout, because they had three more positioned closer to the stage passengers' camp. It was highly unlikely any of the passengers, including the half-breed, would try to turn the tables and bushwhack them, Betajack and Hendricks.

"Two men," said Wiley Scroll, one of Hendricks's boys from Oklahoma. The lone scout stood and walked out a ways from the cedar and the dry wash, cradling his carbine in his crossed arms. The vapor of his breath jetted around his hatted head.

Claw Hendricks yawned and came over from his own spread gear, smoothing a lock of dark red hair back from his scarred, freckled forehead and donning his black opera hat. He thumped his rose-colored glasses up his nose, and said, "Prob'ly grub-line riders out of work since the roundup. Send 'em on their way, Scroll."

"If it's grub-line riders," Scroll said, "they ain't ridin'. They appear to be *walkin'*."

Hendricks had started to turn away, but now he turned to face northwest again. He glanced at Betajack, but the old train robber squinted into the night, even his old ears now picking up the soft thumps of men walking toward him. His old eyes picked up the silhouettes of—sure enough—men *walking* toward the wash. Two men. Walking about ten feet apart. White socks shone in the darkness.

"What the hell . . . ?" said Sonny, coming up behind his father, tucking his tangled blond hair under his hat.

Sonny climbed the bank in three strides. Betajack climbed halfway up, but he lost his footing and lurched backward. Throwing an arm up, he said, "Help me here, damn it!"

Hendricks half turned and he and Sonny quickly grabbed the older man's arms and pulled the grunting, wheezing Betajack on up the side of the wash. "You all right?" Hendricks asked, chuckling wryly as the older outlaw caught his breath.

Betajack gave a caustic snort, jerked his arms out of the younger men's grips, and walked forward until he was standing left of Scroll. Hendricks walked up to stand left of Betajack, as did Sonny, all four staring at the two men now walking heavily toward them, the vapor of their strained breath visible. They were sighing and grunting and breathing hard, dragging their feet. One of the socks of the man on the right had curled down over the end of his foot, and he was half dragging it as he walked.

The two stopped about ten feet in front of Betajack, Sonny, Hendricks, and Scroll. The others were moving up out of the wash to stand around behind them, curious. Calabasas had stopped strumming the mandolin he took with him everywhere.

Hendricks placed his fists on his hips as he said, "*Simms? Soot? That you?* Where's your damn *horses?*"

The beefy gent in a low-crowned sombrero merely hung his head, leaning forward, slouching wearily, thick arms hanging straight down before him.

The black man, Soot Early, said, "Got caught unawares, Mistuh Claw."

"You got caught with your pants down, you mean!" This from Betajack, who stared at both men with his lower jaw hanging.

Sonny laughed.

"Shut up, Sonny," said Betajack.

Sonny scowled.

"You fellas were supposed to be watching that stage so's you could let us know when they pulled out!" Hendricks had lunged forward like an angry bulldog, barking the words. "You were supposed to sit tight, keep an eye on them people!" He pointed in the general direction of the stage passengers' camp. His face was concealed by the darkness, but Betajack knew the man was embarrassed by the negligence of his crew so far, when he'd been wanting so hard to prove what a great outlaw he was. A great outlaw himself and a *leader* to others.

Simms said nothing. He stood with his chin dipped toward his chest, his broad hat covering his face. Soot Early doffed his own hat and held it over his chest as though in supplication to a couple of higher powers. "Mistuh Claw, Mistuh Betajacks, suhs, we wasn't jumped by just anybody. We was jumped by the green-eyed half-breed."

"So?" said Betajack and Hendricks simultaneously, scowling their exasperation.

"His name's Henry, suhs," Simms said, the whites of his eyes reflecting the light of the fire flickering behind Betajack, Sonny, Hendricks, Scroll, and the other men who'd spread out along the bank of the wash. "Yakima Henry."

Betajack looked at Hendricks. "Mean anything to you?"

"Nah," said the big man in the top hat, shaking his head slowly as he stared at the two men standing before him like castigated schoolboys. "Nah, I never . . ." He let his voice trail off before raking his thumb back and forth across the nub of his chin. "Wait a minute. . . . Yeah . . . yeah, I've heard of a Yakima Henry. A gun wolf. Damn near wiped out an entire gang of despera-does down in Arizona, because they stole his horse. Did some work down in Mexico, too, against the *Rura-les*, I heard. Really piled up the bodies." Hendricks nodded slowly. "Yeah, I heard of him."

"All right, so you heard of him. And you left him alive when you could have blown them two green eyes out of his head back in Wolfville!"

"Ah, hell, it don't matter," said Hendricks, holding up his hands, palm out, trying to soothe the old man's ruffled feathers. "He's just one man. A man like any other. True, I made a mistake and he's caused us some problems, but I'll make it good, Floyd. I'll make it good!"

He enjoyed calling Betajack "Floyd" in front of their men, to show how close they'd become.

"Suhs," Early said. "He told me an' Kitchen here to tell you that if you keep after that stage, he's going to see to it he kills the both of you."

Betajack stared blankly at the black pistoleer, as did Hendricks, who gave an uncertain chuckle.

"Good to know," Betajack said, not liking the faint note of apprehension he heard being strummed in the back of his head. Where the hell had that come from? Had he gotten so old he feared the threat of one severely outgunned half-breed? "Good to know," he added, louder, thrusting his shoulders back. "But he's the one who's gonna die hard. No, sir, no man's ever died harder than he's gonna die, and that's *bond*!"

"Pa, that's what you done said—"

"Shut up, Sonny!" intoned both Betajack and Hendricks, making the little blond, oddly feminine coyote flush and scowl at the ground again.

"What about these two damn pullet-brained, tinhorn heel-squatters?" Betajack asked Hendricks, pointing at the two bootless men before him.

"What about them?" Hendricks said, seemingly glad to have the subject changed. "I'll tell you how I handle this sorta thing. This here is how I handle it."

Two of his pistols were in his hands in a lightning flash. They resembled a lightning flash, too. Two lightning flashes lapping simultaneously at Early and Simms, the reports sounding like cannon fire in the quiet night.

Kitchen and Simms screamed and flew straight backward as the .45 slugs shredded their hearts. They hit the ground on their backs, side by side, groaning and kicking their stocking feet as though trying to gain their feet and run.

But they were all done running.

The men behind Betajack and Hendricks muttered and mumbled, shifting around uncomfortably. Hendricks ignored them as he turned toward his colleague and respected mentor. "That how you do it?"

Betajack looked at the two fast-dying and still-quivering men on the ground before him, and grinned. He spared a fond look at his younger partner. "You'll do, Claw. You'll do."

Hendricks took that as a compliment. He spun his smoking pistols and dropped them into their holsters with a flourish.

"Want us to ride over and hit 'em, Pa?" asked Sonny, reclaiming his self-respect. "Hit 'em hard? Kill the half-breed and bring Mendenhour over here so we can stretch some hemp and get back home in time for Christmas?"

"What's the matter, son—you got some sparkin' to do back in Wolfville? Maybe enjoy another visit to the Silk Slipper?" Betajack grinned crookedly at his younger and, as of two days ago, his only boy. "Enjoyed that, did you?"

Betajack always swelled with pride when Sonny showed hints of genuine manliness. Sonny hesitated, shrugged. "Just see no point in draggin' things out. They're stranded over there without a wheel. Now, why don't we go over there and—"

Crack!

The sharp report of the old outlaw's open right hand

slammed across his son's left cheek caused all the killers around him to take one step straight back with sudden starts. Even Hendricks reacted, arching his brows above his glasses.

"Mendenhour done hanged my older boy for no good reason, and you 'spect me to make it *easy* for him? You 'spect me to make it *quick*? So you can get home for *Christmas*?"

Sonny held a hand to his left cheek and stared at his father, who was about three inches taller than Sonny was, and much broader, as well. Floyd Betajack was built like a bare-knuckle fighter—a lightning-fast pummeler—and he had the soul-deep reckless, unpredictable edge for it, too. Sonny knew that when you crossed him, however unwittingly, you just stood there and kept your mouth shut and hoped the storm blew itself out fast, and that you still had all your limbs, both balls, and your tongue on the other side of it.

"No, no," Betajack said. "We're gonna make this slow. That lawyer is sweatin' salt licks over there by now, holed up out in the cold with his wife. He knows we could hit him whenever we want." He shook his head slowly as he stepped forward and looked westward. "No, no. We ain't gonna make this easy on him at all."

Silence except for the milling of the horses in the brush on the wash's far side. The fire snapped and sputtered. A coyote began yammering from maybe a hundred yards away, as though in eerie accompaniment to Betajack's words.

"No, this ain't gonna be easy for Mendenhour. In fact, I know a way to make it even harder." Betajack turned to look at the men standing around behind him, including his sullen younger son and the bearded

Claw Hendricks in his glasses and top hat and long horse-hair coat. "Anyone got a white flag of some kind? Part of a white sheet?"

They all just stared at him, as though he'd gone mad.

That struck him as funny. For the first time since learning that his older boy, Pres, had been hanged by Neumiller and Mendenhour, Floyd Betajack clapped his hands and laughed.

"Forget Christmas, Sonny," he said, tugging the kid's hat brim down over his eyes. "You wasn't gettin' nothin', anyways."

Betajack laughed again. The others laughed with him, albeit nervously. All except Sonny, that is.

Chapter 18

"Come on down here, breed," the shotgun messenger repeated. "Come on down here. Let's chat. Men to breed."

Someone else chuckled.

Yakima sighed, gained his feet, then leaped lithely down off the top of the scarp. He held his Yellowboy in his right hand as he walked down out of the tight corridor of rocks to where Coble and the two drummers, Kearny and Sook, stood at the scarp's edge.

Both drummers wore pistols that Yakima had provided from the Betajack-Hendricks men—the grips protruding from their coat pockets. Coble had his own pistol holstered on his right hip, and one of the new weapons wedged behind his cartridge belt, over his shaggy, molting wolf coat. He held a double-barreled sawed-off shotgun up high against his chest.

He wore a nasty glint in his little eyes as he said, "We wanna get a few things straight, breed."

"All right, let's straighten things out."

"What's your beef with Betajack and Hendricks?"

Yakima canted his head to one side. "What do you think it is?"

The older, fatter drummer, Kearny, said, "We'd like to hear it from you, if you don't mind."

"We noticed you had a mighty full saddlebag pouch," said the other, younger drummer, Kimble Sook, standing to the left of the beefy shotgunner, smiling knowingly. "We was wondering if . . ."

"Shut up, Sook," said Coble, keeping his bright, challenging eyes on Yakima. "We wanna hear it from him."

"All you're going to hear from me is the sound of my fist hammering your face if you don't walk away, Coble. I've had enough of your shit." Yakima slid his hard jade gaze from one drummer to the other standing with the fur of their heavy coats and the brims of their shabby bowler hats blowing in the cold morning breeze. "You two really want in on this?"

Their faces were red from the cold, but they turned a shade darker. Hesitation touched their eyes.

"That how you want it?" asked Coble. "Bare knuckles?"

"That's how you seem to want it," Yakima said.

"All right," the shotgunner said, and lowered his coach gun. "I'll set this down if you set that Winchester down, and then we'll go at it like—"

"Coble!"

The shotgunner stopped and turned to his left. The old man with the tangled beard hanging to his belly, Elijah Weatherford, stood thirty yards away. He held one of the rifles Yakima had hauled in. He was scowling bright-eyed at the shotgunner, who barked, "Can't you see I'm busy over here, old man?"

Weatherford jerked his head to indicate behind him,

where Adlard and Mendenhour stepped out from the mouth of a corridor in the caprock and stared toward Yakima's party.

"Adlard's headin' out to fetch the wheel. Maybe you could take up your business later?"

Adlard said something to Mendenhour, then beckoned to Coble and started down the hill toward the crease, where the horses were picketed amongst the aspens and pines.

Coble looked at Yakima. "We'll talk again"—his eyes flicked at something in the niche behind Yakima—"'bout you and the gold."

Yakima glanced over his right shoulder. The pouch about the size of a five-pound sugar sack sat on the ground, leaning against a side of the stony niche, where Yakima had put it before he'd delivered the saddlebags to the passengers. He looked back at the shotgun messenger, who grinned foxily.

"So it is gold," Coble said. "I figured that hump in one of your saddlebag pouches was either that or a man's head. Just a hunch, but I'm right, ain't I?"

Yakima felt his jaw harden. "You're playin' it mighty close to the edge, Coble. But, yeah, anytime you like."

Coble turned and stomped away. The drummer glanced warily at Yakima and then hurried along behind him. Meanwhile, the old prospector walked toward Yakima, the ends of the thick green scarf tying his wool watch cap to his head blowing in the breeze.

"Don't tell me you're in with them," Yakima said wearily.

"I ain't in with nobody. But you'd best watch your back, mister."

"Tell me somethin' I don't already know—Weatherford, ain't it?"

He nodded. "You're Yakima Henry?"

Yakima frowned, puzzled. "That's right."

Weatherford gave him a look of vaguely fond remembrance.

Yakima stared at him, the wind blowing the half-breed's long black hair around the scarf he had tied over his ears and knotted beneath his chin, strands touching cheeks he could no longer feel because of the cold. "You got me at a disadvantage, friend."

"I was one of the freighters drifting through Thornton's Roadhouse now and then. Seen you workin' there. I was there, in fact, the night them fellas tried to cut that whore you saved and ended up havin' to shoot your way out of the place with, on account o' the white men you sent to Glory." Weatherford looked around, closing his shaggy gray brows down over his liquid blue eyes, puzzled. "What was her name? Hell, some mornin's I wake up and can't remember my own till I've had a cup of whiskey."

"Faith."

Weatherford's eyes blazed. "That was the one! A favorite around Thornton's. Whatever happened to her?"

"Died."

Yakima's voice was flat, dull. It betrayed little of the sorrow that had staked out a permanent claim in his heart over these three long years since he'd buried her on the ranch they'd been starting in Arizona, before Thornton's bounty hunters had taken her, and Thornton himself had killed her.

"Ah, that's too bad." The old man studied Yakima. His eyes said he wanted to ask how it had happened, but he'd been alive long enough to know that some questions were best left unspoken. Instead, he just said with a sigh, "Well, that's the way of it. This is probably the end of us. I spent the past two years steering clear of both Claw Hendricks and Floyd Betajack while I worked my hole over on Ute Creek, and now here when I'm headin' up to Belle Fourche for my first Christmas in eight years with my only daughter, they're dustin' my trail. Thrown in together. Imagine that."

"I don't have to," Yakima said.

"And all because of Mendenhour."

"That's a fact."

"If we was smart men, Mr. Henry, we'd throw that lawyer to 'em. Let 'em feed on his uppity carcass." Weatherford gave a foxy grin.

"I've thought about it," Yakima said.

"Ah, hell," the oldster said, covering a yawn with a buckskin glove through the holes of which shone another, second wool glove in nearly the same disrepair as the first. "I reckon this is the price we pay for law and order on the old frontier, ain't it?"

"I reckon." Yakima thought about what the two cutthroats had told him about the man Mendenhour had hanged. What if what they'd said were true—that Pres Betajack had been innocent of the crimes he'd been accused of?

Weatherford turned and sauntered off along the scarp, back in the direction from which he'd come, toward where the women must be holed up. Stopping, he looked back at Yakima. "Adlard and Coble are headin' off to fetch a wheel. I reckon now is when they could hit us."

"You know how to use that thing, Mr. Weatherford?"

"This here?" Weatherford held up the rifle and ran

an appreciative hand down the barrel. "Hell, in the Little Misunderstandin' Between the States, I could knock the tail off a rabbit with what compared to this would be considered a slingshot."

Yakima nodded. The man sauntered off along the scarp, then strode carefully, a little awkwardly down the hill and into the crease where the stage horses were tied to a long picket line.

Yakima was about to head back up to the top of the escarpment to keep watch over the area when he saw another figure move toward him from out of a niche in the rock wall capping the bluff. Glendolene walked toward him with a smoking cup in one hand, his saddlebags thrown over the opposite shoulder. The wind and the gray light of morning silvered the fur of her long bear coat that was almost the same deep, rich color of her hair.

"Thanks for your possibles," she said as she approached, regarding him thoughtfully.

He took the bags from her, draped them over his own shoulder. Offering the cup, the steam from which drifted up like pale snakes to caress her smooth, cold-reddened cheeks, she said, "I thought you could use a hot cup of coffee. Fresh brewed."

"Thanks."

He stared at her through the steam of the cup. She stared back at him. Her lips quirked a wry smile, and she shook her head slowly. "Funny, isn't it . . . ?"

"I'm not laughing."

Her eyes acquired a wistful cast as she said, "Yakima, I—"

Her husband's voice cut her off. "Glendolene?"

She swung around with a start. Mendenhour was

poking his head out of the niche from which she'd come. He held the second rifle that Yakima had brought back to the group.

"I'll be right there, Lee," she said, glancing once more at Yakima before walking back along the edge of the scarp.

Yakima watched her go. Mendenhour stood beyond her, facing Yakima, a scowl on his face as he regarded the half-breed curiously, puffing on a fat cigar. Yakima pinched his hat brim to the man, then turned and walked into his niche and picked up the sack of gold. He stuck it into his saddlebags, buckled the strap over the pouch, then walked out of the niche and down the hill to where Wolf grazed from a picket pin, about fifty yards south of the stage horses.

He saddled the horse, tossed the saddlebags onto its back, and stepped into the leather. He rode up the grade and back onto the trail where the stage sat, tongue drooping, unharassed. Looking around carefully for any sign of the stalkers, wondering how well Betajack and Claw Hendricks had received his message, he put the horse off the trail's west side and booted Wolf into a lope.

Twice, he circled the stage from about half a mile out. On the second trip, he approached the hill with its caprock from the east and reined up when he saw a figure sitting on a rock outside the escarpment, on the backside of the bluff from the crease in which the stage horses had been staked. He could see the long buffalo coat and her long hair blowing in the wind beneath her fur hat.

She turned her head toward him. Her face was a pale oval beneath her hat from this distance of seventy yards or so. He held her gaze, as she held his. Wolf snorted, stomped, lowered his head and shook it, jangling the bit chains. She continued to look toward him.

He felt a tightness in the pit of his gut.

He heard the soft chime of her laugh from one of their nights together in the line shack. He heard her groan. Saw the firelight caressing her bare breasts as they'd lain together on the floor in front of the hearth.

He reined Wolf around the north edge of the bluff, dropped into the crease between the hills. At the bottom of the crease, he stopped.

Mendenhour, Weatherford, and the two drummers were out there, standing near a small fire to keep warm while they guarded the horses, their pistols shoved into coat pockets. Mendenhour was smoking his cigar, looking awkward and out of place out there in his tailored sheepskin coat, beaver hat, new brown boots, and carefully trimmed beard. His hands were gloved in the finest leather. His hat was being dusted by a very light snowfall from a sky the color of wood smoke.

The others just looked cold and fearful and generally miserable as they awaited the new wheel for the stage.

Yakima put Wolf up the slope and back onto the trail. He looked around carefully, ready to reach for the sheathed Yellowboy at any time, but nothing moved out there amidst the bluffs and sage-stippled hogbacks rolling in nearly all directions to dark blue mountains. What were Betajack and Hendricks waiting for?

Had Yakima's promise scared them?

Doubtful. It might have given them pause, though, if one or both were aware of his history. If they came now, they'd no doubt get exactly what they wanted, but he'd be damned if they wouldn't get him at a hefty price. They probably knew that.

What was their plan?

A man shouted to the north, and Yakima cast his gaze in that direction. A buckboard wagon was coming around a bend in the trail, pulled by a big roan and trailing two fresh stage horses, all three horses galloping as the driver, Charlie Adlard, hoorawed them loudly and cracked the blacksnake over the roan's back.

Yakima turned to look into the crease beyond the sloping trees. He gave a quick whistle, and the prosecutor and the others looked at him. Yakima jerked his head and they appeared to get the message that the wheel was on its way.

Ten minutes later, Adlard and Coble had pulled the wagon to a halt near the back of the stage and were wrestling the new wheel onto the axle. Mendenhour, Elijah Weatherford, and the two drummers, Kearny and Sook, were guiding the three women up the slope toward the stage.

When Adlard and Coble had the wheel in place and the hub screwed on over it, they fetched the horses from the crease and were hitching the team to the stage when Yakima spied movement to the west. He turned to see a dozen or so riders in long dusters or fur coats and capes moving toward the stage, all strung out in a long, uneven line.

The other men from the stage saw the riders and came around to where Yakima sat on the trail beside the team.

"Well, this is it, isn't it?" said Mendenhour darkly, retrieving his rifle from where he'd leaned it against the stage's left-front wheel. "Glendolene, take the women back to the cavern!"

"Hold on." Yakima watched the riders stop about a hundred yards out from the stage. They sat their horses about five yards apart, staring toward him and the stage passengers with menace.

Sally Rand sobbed. Her husband guided her to the other side of the stage. Glendolene and Mrs. O'Reilly stood near Mendenhour, staring in the direction of the menacing-looking riders, their shoulders set with both fear and curiosity.

The drummers stood together near the rear of the stage, looking jumpy and ready to take cover if shooting started. Coble grabbed his shotgun out of the driver's box. Then with a grunt he exchanged it for his rifle. The driver, Adlard, stood near the team, tugging at his beard and scowling toward the line of riders.

Mendenhour glanced at Yakima. "What the hell are they doing?"

"Hold on," the half-breed repeated slowly as one rider moved forward from the pack.

This rider walked his horse, a steeldust, toward the stage, lifting a rifle. A white flag had been tied to the barrel.

"I'll be damned," Yakima said wistfully. "Looks like we got us a truce."

Chapter 19

Oh, sweet mercy, Glendolene thought as she watched the lone rider moving toward her and the others, raising the white flag. Now what?

A crawling sensation between her shoulders told her the man wasn't about to make peace. She looked at her husband, who stood slightly ahead of her, holding the rifle up high across his chest in his gloved hands. Lee Mendenhour was a capable man. As he himself had said, he'd grown up out here, and he knew how to ride and shoot as well as most men.

Still, she felt comforted by the presence of the man whose name she hadn't known until yesterday, Yakima Henry. She'd been horrified to see him out here, away from the shack, removed from their intimate time together, but then she'd realized what he'd done. Without him, they'd likely all be dead.

But why was he remaining here, in harm's way? He didn't need them. He had a horse. He could have left them a long time ago, possibly been halfway to his destination by now.

She glanced at him. He was looking at her. She

shrank from his gaze. Sometimes, the awkwardness of them being here together in Lee's presence was too much for her to bear. But she kept her eyes on his, trying to read his mind.

Why?

Yakima stared back at Glendolene as the rider with the white flag moved toward them slowly, with maddening steadiness. Mostly, Yakima was here for her. She was a beautiful white woman, but she was much like him in many ways. Separate from the others, including her husband. Maybe even partly separated from herself.

She was alone.

Her dark brown brows wrinkled slightly as her eyes bored into his, trying to decipher his own thinking. Yakima turned away from her. He was about to touch his moccasin heels against Wolf's ribs, intending to ride out and meet the man with the white flag away from the group, when Mendenhour said, "Hold on. I want to hear what he has to say."

Yakima eased his weight in the saddle. He swept the area around him with his gaze, making sure they weren't being surrounded. But, then, there were nearly a dozen riders out there beyond the man riding toward him. That man was Betajack, he saw now, as the outlaw rancher rode within fifty yards and kept closing, his pale breath tearing in the wind, the tattered white swatch buffeting wildly at the end of his rifle barrel.

Betajack drew back on his steeldust stallion's reins about thirty yards from the group. His red face, sandwiched between roached gray muttonchops, was expressionless. It looked like a dark red inverted V, with his two eyes appearing colorless near the top of the V, just beneath the black brim of his Texas-creased Stetson under which he wore a thick red scarf covering his ears. The scarf was knotted behind the man's left ear.

"Say what you have to say, Betajack!" Mendenhour yelled above the steady rustling of the wind.

"Here it is!" the old man with a killer's cold eyes returned. "We're leaving the outcome of these unfortunate events up to you, Mendenhour. We want only you and you alone. If you turn yourself over to me and my boys before sundown today, we'll let the others in your party go free. They can continue on to their destinations without further harassment from us. They'll live to see Christmas."

The old outlaw leader shook his head slowly, ominously. "If you don't turn yourself over to us before the end of the day, we're going to kill every last one of you people." He threw his free arm forward, extending an angry finger. "Including the women!"

He slid his angry his finger toward Yakima.

"And I don't give a shit how many notches that redskin has on his belt—he won't be able to save you!"

Betajack began to turn his horse.

"Hold on, Betajack!" Mendenhour started forward. "You got no right—"

"I got every right!" the rancher shouted shrilly, face turning even darker. "You killed the wrong son, you son of a bitch. My boy was not rustlin' them horses. He bought 'em and paid for 'em!"

"That's not what the man he stole them from said!"

"That's because Denton Calhoun was told to lie for the good of your precious county!"

"Hold on, goddamn it!"

"That's all I got to say, Mendenhour!" Betajack gave a single fierce nod. "Sundown today or everyone dies."

He reined the steeldust around and hammered his spurred heels into the horse's flanks. Horse and rider galloped away, hoof thuds dwindling beneath the wind's steady sigh.

Yakima and the others watched as Betajack rejoined his crew. He rode through the group and continued riding west, the others turning their horses and following him until they disappeared into a distant swale.

Yakima looked at Mendenhour. The others were looking at him, too. The attorney continued staring toward the killers.

"Well, that seals it," he said with what Yakima detected as a melodramatic air. "I'll stay here. All you people, including you, Glendolene, go ahead and board the stage." He looked at the driver. "Charlie, get these people out of here!"

"No!" Glendolene grabbed his arm. "Lee, you can't. They'll hang you!"

"That seems to be the idea, yes," said Mendenhour.

"Mr. Mendenhour, you simply can't," said Mrs. O'Reilly. "You can't let those brigands win. You ran for office on the platform of law and order. By turning yourself over to those men, you'd only be allowing them to win the battle. Why, if Betajack hangs you, he'll think he owns this county again. He'll terrorize us all the way he was doing five years ago. We won't be able to hire *a single decent lawman!*"

Mrs. O'Reilly swept her gaze across Adlard, Coble, Weatherford, and the two drummers, Kearny and Sook, all of whom were looking around sheepishly, obviously reluctant to get behind the two women.

"Charlie, you tell him!" Mrs. O'Reilly said. "Tell the man to get on board the stage and stop this foolishness." She looked at Coble. "Mr. Coble, surely *you're* not considering allowing Mr. Mendenhour to remain here so those brigands can *hang* him?" She looked at the others, including Yakima. "Why, what kind of men *are* you, *anyway*?"

Yakima looked at the other men. They all fidgeted like boys caught trapping rattlesnakes in the girls' privy at school. Mendenhour waited, staring west, a false look of bravery on his face. His doubtful eyes and mottled pale cheeks gave the lie to it.

Glendolene turned to Yakima. "Please," she said. "Yakima . . . don't let him do this."

"It ain't my decision," he said.

"Glendolene, please," Mendenhour said halfheartedly. "Get aboard the stage. All of you, please. Adlard . . . ?"

"I . . . I reckon we'd best all get aboard the stage, Mr. Mendenhour," the jehu said, unable to conceal his eagerness to get moving.

"Yeah, I reckon," said Coble in much the same tone, unable to meet the castigating gaze of Mrs. O'Reilly. He glanced at the two drummers, who merely stood staring at their shoes. "Reckon we'd all best get back on the stage, Mr. Mendenhour."

Weatherford chuckled as he blew cigarette smoke out his nose. They all looked at him dubiously.

Glendolene turned to the driver. "Mr. Adlard, you can't do this. You cannot leave my husband behind! What kind of a *man* are you?"

Mrs. O'Reilly said, "Indeed!"

Adlard looked stricken. He stared back at Glendolene and then, flushing deeply, he glanced at Coble, who gave a ragged sigh and cast his troubled gaze into the distance.

"Ah, shit," muttered one of the drummers.

Adlard looked at Mendenhour. "I reckon we'd *all* best get aboard the stage, sir."

Mendenhour scowled, pretending to think it over. Finally, as though he were outnumbered, he said, "All right, all right!" With exaggerated reluctance, he took his wife's arm. "Glendolene, let's get you on board. You, too, Mrs. O'Reilly."

Meanwhile, Sally Rand was weeping on the stage's other side, in the arms of her honyocker husband, Percy.

As he led his wife around the rear of the stage, Mendenhour stopped and looked up at Yakima. Yakima returned the gaze, saw the fear and humiliation painting white splotches across Mendenhour's windburned cheeks. The half-breed found himself feeling sorry for the man. If he were in Mendenhour's place, he would send the stage on and go down fighting. He'd be damned if he let them hang him.

But Mendenhour was a civilized man. And he was scared shitless.

Betajack had really done a job on the attorney. On the stage passengers, too, who now had to wrestle with their own courage or lack thereof. The old killer was one crafty son of a bitch.

Mendenhour said, "Will you stay with us, Mr. Henry?"

Glendolene's eyes were on him, faintly beseeching. But he'd already made up his mind. He might not share the prosecutor's views, but he wouldn't throw him to the wolves. After all, he himself had been saved by a man who hadn't even known him.

"I said I would, didn't I?"

He touched heels to Wolf's flanks, put the black on up the trail.

Chapter 20

It was dark when they pulled into the overnight Hamburg Station on Seven-Mile Creek, in the foothills of the Big Horn Range. Yakima rode in ahead of the stage, putting his tired horse up to the hitch rack fronting the two-story, boxlike adobe brick shack sitting to the right of a broad wood-frame barn and several corrals.

Surrounded by a stone water trough, a windmill rose from the hard-packed front yard, the blades clattering in the brittle breeze.

A lamp hung outside under the station house's porch beams, swinging, shunting shadows across the porch's weathered boards and the half dozen saddled horses standing at the two hitch racks, heads hanging. A man was laughing inside, the sounds muffled by the breeze sawing against the shack's brick walls and at the edge of the shake-shingled porch roof, causing a tin cup hanging by a string from a nail to bang irregularly against a tin washtub mounted on a wooden stand beside the closed front door.

Judging by the number of horses and the sounds

from inside, the overnight station doubled as a trail house of sorts. Yakima could smell the whiskey and the stale beer and tobacco smoke of the place as he swung down from Wolf's back and looked around.

He hadn't been surprised that he and the stage had traveled throughout the day, making their slow, steady way toward the Dakota line, unharassed by Betajack and Hendricks. The outlaws would live up to their word. They'd probably enjoyed the tension that even Yakima could sense inside the stage amongst the passengers traveling with the man who could very well get them all killed if he hadn't turned himself over to the killers by sundown.

The driver, Charlie Adlard, and the pugnacious shotgun messenger, Melvin Coble, had displayed grave, brooding looks as they'd maintained their perches atop the rocking, swaying coach, bandannas lifted against the choking dust kicked up by the six-hitch team. They'd gone through three team changes that day, finding little help for their predicament at any of the remote swing stations. The men and women who worked at such places were mainly stalwart, workaday folk, some young, some old—and none up to the formidable task of helping fight back the breed of wolf that was trailing Mendenhour and the others.

If it had been earlier in the year, the women, and maybe even some of the men who didn't mind losing face, might have stayed at one of the stations and simply awaited the next coach through. If they'd had the money for prolonged lodging, that is. And if they didn't have families waiting for them. But there wouldn't be another stage through until after New Year's, and the trail could be socked in with snow at any time, so they all felt compelled to continue on in the small, dusty Concord that some of them, if not all, must have been starting to see as a wheeled coffin.

It was good dark. Time had run out for the prosecutor as well as the others. Yakima could see that now in the faces of Adlard and Coble as they pulled the stage into the yard and the shunting light of the swinging oil lamp found them, their eyes harried. Adlard swung the coach up close to the station house and hauled back on the ribbons, standing up in the driver's boot and yelling, "Whoooo-ahhhhhhhh, now!"

The horses lurched forward against their harnesses, eager to get to the barn. But the jehu yelled at them again and set the brake, snugging the wooden blocks taut against the left-front wheel.

Adlard had wanted to get the coach as close to the station house as possible, so the passengers could get inside quickly without being overly exposed to possible snipers. He likely hadn't thought about the possibility of Betajack and Hendricks awaiting them inside. Yakima had. That's why, as the passengers began tensely destaging, the half-breed shucked his Yellowboy from his saddle boot, levered a round into the chamber, and mounted the porch steps. He opened the door and moved on inside the smoky, dark, cavelike room before him, holding the Winchester's butt against one hip, thumb caressing the hammer.

The place was filled with shadows, and even as his eyes adjusted to the murky, smoky twilight, he could still see only mostly shadows of men hunched around tables to his right, around and beyond a large stove that stood in the middle of the room and slightly to his left. To the far right was the bar, and three men in unbuttoned fur coats stood chatting, elbows on the planks stretched across several beer kegs.

At least, they had been chatting until Yakima had come in. Now most of the men near the room's front were looking at him, including two civilians and one army officer with a thick dark red dragoon mustache playing cards at a table between Yakima and the stove. One of the civilians—a blond, freckled man with a handlebar mustache—wore the moon-and-star badge of a deputy U.S. marshal.

"Stage here?" he said, critical eyes raking Yakima's tall, broad frame.

"Tom Kelsey!" The prosecutor had stepped in behind Yakima. Mendenhour walked around him now, striding toward the seated lawman. "Tom, you don't know how good it is to see you!"

"Mendenhour!" the blond lawman said. "Or I reckon I should say *Prosecutor* Mendenhour!"

He laughed affably, showing square yellow teeth beneath his mustache as, closing the fan of cards in his right hand, he slid his chair back and rose, twisting around to face Mendenhour while canting his head toward the other civilian and the army officer. "Raul Arenas."

"Ah!" Mendenhour said, leaning forward to shaking the hands of the other civilian—a tall, dark man with a black mustache flecked with gray. "Another law dog—just what we need!"

As this man rose from his chair, Yakima saw that he, too, was wearing a deputy U.S. marshal's badge, and that he sported at least two pistols, one positioned for the cross draw on his left hip. Both federal lawmen also had rifles leaning against the table, near their chairs, while the redheaded soldier—a major—had a Spencer carbine resting across an empty chair flanking him, between him and the dark-eyed badge toter, who appeared to have some Mexican blood and also wore a nasty scar across the side of his nose.

"Major Demarest!" Mendenhour said when he'd shaken the dark lawman's hand. His voice was rising with even more unbridled relief. "Matt, what are you doing this far from Camp Collins?"

"Headin' north to spend the holidays with my brother at Fort Lincoln," Demarest said, rising and smiling around the quirley that dripped ashes onto his playing cards as he gained his feet awkwardly. There were several shot and beer glasses on the table, as well as a half-empty bottle.

"Hope I can make it before the snow flies." Major Demarest canted his head toward the open front door behind Yakima, through which the other passengers were entering the station house warily, stiffly tentative. "I take it the stage is here. Good. I'll be hoppin' aboard tomorrow. See no reason to ride horseback all the way to Mandan."

"Good! Good!" Mendenhour rubbed his gloved hands together and looked around nervously at the passengers and Yakima, and then said, more quietly as he crouched over the lawmen's and the soldier's table, "Do you men think we could have a word outside? We've encountered trouble along the trail, and . . ."

That was all that Yakima heard. Or all that he listened to. Mendenhour was about to request help, and Yakima felt a mild relief tempered by his knowing how many wolves were on the prosecutor's trail, as well as the breed of wolves. More important to him just now was his horse. He turned, ran into someone standing behind him, and looked down to see Glendolene stumbling back a step.

"Whoa!" he said, grabbing her arm with his free hand.

She looked up at him. "Sorry."

Unsteady from the long, jouncing ride, she now stepped too far forward and placed a hand on his chest, over his buckskin mackinaw to steady herself. He watched as a flush rose in her smooth, tapering cheeks, and her brown eyes sparkled in the light of a near lantern, beneath the brim of her fur hat. She looked at her hand on his chest, then lowered it and stepped back, but her lustrous eyes remained on his.

Just loudly enough for him to hear above the rising hum of conversation reverberating around the room, she said, "Are we safe here, do you think . . . Mr. Henry?"

"Glendolene," the prosecutor said, turning to her as the two lawmen and the soldier gained their feet, wearing serious expressions now despite the drink-bleariness of their eyes. "Why don't you and the other ladies inquire about the accommodations while I step outside for a moment?" He moved around Yakima and smiled down at his wife. "I think we've just been given an early Christmas present."

She glanced from her husband to Yakima, who stepped past her and outside. As he closed the door behind him, Adlard and Coble were moving up the porch steps while three hostlers from the station were leading the spent team toward the large barn on the north end of the yard. The barn's doors were thrown open, showing light from a lantern inside. A small, crude log shack flanked the barn. Its windows, too, were lit. Likely where the hostlers who worked for the stage company were housed.

Neither the driver nor the shotgun messenger said anything as they climbed heavily onto the porch. The driver said, "I sure could use a drink," and walked past Yakima.

Coble stopped in front of the half-breed. He was a couple of inches shorter. He stared up at him with his customary bulldog scowl.

"Come on, Mel," Adlard said wearily. "Get your ass in here and quit spoilin' for a fight!"

He was holding the door open. Someone from inside said, "Hey, close the damn door! You born in a barn?"

The driver went in. Coble brushed stiffly past Yakima, like a dog with his hackles and tail raised, and followed Adlard into the station house.

Yakima looked around. The stage still sat in front of the station house, where it would likely remain overnight, giving the passengers a short walk from the cabin. Nothing moved around or beyond it except for the hostlers just now leading the team into the barn, one man standing back ready to pull the doors closed.

He walked into the yard and stood behind Wolf, staring out at the cool, breezy night in which a few snowflakes blew this way and that, and the windmill hummed. The tin cup continued to rap against the wash barrel.

Yakima stared off across the dark hills to the west, feeling that eyes were on him. Snowflakes brushed his eyes. One stuck in his lashes. Behind him, the station house door opened. Voices spilled out, as did a rush of tobacco smoke and the fetor of beer and whiskey.

Yakima glanced behind him to see Mendenhour step
out with the two marshals and the major.

As the other men stopped on the porch to converse,
Yakima led Wolf over to the barn. He tended the horse
slowly and thoroughly, giving him a good rubdown
before putting him up in an empty stall with a blanket
thrown over him, to leach the chill from his bones. The
hostlers tending the stage horses talked amongst
themselves, snorting and laughing in the way of men
doing rote work.

Yakima draped his saddlebags over his shoulder,
picked up his Yellowboy, gave the black a parting pat,
and left the barn, heading back to the station house.
Mendenhour and the others had gone back in. Yakima
went in now, too, and walked up to the bar. Earlier,
he'd smelled food cooking, and he asked the broad-
chested man—flat-faced and with long blond mustaches—behind the bar, if he could get a plate.

The man planted his fists against the bar and
squinted his suspicious, heavy-lidded eyes as he took
the half-breed's measure. "Can you pay for it?"

Yakima ignored the angry burn behind his ears and
blinked slowly. "I can pay."

"One dollar for steak and beans."

Yakima reached into his buckskins and flipped the
man a silver dollar. The man inspected the coin, tossed
it into a tin pail on a shelf behind him, and yelled
through a door left of the cracked back bar mirror.
"Another plate, Rosey!"

Then he shuffled away to answer the call of a man
standing to Yakima's right.

Yakima turned and headed for a free table on the
room's far side, noticing a couple of girls in corsets and
bustiers working the room toward the stairs climbing

to the second story and, presumably, the stage passengers' sleeping quarters. There was a blonde and a brunette, and colored feathers danced in their hair as they made conversation with a couple of prospective jakes who looked like cowpunchers in their battered Stetsons and woolly chaps.

Adlard and Coble sat at the table to the right of the one Yakima headed for. The driver was slumped back in his chair, enjoying a beer and a shot, while Coble was hunkered over his own beer and shot, eyeing Yakima devilishly. The man's eyes drifted from the half-breed's face to the saddlebags, then drifted away, and he brushed a hand nervously across the thin sandy-brown mustache mantling his chapped pink mouth.

Yakima ignored the man, though he didn't at all like the interest Coble had taken in his pouch, which the shotgunner had rightly assumed was filled with gold. That was a particularly vexing complication he didn't need on top of the other more obvious one.

He was trying to help this crew to safety, and one of them wanted to rob him.

Again, a voice pitched with incredulity said in his mind, "What the hell are you doing here, fool? Get the gold to Belle Fourche and hightail it to warmer climes!"

He sagged into a chair at his table, facing the room at large. He set his rifle on the table to his right, draped his saddlebags over a chair back to his left, and watched the lawyer walk toward him.

"Ah, shit," Yakima said, aloud to himself. "Now what?"

Chapter 21

Mendenhour looked considerably more confident than he had only a few minutes before. His eyes were shiny, as well. He'd been drinking with his U.S. marshal and cavalry pals, and he was teeming with vim and vinegar.

It made Yakima's shoulders contract with edginess.

Mendenhour stood over Yakima in much the same way he'd done when Yakima had first met the man. His face with its close-cropped cinnamon beard was set with arrogance, and he set the beringed knuckles of his right hand lightly atop Yakima's table, near the octagonal barrel of the Yellowboy.

"Mr. Henry," he said, "while I do appreciate your help with the trouble out on the trail, I'm afraid we'll no longer be in need of your services."

"All right."

The prosecutor seemed surprised by the half-breed's casual response.

"You may ride on first thing in the morning," Mendenhour added, as though to make sure the half-breed understood his meaning.

"Fine as frog hair," Yakima said as a portly older woman in a shapeless dress and blood- and grease-stained apron set a plate heaped with a bloody steak and smoking pinto beans on the table before him.

He rolled up his shirtsleeves. Mendenhour remained standing over him, staring down at him with faint consternation.

"I just want you to know," the man added, dipping his head lower and softening his voice so that no one around them could hear, "I've seen the way you've been regarding my wife, and I disapprove of it."

Yakima looked up at him. "Yeah, well, it's hard not to look at a woman like that. Hard to not want her, in fact. But I do apologize for gettin' your neck in a hump. Now, maybe you'd best go sit down with your pals over there, before you get in over your head here. Me? I'm hungry."

Yakima glanced at the table on the other side of the stove, where the two marshals and the soldier sat regarding him over their shoulders and talking amongst themselves. He pinched his hat brim to them and then took up his knife and his fork and cut into his steak.

Mendenhour continued to hover over him, ever so slightly unsteady on his feet. Slurring his words just a little, he said, "Kelsey and Arenas say they've seen your face on wanted dodgers."

Yakima didn't look up at the man. He'd figured he was wanted somewhere or another, after all the men he'd been forced to turn toe-down. Not many men with Indian blood could kill a white man, however much said white man needed killing, without finding himself wanted by the law.

"Wouldn't doubt it a bit," Yakima said, chewing,

lifting his head to cast Mendenhour an insolent grin. "Now, 'less you and your men want to push the matter, I suggest you wander on back to your table. Best get to bed soon. You're going to need your beauty sleep, Mendenhour. Gettin' help from them federals is all fine and good, but it ain't gonna do you much good come tomorrow, when you're out on the trail with the father of the man whose neck you stretched doggin' your heels. *Your* heels and the heels of innocent folks who've found themselves in the regrettable position of sharing the same stage with you."

"Don't talk to me in that tone, Mr. Henry."

"You know, Mendenhour, Betajack claims his son didn't deserve that necktie party," Yakima added, his temper burning as he continued talking and forking beans and meat into his mouth and staring gravely up at the arrogant man glowering down at him.

Mendenhour's gaze wavered for a split second. For that half second, doubt shone in his eyes—a weakness in the chinking of the prosecutor's certainty that he had indeed hanged the right man. Yakima reflected that Mendenhour's intentions had likely started out honorably enough, but he'd become corrupted by the same thing that corrupted most men. Power. By a totally dunderheaded sense of his own infallibility.

"I have a feeling we'll meet again, Henry," Mendenhour said tightly. "Most likely in a court of law."

"We could at that."

Mendenhour moved back to his table and sat heavily down in his chair. Yakima continued shoveling his food into his mouth and trying to keep his mind off the man only to have another man piss-burn him nearly as much. It was Melvin Coble, chuckling as he held the brunette doxie on his lap to Yakima's left and about ten feet away. The shotgunner held the girl's back tight against his chest, and he was hefting her breasts in his hands, through her pink bone corset trimmed with black lace, and staring over her head at Yakima.

"Guess you sorta been given the rail, ain't ya, breed?"

The girl regarded Yakima crookedly, feathers bouncing in her hair as Coble blew on them and then continued to laugh. Meanwhile, Adlard merely stared disgustedly down at his beer.

Behind the jehu, the blond whore was pulling one of the two other men in the room up out of his chair. The man resembled a puncher, with his woolly chaps and fleece-lined denim jacket, but Yakima saw now that he was wearing two big pistols in tied-down holsters low on his leggings. When his jacket flapped open, Yakima caught a glimpse of yet a third pistol holstered under his right arm.

That was a lot of weaponry for a cowpuncher, most of whom had little use for that many guns, and preferred to ride light in their saddles.

Oh, well—Yakima had had enough. It was time to ride on out of here. He'd do so first thing in the morning. Glendolene had married the man. What could he do if Mendenhour was bound and determined to get her killed?

Trying his best to ignore the jeering shotgunner, Yakima nudged his empty plate away, rose from his chair, slung his saddlebags over his shoulder, scooped his rifle off the table, and headed for the door.

"Night, now, breed!" Coble called behind him. "Enjoy the barn!" Less loudly, he said to the whore, "Why, a man like that's only fit to sleep with hosses. . . ."

Then Yakima was outside, and the door was closed on the station house din. He walked heavily off the steps, the saddlebags with their heavy bag of gold bouncing against him. Snow was falling harder than before. A white dusting lay on the ground, tempering the night's stormy darkness. The wind pelted the half-breed's face with the cold flakes.

From above and behind him rose a girl's cackle. As he stepped out away from the station house, he glanced up to see a female shadow jostling with a man's hatted one in a second-story window. A whorehouse and overnight station. He wondered how much sleep the stage passengers would get tonight.

As for himself, he figured he'd sleep pretty well despite the edginess clawing its cold fingers up and down his back. Betajack and Hendricks might be close, but he wasn't going to worry about them anymore. They were after Mendenhour. Let them have him. Now he began to see the ludicrousness of his ever getting involved with Mendenhour and the other passengers in the first place.

All for a pretty woman he'd enjoyed a few good times with in a remote line shack. A married woman.

Time to move on, Henry.

He went into the barn. Using the soft snow light pushing through the open doors and the sashed windows, he lit an oil lantern hanging from a ceiling post. He closed the doors and was heading for Wolf's stall, intending to throw down with his horse, as he usually did, but he saw a door off to the right of Wolf's stall. It was a low, brittle wooden door with a steel latch and a scrap of cracked mirror hanging by a tattered length of twine from a nail on the outside.

There was a small room behind the door—one with

a cot and a small, cold, bullet-shaped stove and a long shelf running along the outside wall. There was a blanket and a lumpy straw pillow covered in stained ticking on the cot. A small milking stool and a saddle rack were the only furniture beyond the cot. The pent-up air in here was musty; it smelled like leather, wool, and mice shit. There was enough wood in the box beside the stove for a fire.

Yakima decided to sleep on the cot, with the comfort of a fire. It was likely to be his last bed in a warm room for a few days, until he reached Belle Fourche. When he'd opened the stove's flue and got a fire going, he threw his blanket roll onto the cot, kicked out of his boots, and stripped down to his balbriggans.

He stretched deep, throwing his arms up as far as he could get them under the low, soot-crusted ceiling, and scratched his broad chest through the threadbare underwear top. He gave his head a vigorous scratching with both hands, then hung his shell belt and holstered .44 on a stout nail over the cot and dropped onto the makeshift bed with a weary groan. He drew his blanket up, turned onto his side, and drew a deep breath.

He froze, the breath still in his lungs, and lifted his head to listen.

He'd heard something. He heard it again—the crunch of a light foot coming down on straw. Through the cracks in the door's vertical boards, a shadow moved. Yakima reached for the .44 but froze with his hand a foot away from the horn grips when a girl cleared her voice, and said, "Mr. Henry?"

"Glendolene?"

"Who?" the girl said with an amused chitter.

Then he felt foolish. Of course it wasn't her. He went

ahead and slid the Colt out of its holster, rose from the cot, and walked over to the door. He'd turned his lamp down, but he'd left the stove's small, dented door open, so there was enough umber light to see the face that appeared in the gap when he opened the door a foot.

The brunette from inside the station house stood before him, in a long wool coat that she held close at her throat. She still had the feathers in her hair. On her feet were fleece-lined, buckskin slippers.

"I'm Angie."

"So?"

She chuckled as though delighted by the response. "I thought you might like some company."

"What gave you that idea?"

Her coquettish smile turned into a pout. "Don't you want company? I'm very cheap. Business was slow tonight, so I'll give you a roll for a dollar." She shifted her weight from foot to foot, enticingly rolling her hips.

"You would, would you?"

"Sure."

"How 'bout fifty cents?"

She nibbled her upper lip. "Well . . . okay."

Yakima threw the door open wider and stepped to one side. "Come in."

Smiling up at him alluringly, she sauntered through the doorway. Yakima drew the door closed.

"If it's all the same to you, I'd just as soon you'd put the hog leg up. That ain't the . . . uh . . . *instrument* you're gonna need for what I got in mind for you, Mr. Henry."

Yakima set the Colt on the shelf to his right. Standing before him, the girl opened the coat from which the buttons appeared to have been torn. She tossed it aside and stood before him in the pink corset that shoved her breasts up nicely. There was a small mole on the top of the right one. She wore a silk choker around her pale neck; it was trimmed with a small turquoise stone set in tin painted to pass for gold. She was a pretty girl for these parts.

She kicked out of each slipper in turn. Then, staring up at him as though to mesmerize him, she began unlacing the front of the corset. It spilled away from her breasts and dropped to the floor. He watched her as she sat down on the edge of the cot and unsnapped her stockings from her garter belt and slid them down her legs.

All the while she kept her cool, seductive eyes on him.

When she was pale and naked, wearing only the choker, she rose from the cot to stand before him once more. Chicken flesh rose across her breasts and down her soft, pale belly.

"You like?"

"Take your hair down."

She reached up and removed the pin from the light brown bun atop her head. She tossed the pin onto the shelf, shook her head, and the hair spilled in a messy mass across her shoulders, curled ends dancing across the full, pale, pear-shaped breasts.

"Your turn," she said in a husky-sexy voice.

"Hold on."

He rammed his shoulder against the door behind him. There was a grunt as the door slammed into something yielding, sending the chunky figure stumbling backward into the shadows, though the light from Yakima's fire flashed on the pistol in Coble's fist.

"Goddamn you!" Coble cried.

Just before he got the Schofield leveled, Yakima kicked it out of his hand.

"Achh!"

It smacked against the barn's low ceiling. Wolf whinnied to Yakima's right. Half a second later, as Coble crouched over his right wrist, clutching it with his other hand, Yakima slammed his fist against the man's jaw. There was a sharp *smack* as the man flew back and twisted sideways before he hit the straw-littered floor, near a ceiling post hung with moldy tack.

"You son of a bitch!" the man snarled, grabbing a pitchfork sticking up out of a hay mound.

As he gained his feet clumsily and came at Yakima, the half-breed sidestepped the man's thrust easily and hammered Coble's face twice quickly with his left fist—*smack-smack!* As the man groaned and turned away from Yakima, the pitchfork wilting in his hands, Yakima grabbed him by his hair and slammed his head against a side of the ceiling post that was free of tack. He slammed it three times hard, hearing the soft thuds and smacks of Coble's nose connecting with the oak. Then he released the man's head.

As Coble sagged to his knees, blood glistened against the side of the post where his face had connected with it.

Yakima grabbed the man under his arms and half carried, half dragged him to the half-open front doors. He tossed him out into the night. Coble hit the ground with a sobbing cry of misery, covering his face with both hands and curling his knees toward his belly.

Yakima turned and walked back to his room. The girl stood back by the stove, fidgeting nervously.

"Look," she said. "We can still . . ."

"Get out."

"It was Melvin's idea! He said you had enough gold, we could each just take a handful and get the hell out of here before those men after Mendenhour kill us all!"

"Get out," the half-breed repeated.

"All right! All right!"

She quickly gathered her clothes, few as there were, and ran out of the room and into the barn's deeper darkness. Yakima slammed the door. He walked over to stand in front of the stove, getting himself warm again before dropping his Colt back into its holster and sagging onto the cot with a weary groan and a grunt.

Gonna be damn good to get out of here. . . .

Chapter 22

Yakima was up early the next morning, when the dawn was still a faint pearl wash in the east, beyond the frost-crusted windows of the barn's windows.

He didn't bother with a fire but merely dressed in the misty darkness of the little room, then carried his rifle and saddlebags and blanket roll out to where Wolf stood, snorting and stomping in his stall. The black had heard Yakima get up, knew they'd be on the trail again soon, and he, like his rider, was pleased as punch at the prospect.

Yakima set his gear down beside the stall, then walked to the front of the barn and opened the doors. Smoke curled from the chimneys poking up out of the station house's second-story roof. He couldn't see any light on in the place yet, but the smoke meant someone was likely up fixing breakfast.

It was gray and cold. About an inch of feathery snow had fallen overnight, but the faint dark smears of Coble's blood were still visible in front of the barn doors. His boot prints as well as the girl's smaller slipper prints trailed off toward the station house—very faint outlines under the snow that had fallen after they'd taken their leave.

Judging by how close the girl's prints were to the man's, she'd probably helped him back to the station house. Coble's boot toes were pointed inward, and they'd raked across the ground. He likely wouldn't have made it back to the house by himself; he'd have died out here and frozen up like marble.

Yakima knew it was not to his credit that the idea amused him.

He went back into the barn, led Wolf out, tied him to a post, and saddled him. He'd just tossed the saddle-bags over the horse's back and shoved his rifle into the boot when a woman screamed. He jerked the rifle back out of the boot and ran into the yard as the woman screamed again. He looked around. The scream had come from behind the station house.

Running that way along the side of the house, he heard men yelling and boots thumping in the house's second story. The screams had alerted others. Yakima ran around behind the station house, skirting a large L-shaped stack of split firewood. Beyond, at the end of a worn path, stood a two-hole privy. Up a low, brushy knoll behind the privy, Glendolene stood in her fur coat, staring farther up the knoll.

At the top of the knoll jutted a large, sprawling, leaf-less cottonwood. From one of the tree's arcing branches, on its left side, a man hung from a rope, his body twist-ing slowly in the slight, sighing wind.

Yakima ran up the knoll. Glendolene turned to him, one hand over her mouth, eyes wide. She gave another frightened start when her eyes found him, but then she lowered her hand and pointed toward the man hang-ing from the tree.

Yakima ran past her and stopped to stare up at the slack body of Mel Coble. The shotgunner's face was bruised and swollen, his lips cut, his left eye swollen shut. That brow had a crusty cut angling through it. His chin was tipped toward his chest, and his wide-open eyes gazed dumbly at the ground, his lower jaw hanging slack.

Coble wore only his long handles and wool socks.

Slowly, he turned from right to left in the breeze. He'd turned nearly a complete circle at the end of the rope when the bartender from last night came running out the back door of the station house, hatless, an apron around his broad waist. His mouth opened beneath his long blond mustaches when he stared up the hill past Glendolene and Yakima at the shotgunner hanging from the cottonwood.

"Glendolene?" Mendenhour called from inside the station house, amidst the thudding of several pairs of boots. "Glendolene, what in holy blazes . . . ?" he said again as he ran out the back door.

He wore only his suit without the jacket, and suspenders. He wore no hat. In his right fist was a Colt .45. He ran past the bartender and stopped five feet from the back door, staring up the knoll at Glendolene and then at Yakima before his eyes widened as they settled on Coble.

The barman said, "Who is that? Is that Coble hangin' there with his neck stretched? Who did that?"

Yakima only vaguely heard the man. He was walking around on the other side of the tree, noting two sets of boot tracks and the lighter prints of stocking feet. Coble's feet. He'd been dragging his toes again, only this time he probably hadn't been conscious when the two men who'd hanged him had dragged him out here, most likely from the privy where he'd probably gone to be sick after the beating Yakima had given him.

Looking up at the dead man again, he saw a bloody splotch at the back of Coble's head. Yakima didn't remember hitting the shotgunner anywhere but on his face. Whoever had hanged him had likely knocked him over the head first, so he couldn't make any noise and alert the others.

Yakima followed the tracks down the far side of the knoll. There were only the boot prints here. At the base of the knoll and in a sparse grove of cottonwoods, he saw where two horses had been tied. The tracks were a couple of hours old; only a little snow obscured them.

He walked back up the knoll. More people had emerged from the station house, including the two lawmen and the army major. They were standing around with Mendenhour, holding pistols or rifles, and looking bleary-eyed and befuddled as they stared up at the hanged shotgunner.

"Any tracks?" asked the lawman named Kelsey. The white of his eyes were mostly red beneath the brim of his Stetson.

"Two horses," Yakima said. "Two men, two horses. They hanged him and rode out."

"Who?"

"Him!" a girl yelled in the direction of the station house, and Yakima turned to see the brunette from last night holding a blanket around her shoulders and pointing up the hill at him. "The breed done it! Beat the shit out of Mel last night, but that wasn't enough for him. He had to go an' hang him, too!"

Even Mrs. O'Reilly and the drummers and old Elijah

Weatherford were outside now, looking bleary-eyed, confused, and fearful. They all looked at the whore and then turned their heads slowly toward Yakima.

"What's this?" asked the Hispanic lawman named Arenas.

Yakima nodded. "I did that to his face, but only after he tried to feed me a chunk of lead. But I sure as hell didn't hang him. Didn't see the need."

"If not you . . . ," said Mendenhour testily.

Yakima walked past Glendolene and over to the privy, circling it slowly with his rifle on his shoulder. When he walked back around to the corner nearest the hang tree, he said, "They followed him out here from the station house. Early this morning. Probably waited till he was done with his business, then beat him over the head and hanged him."

"Why?" said Glendolene, scrunching her face up, aghast.

Yakima shrugged. "To show what they're capable of. And to show"—he looked at Mendenhour—"what's comin'."

"He did it," the whore shrieked, pointing at Yakima. "I swear he did!"

The lawmen, the major, and Mendenhour all stared at Yakima. He looked at the other passengers. They were staring at him, too.

Yakima turned back to the lawmen. "There were two well-armed men in the station house last night. I'm betting they were from Betajack's and Hendricks's crew. And I'm betting they're not all that far away."

The men standing around the swinging feet of Mel Coble all looked at each other curiously.

Arenas said in his deep, gravelly voice, squinting at

Yakima, "Don't know if I'd believe a man with paper on him. Especially one who done that to Coble's face last night. I'd say we have the hangman right here, fellas. Maybe we'd best throw the cuffs on him, haul him over to Broken Jaw, toss him in the lockup, report this business to the prosecutor over there."

"That's crazy!" Glendolene said. "He wouldn't have hanged this man. Why, he's done nothing but help us. Lee, for goodness' sake!"

Ignoring his wife, Mendenhour glared at Yakima and said tightly, "I believe I told you last night, Mr. Henry, that your services will no longer be required."

"Pshaw!" said Mrs. O'Reilly. "What kind of way is that to treat a man who saved our lives when he sure as sin on earth didn't have to?"

Boots scraped and thudded inside the roadhouse, and all heads turned to see the stage driver, Charlie Adlard, poke his head out the door, dirty gray hair hanging in his eyes. His weathered, papery cheeks sagged beneath his salt-and-pepper beard.

"What . . . what's goin' on out here?" he asked in his gravelly voice, still a little slurred from all the tanglefoot he'd consumed the night before.

The drummers chuckled at him. The others ignored him.

Yakima ignored him, as well. He looked at Glendolene, who had kept her eyes on him. She was smiling sadly, with understanding, her eyes boring right through him.

Go, she seemed to be saying. *You've done all you can for us.*

Yakima glanced once more at the lawmen, the soldier, and the prosecutor, then turned and walked away, holding the Yellowboy straight down in his right hand.

Behind him, Mrs. O'Reilly clucked her disapproval.

Crows lighted, cawing, from a copse of winter gray deciduous trees and a smattering of conifers sheathing a creek at the base of a low sandstone ridge that stood about a hundred yards from where Deputy U.S. Marshal Tom Kelsey and Major Matt Demarest sat their horses.

As their horses foraged freeze-dried clumps of needle grass and brome rising above the snow now glittering like sequins in the early-morning sunshine, both men studied the flock of squawking birds as it rose, resembling a thin black kite, nearly straight up, then flattened out toward the west before banking and careening straight south over the ridge.

"What do you think about that?" Demarest said, nibbling at the frost riming his thick red mustache.

Kelsey lowered his gaze from the crows to the tracks pocking the snow-dusted terrain before him. The two sets of shod hoofprints trailed nearly straight out from beneath him and the major. They rose and fell over the cactus- and sage-pocked hills toward where the crows had lit from the cottonwoods, aspens, and ponderosa pines.

Kelsey and Demarest had left the station house half an hour ago, following the tracks leading away from where Mel Coble dangled from the cottonwood. They'd left Kelsey's partner, Raul Arenas, back at the station house to help cut Coble down and get him buried and then to take the man's place as shotgun messenger aboard the stage.

Kelsey felt as though he had no choice but to follow

the tracks, and he was happy when Major Demarest, who was on furlough from Camp Collins in Colorado Territory, south of Cheyenne, had volunteered to ride along. What Kelsey intended to do if he ran into Floyd Betajack and Claw Hendricks's large gang out here, he had no idea. But he'd been outnumbered before, albeit by less seasoned cutthroats, and he hadn't been about to let that deter him.

Especially not when Lee Mendenhour's beautiful, brown-eyed wife had been there to witness any sign of cowardice displayed by the lawman, he mused now with a wry chuff. Tracking two murder suspects, when they could very well be part of a larger, notorious, and particularly savage gang that had been running rough-shod around northern Colorado and southern Wyoming territories for years, was the price a man paid for wearing the badge.

"I suspect somethin' spooked them birds," Kelsey said, reaching behind to poke a hand into his left-side saddlebag pouch, pulling out his field glasses.

He slipped the glasses from their leather case and lifted them to his eyes. Quickly, he adjusted the focus until the trees and the cold creek meandering through them clarified. Breath vapor washed in the air around his pearl Stetson sitting over the white scarf into which Kelsey's girl, Sandra Felix, had crocheted little green Christmas trees, fashioning it for him special in Cheyenne. He'd been heading back that way to spend Christmas with her and her family in their little frame house on Cheyenne's eastern outskirts, but now he'd likely be a day or so late.

That frustrated the deputy marshal, because he'd been looking forward to Mrs. Felix's plum pudding and stealing kisses and a few other things out in the icehouse from the woman's buxom daughter, who was not nearly as chaste as she let on when in the presence of her well-heeled parents and brothers, one of whom was studying mining law in St. Louis.

"Anything?" Demarest asked.

Kelsey shook his head. "Nothin'." He returned the glasses to their case and dropped the case back into his saddlebag pouch. "I reckon we'd best check it out." He was about to nudge his buckskin gelding with his spurs but stopped and turned back to the major. "You know, Matt—there ain't no reason for you to be here."

"What're you talking about? I'm as federal as you are. And aren't there federal warrants out on them coyotes' heads?"

"There are. But if Mendenhour is right and Betajack's gang and Claw Hendricks's gang have gotten together . . ."

"We'll be ridin' into a shit storm."

Kelsey smiled grimly. The major showed his teeth beneath his mustache. He laughed, and then Kelsey laughed, too. "I reckon there ain't no turnin' back to either one of us. But you know what I think?"

"What's that?" asked Demarest.

"I think the half-breed killed Coble. Not that Coble didn't have it comin'. I never liked the son of a bitch myself. But that breed's a killer. He's killed before, plenty of times. And once killin' gets in a red man's blood, there's just no stoppin' 'im till he's dangling from a tree."

"What about the two men who obviously rode out from the station house?"

"Prob'ly just got up early to ride back to their outfit. The Steamboat Butte Ranch is out this way, and I believe I remember seein' them two punchers herdin' cattle down around Crazy Dan Creek."

"You think they just seen Coble hangin' there and rode over to investigate?"

Squinting one eye, Kelsey nodded. "That's what I'm thinkin'. They prob'ly lit a shuck out of fear they themselves would get blamed."

"All right, then," Demarest said. "Let's go check out them trees and call it a day. Then I reckon we'd best run that breed down, cuff him, and hold him at the jail in Broken Jaw. After Christmas, we'll sift through the warrants he's got on him."

"Fair enough."

As the men gigged their horses forward, Demarest said jovially, "How's that girl of yours?"

"She's gonna be mad when I'm late gettin' to Cheyenne for Christmas. Why couldn't that damn Mendenhour have waited till after New Year's to hang Betajack?"

Demarest laughed. "Hell, he's been sharpenin' his horns ever since he was voted to the office down there in Big Horn County. Old Wild Bill got him voted in—you can be sure of that. Gonna get himself killed, though, sooner or later. I'm not sure this country is ready just yet for his brand of law and order."

"It ain't!"

Both men reined their horses up sharply, startled by the voice that had seemed to emanate from the air around them. They looked around wildly, Demarest closing his hand around the stock of the Winchester jutting from his saddle boot. He froze when he looked behind him, as did Kelsey, to see ten or so hard-looking, well-armed men in furs and skins and dusters step out from behind tree boles. One of the party was old Floyd Betajack himself, his craggy face beet-red from the cold. Another taller, younger man just stepping out from behind another tree to the old man's

right was none other than Claw Hendricks in his trade-
mark black opera hat and rose-colored glasses.

Both his holsters belted around the outside of his
horsehide coat were empty. The long-barreled .45s
were in his gloved hands, aimed straight out from his
belly at the lawman and the major. He smiled. Most of
the other men, including old Betajack, just looked
stony-faced in their hats and scarves, their mustaches
and beards rimed with frost. A scrawny, blond, coyote-
faced kid flanking Betajack gave a lewd snicker.

"You two doin' anything for Christmas?" the old
man asked tonelessly.

Silence.

One of the horses snorted.

There was a very faint dribbling sound, and Kelsey
looked over at Demarest. The major sat tense in his
saddle, lips and mustache bunched angrily, eyes hard
beneath his thick red brows. Then Kelsey saw that
urine was dribbling down from inside the cuff of his
left dark blue uniform pants to splatter onto the toe of
his worn cavalry boot.

That more than anything else caused the deputy
U.S. marshal to realize he wouldn't be heading back to
Cheyenne this Christmas. Or ever again.

"Yeah," he said, his own voice as toneless as Floyd
Betajack's had been, making the statement an eerily
emotionless observation. "Yeah, I reckon we're dyin'."

The killers stared at him. A few smiled. A few
chuckled. The wild-looking blond kid flanking Betajack gave a coyote-like whoop.

Betajack blinked slowly. Hendricks grinned.

His guns blossomed like twin poinsettias in a sunlit
Christmas window.

Chapter 23

Crows lighted from a copse lining a boulder-choked canyon gap off the right side of the stage trail.

Staring out the right window as she faced forward in the rocking stage just now slowing to climb a hill, Glendolene felt her heart quicken. But then she saw what had frightened the birds—four shaggy, red-brown, white-faced cows running up a slanting hill climbing the north side of the canyon.

Behind the cows came a young man in woolly chaps and a ragged blanket coat with the collar turned up. He was riding a fine chestnut gelding with one white stocking. Glendolene could tell that the rider was young because he was only about fifty yards away, and his pale face beneath his Stetson's brim shone pink and hairless in the coppery light of the setting sun.

He was whistling shrilly and waving a coiled lariat at the cows that he was hazing out of the canyon, and now he turned toward the stage, shouted something that Glendolene couldn't hear above the coach's thundering clatter, and waved his arm broadly over his head.

Atop the stage, the driver, Adlard, shouted something in return, and the young man smiled and then returned his attention to the cows. The crows were a thin line, ever thinning against the steel gray sky, as they drifted off up the deep, narrow canyon to the east. Glendolene eased back in her seat and turned forward to face her husband, riding opposite her in the carriage, facing the stage's rear.

Mendenhour had heard the young man's whistle, and he was just now turning his head away from the window, flushed with anxiety. He had a Colt pistol with gutta-percha grips stuffed down in the right coat pocket, and he must have grabbed it when he'd heard the whistle. Now he released it, glancing sheepishly at Glendolene and then returning his gaze to the dun-colored hills striding past beyond the window.

Glendolene kept her eyes on Lee. He'd been oddly quiet and contemplative all day as they'd ridden through this vast land, stopping occasionally and briefly to rest the horses or to have a fresh team hitched to the stage at one of the two relay stations the trail had passed through so far this day, their second full day on the trail. Glendolene couldn't help wondering if he suspected the truth about her and Yakima Henry.

But no, he couldn't have. The idea would have been so far out of the realm of what he thought her capable of doing that it wouldn't have occurred to him. Such a possibility would have seemed just as fantastic to her only a few months ago, before she'd run into the dark-skinned, black-haired loner with the coal black stallion at the line shack.

No, that wasn't what was bothering Lee. Such a suspicion was merely her own guilt needling her.

As she studied him now she saw not only the trepidation in his eyes about when and where the killers would strike again, but—maybe she was only imagining this, too?—whether he'd done the right thing in hanging Pres Betajack. Glendolene never would have thought him capable of killing a man without the utmost evidence convicting him of the crime he'd been accused of, but coupling his grim, sheepish demeanor with what Floyd Betajack had accused him of earlier, she was beginning to wonder.

And worry.

The man she'd met in Omaha would have done no such thing. Lee Mendenhour had been serious, but his seriousness had been tempered by a playful sense of humor, even a loquacious frivolousness at times. Most of all, he'd been fair and just to an idealistic degree, and he'd wanted nothing more than to bring that fairness and justice home to Wyoming.

She had thought that for the first few months after he'd become the county's prosecuting attorney, he'd retained those ideals. It was later when she'd noted a change in his temperament—a sternness and remoteness, like that of a man who sees he's waging a tough battle and must summon all his strength to fight it.

All of his strength while subjugating his sense of justice?

She felt sick and hollow when she considered the possibility that Lee's desire to run Betajack's gang to ground had caused him to be negligent in making sure that the man he'd caused to be sentenced to hang had been genuinely guilty of stealing those horses.

After their romantic affair in Omaha, what kind of man had she really found herself married to?

"What are you thinking about, Glen?"

Suddenly, she found that he was returning her penetrating, faintly quizzical gaze. Again, her heart quickened. Guilt racked her for the thoughts she'd been entertaining as well as about her indiscretions that, after the first one, had been not only premeditated but anticipated with eagerness and downright longing. "I was . . . thinking about Uncle Walt and Aunt Evelyn, hoping they're not going to too much trouble with us coming for Christmas."

He stared at her with the same expression. Inwardly, she flinched from it and was relieved when Mrs. O'Reilly sitting to her left said, "What are we all doing for Christmas?" as though to relieve the tension that was almost palpable inside the coach.

No one said anything. The two drummers, sitting facing each other and playing cards on a small trunk they'd upended in the aisle between them, merely glanced at each other and continuing playing. Old Elijah Weatherford was dozing, chin on his chest, to Mrs. O'Reilly's left. Sally Rand and her husband, Percy, sat to Lee's right, across from Mrs. O'Reilly. They both looked the most fearful of all the passengers.

"How 'bout you, dear?" asked Mrs. O'Reilly, smiling at the plain-faced young woman, who looked at her with her stricken pale blue eyes, as though she thought she could die at any time. And she was probably right, Glendolene thought. One bullet through the thin walls of the coach could kill two, possibly even three of them. All because of Lee. . . .

"*Me?*"

"You and your husband. What is his name, again?"

"N-name's Percy, ma'am," the young man said in his shy, country manner. He leaned forward, his large hands in their deerskin mittens hanging down over his slender knees.

"What are your plans for Christmas, if I my ask?" said Lori O'Reilly. "Don't you just love this time of the year?"

Sally Rand tried to smile, but the look came off as more of a wince. Christmas, it seemed, was the last thing on her mind. Obviously, Lori was just trying to get her mind back in the holiday spirit and off Betajack and Hendricks, but Glendolene knew from her own attempts at it that was like trying to get a thousand-pound horse off your foot.

"We're going home to Percy's family place up on the Missouri River," said Mrs. Rand, almost too softly to be heard above the loud squawking of the stage's thoroughbraces. "We won't make it for Christmas, but we hope to arrive by New Year's."

"And what will you do there?" Lori continued to prod the young woman.

"Oh, I don't know. . . ."

"Probably sit around and do my old man's chores while he stumbles around drunk," said Percy Rand, chuckling with what appeared genuine mirth. He was at least trying to distract himself, however awkwardly, Glendolene thought.

"Percy!" Sally scolded the young man.

Percy shrugged his broad, bony shoulders, flushing and dropping his eyes to his thick-soled boots in embarrassment.

"Drinking problem, has he?" said Lori. "My pa was the same way. I reckon your ma has to carry most of the load, eh, Percy?"

"Oh, she has to!" Sally said, wrinkling the skin above the bridge of her nose. "That old George Rand—

all he does is drink and, like Percy says, stumble around drunk. We was gonna ranch with him, but we pulled out when Percy heard about good homestead land up near the Snowy Range. All his pa done was boss him and didn't do nothin' else but drink up any profits we saw. We proved up on the place in Wyoming, but . . ." A corner of her mouth slanted up, and she let her voice trail off, looking a little shameful about her outburst.

Percy appeared to harbor no offense. "Blackleg," he said, by way of explanation. "Two years of it broke us. Now . . . we're heading back to old George's ranch."

"Ah," Lori said. "To eat some humble pie, which I'm sure George will serve up aplenty." She chuckled. "But I'll bet deep down he'll be very happy to see you back. Why, I bet he's let his own place fall into ruin. You two will get it back in shape in no time."

Sally Rand's eyes brightened slightly as she said, "I'm with child." She looked around a little sheepishly at the other men. Old Weatherford must have been sleeping lightly, because he lifted his chin just then, and opened his eyes that shone in the salmon light pushing through the windows on the other side of the coach from Glendolene.

He smiled, his handlebar mustache above the bib beard lifting until the upswept ends nearly encircled his nose.

"Congratulations, my sweet!" said Lori, leaning forward to clasp her knit-mittened hands around those of Sally Rand. "Congratulations, indeed. I bet it'll be such a help to have Percy's mother around."

"Oh, she's very happy," said Sally.

"Congratulations," Glendolene said, genuinely happy for the girl, who appeared genuinely happy herself, riddled with none of the misgivings that Glendolene herself was feeling about bringing her own child into what might very well be a loveless marriage. If a marriage much longer at all. She felt tears fill her eyes, and her voice pinch, as she said, "I wish you every happiness."

She turned away quickly. As she did, tears dribbling down her cheeks, she saw Lee regarding her incredulously. Quickly, she brushed her tears from her cheeks and gave her gaze to the countryside rushing past now as they stormed down a hill, toward what must have been the overnight station—another grim collection of crude gray buildings and corrals—nestled along a creek in a broad bowl below.

The sun went down, and twilight filled the now-silent coach. Outside, snow the size of buckshot fell at a slant. Glendolene felt the growing cold penetrate her womb. She shuddered against it.

Yakima hunkered low against his saddle, drawing his buckskin's collar up to his ears. The fire popped before him. The falling snow sizzled in the orange flames, melted on the stones surrounding it.

He was camped just off the stage road, about half a mile south of the station at which he'd seen the coach pull up to a couple of hours earlier. He'd wanted to ride on, but he hadn't been able to. Something had held him back, keeping the clattering of the iron-shod wheels and the thudding of the horses' hooves just within his hearing.

Holding a tin cup of steaming coffee in his left hand, he shivered against the cold that blew into this hollow he'd found in some glacier-strewn rocks and stared into the darkness beyond the fire. It wasn't her that held him back. He'd just started to realize that a while ago, after he'd set up the camp.

In the shadows to his left, Wolf whinnied.

Yakima jerked his .44 out of its holster, raking the hammer back, managing to hold on to the cup in his opposite hand, but feeling the hot coffee dribbling down the sides and wetting his gloves.

"Hal-looo the camp," came a call from the darkness on the other side of the fire.

Chapter 24

Yakima set his cup on a rock, then rose and stepped far wide of the fire, keeping the pistol aimed toward where he'd heard the call.

"Name yourself," he said.

"Donny Pearl. I'm friendly as long as you are. Seen your fire. Got a question for you, mister."

"Ride in slow."

The thud of several sets of shod hooves sounded. To Yakima's left, Wolf nickered and stomped, pulling against the short picket line his rider had strung between two ponderosas. One of the approaching horses whinnied. The stranger said, "Now, Winslow, you act your manners. No one wants to hear a lick out of you this night."

Shadows grew back where the hollow opened. They came on through the trees until the rider drew rein on his blaze-faced chestnut gelding, whose brown eyes glowed in the firelight. The rider was a young man in a blanket coat and cream-colored woolly chaps that were missing several tufts of wool, showing the sheepskin beneath. The kid—clean-shaven, sandy-haired, not yet twenty—had an old carbine in the brush-scarred scabbard on the chestnut's right side, but all he held in his hands were the horse's reins and the reins of two horses he trailed.

The two spare horses flanked him; Yakima could make out only their outlines. Packhorses, they appeared; packs were slung over their backs.

"What're you doin' out on such a night, Donny Pearl?" Yakima asked the young man.

"I'm a maverick hunter for the Five-Star Ranch over west."

The kid stopped, expressionless. Since he appeared to be waiting for Yakima's prompting, the half-breed said, "All right."

"What about yourself?" the kid asked, haltingly, a little tense about asking a stranger—especially a big one holding a cocked Colt in his fist and who obviously had a good bit of Indian blood—impertinent questions.

"Fair enough," Yakima said. "I'm Yakima Henry. Makin' my way to Belle Fourche."

"Fer Christmas?"

Yakima had to snort at that. The kid obviously felt much more strongly about Christmas than he did. Than he ever had, most likely, since he'd spent most of his Christmases alone. "Well, I was hopin' to make it before Christmas, but at the rate I'm goin', I'll be lucky to make it before *next* Christmas."

"Last Christmas wasn't much, but this Christmas Mr. Condit—he ramrods the Five-Star—said he's gonna turn ole Winslow here over to me. Winslow's from Arizona. Fact, I named him when I was trailin' him up here. He was just a colt."

"Congratulations," Yakima said, realizing that the

boy was prattling on because he was nervous about the pistol held in his hand, though he'd depressed the hammer.

He dropped the popper into the holster but kept the keeper thong free, still wary of a trap to be sprung by Betajack and Hendricks. "He's a fine horse. What're you trailin' back there, if you don't mind me askin'?"

Donny Pearl glanced over his shoulder, making the frozen tack squawk. "Thought you might know about these two fellas I found strapped over their horses. Thought maybe they was ridin' with you. They're shot up bad. So bad they're dead," he added without humor.

Yakima moved slowly forward. He wouldn't put it past Betajack or Hendricks to send a few of their hard cases in to bushwhack him. Slow-talking Donny Pearl seemed like a thirty-a-month-and-found cowpuncher, but Yakima had known men who talked just as slow with plenty of blood on their cold-blooded hands. Keeping the kid in the periphery of his vision, ready for any sudden movements from him or the two men draped over the horses behind him, Yakima stopped in front of the buckskin that was directly behind the chestnut, which stood with its tail arched.

The man wore no hat. His head and arms hung down over his horse's left front stirrup. Yakima squatted, lifted the man's head by his hair, was taken by no real surprise when the slack-jawed face of Deputy U.S. Marshal Tom Kelsey stared back at him, eyes half rolled back in his head. His neck was bloody from a ragged hole in his throat. The blood was frozen. His face was pale blue.

Yakima walked over to the second horse. He didn't have to lift the man's head. The red hair dusted with dandrufflike snow granules, and his dark blue cavalry uniform told the half-breed that the carcass belonged to Major Demarest of Camp Collins in the Colorado Territory.

"Yeah, I know who they are," Yakima told the kid, looking off into the darkness and pricking his ears. Nothing out there, as far as he could tell, but the wind and the faint ticking of the steadily falling snow.

"Sorry about that," the kid said. "That's a rough way to go. You know who shot 'em?"

"Yeah, I do."

"They still out here, you think?"

"Yeah. You got a place to throw down tonight?"

The kid jerked his head back and hooked a thumb over his shoulder. "Line shack just west of here. I already got my mavericks corralled over there."

"Best head back to 'em, then. The crew that killed these fellas are nasty sons o' bucks, so take her easy and don't stop for no one."

"All right, then."

Donny tossed Yakima the two sets of reins.

"Sorry about your friends, mister. I hope you don't end up the same."

"Yeah, me, too." Yakima doubted that Donny had heard him above the thudding of the chestnut's hooves, though he heard the kid's raised voice when he called as a final, parting thought:

"Merry Christmas!"

Later that night, on her cot in the rear sleeping quarters of the Hawk's Bluff Overnight Station, Glendolene Mendenhour slid her hands inside the coarse wool blankets, inside her silk nightgown, and over the firm, warm mounds of her breasts. She cupped each orb gently, the way Yakima Henry had cupped them when he'd made love to her in the remote line shack far, far away from the odd stranger who was her husband.

Far from the ranch and the whole rest of the world. . . .

She ran her thumbs across her nipples, remembering him lying between her spread knees on that cot so similar to the one she lay on now. He'd thrust against her rhythmically, nuzzling and then caressing her breasts, softly kissing her forehead, her nose, cheeks, lips, ears. His mouth left a hot dampness wherever he pressed it against her.

Her belly was filled with warm, sweetly churning, tingling nectar. Sheathed in the hot, tangy, leathery smell of him, feeling his calloused hands tenderly roaming across her body, instinctively knowing where to go to pleasure her so sweetly, she was ensconced by his muscular arms and powerful legs in a gradually building orgasmic fire.

She'd breathed deeply, sighed, sobbed as she'd enjoyed the almost unbearably thrilling caress of his maleness sliding in and out of her, the ironlike yet yielding strength of his legs and arms and hips bouncing her lightly up and down, her bent knees and her feet lurching wildly with each exquisite, savage hammering.

After a time, she gave an especially loud groan of sensual agony, swept the pillow out from beneath her, and pressed her head hard against the cot, turning her face to one side, squeezing her eyes closed, and biting her lower lip until it hurt.

He stopped suddenly. She looked up at him. His eyes were dark, far away, jaw tight.

He tensed his long, hard body, gritting his teeth, and then he began shuddering and bucking savagely against her, causing her to gasp and scream as he filled her to overflowing, until her own sweet honey boiled up out of her like a warm rain boiling over the banks of a spring arroyo.

Here in the station house in Wyoming, beneath her palms, her nipples jutted hard as pebbles.

Her own muffled scream of orgasm rose.

"Glen, what is it?" Lee's voice, so harsh and unexpected.

She gasped, lifted her head with a start, realizing that one of her hands had drifted lower, that it had become his hand—Yakima's hand—and that she hadn't merely imagined that she'd screamed.

"Just a dream," she said. "Just a dream, Lee." She was trying to quell her own raspy breaths raking in and out of her lungs. "I'm sorry if I woke you."

The cot to her right squawked, and she saw him rise to a sitting position and reach across the dark space between them. Automatically, she recoiled at the prospect of him touching her.

"Glendolene, for chrissakes . . . !"

"I'm sorry," she whispered, hearing the snores of another passenger—probably Weatherford—beyond the curtain partition to her left. "Just a little jittery, I guess."

Something moved in the darkness ahead of her cot. Ambient light from the room's two windows winked on what looked like a gun barrel. Suddenly, the blanket curtain was pulled back and a figure lurched into the Mendenhours' sleeping crib.

"Quiet, both of you!" one of the drummers hissed, extending a revolver at Lee, whom Glendolene heard gasp as he jerked his head back, sitting propped on his outstretched arms. "One sound, and I'll go ahead and drill a hole through Mendenhour's head!"

Glendolene's heart hammered. For a few seconds she couldn't catch her breath or wrap her mind around what was happening. The reek of moldy fur coats, sweat, and alcohol wafted against her. To her left, old Elijah's snores faltered and then resumed their long, regular sawing. At the same time, the shorter, plumper drummer—the older man, Kearny—took another step until he was standing over the end of Lee's cot. Another shadow moved, and then Glendolene saw the young drummer, the bespectacled Sook, step quickly into the crib behind Kearny and extend a pistol straight at Glendolene's head.

The whiskey stench grew stronger, burning her nostrils.

She stifled a gasp, lurching back against the wall behind her, banging her head slightly, covering her mouth with her hand. "Oh, God!"

"Shut up," Sook rasped. "One peep out of you, Mrs. Mendenhour, and Mendenhour is gonna buy a bullet through his head. You got it?"

Glendolene stared at the round, nickel-sized hole of the pistol barrel held level with her nose. She nodded.

"What the hell are you two men up to?" the prosecutor whispered, his voice quavering with fear and exasperation.

"All you gotta do is get up and throw your coat and your boots on. That's it. One more word, and I'll shoot you. Either of you yell for help, you're liable to get someone else killed."

"It's just easier this way, see?" said Sook. The gun he held on Glendolene shook in his clenched fist. "You just stay here and keep quiet as a church mouse, Mrs. Mendenhour. All right? Nod if you understand."

Glendolene hated the fear that paralyzed her. Sobbing into her hands she held cupped over her mouth, she nodded.

"Christ!" Lee raked out, sliding his enraged gaze between the two men.

Glendolene's heart hammered and her hands shook as she watched Lee fling his covers back and drop his legs to the floor. Helpless and horrified, she sobbed silently into her hands as her husband dressed in jerky, angry, defiant movements. Sook held his gun on Glendolene, and Kearny held his on Lee until he'd thrown his long sheepskin coat on over his long underwear and pulled his boots on. He reached for his hat.

"No need," whispered Kearny, wagging his gun at the open doorway behind him. "Let's go."

Lee glowered at the two men. He glanced at Glendolene. Kearny gave him a shove out the door. Glendolene sobbed louder into her hands. She wanted to call out for help from the others, but Kearny and Sook, being drunk and obviously feeling desperate, might shoot anyone who tried to stop them.

Gradually, she got herself calmed down. She dropped her feet over the side of the cot and reached for her coat. She had to follow them. Whatever Lee might or might not have done, she had to do what she could to keep him from being thrown to the killers. She started through the opening in the blanket curtain, remembered something, and turned back.

Lee's pistol jutted from a holster hanging from a nail in the wall near his cot. Glendolene stared at it. She hadn't fired a gun in years, but she grabbed it, hefted it in her hand, then lowered it to her side and walked out of the crib.

Sook opened the dark station house's front door and gave the prosecutor a hard shove. Mendenhour stumbled over the threshold and out into the yard dusted with new snow. The wind bit him, blew the tails of his coat around his legs clad in only his long handles.

As he got his feet back under him, he spun around, rage searing him, and said, "Goddamn you cowards to hell!"

Kearny stepped toward him and rammed the butt of his pistol against Mendenhour's jaw. The prosecutor gave a cry, spun forward, and dropped to his hands and knees, raking the heels of his hands in the sand and gravel fronting the low-slung station house.

Mendenhour groaned. Fear, desperation hammered him. He'd never known terror this intense, though he'd started to be aware of it when he'd seen Betajack, the man who most wanted to kill him, riding toward him under that white flag.

And now he realized, to his own added horror, that what in the past had allowed him to act so bravely in the face of rampant crime had been knowing that he had his own father, Wild Bill himself, and Neumiller and other lawmen behind him. Now, out here in this vast, stormy land, he had no one, and the horror conjured a strained sob from deep in his thundering chest.

His eyes filled with icy tears that dribbled down his cheeks, and, as he remained on his hands and knees, wanting only to stay here and not have to face that dark, snow-stitched horizon beyond, where his killers waited, he heard himself blubber, "Please . . . please . . . I'll pay you."

"You'll pay us?" Sook said with a laugh that the wind strangled. He kicked the prosecutor hard in the ass with the toe of his boot, and Mendenhour flew forward with a yelp of agony. He lay belly-down on the hard, snowy ground. "You'll pay us to die for you? Ha!"

"Too late to try to buy your way out of this, Mr. Lawyer," said Kearny, squatting beside Mendenhour, "even if you did have enough money on you to pay us to die *with* you. You heard old Betajack. He gave you one day to turn yourself over to him, or he'd not only kill you, but he'd kill us all."

"Get up!" Sook snarled. "Get your ass up and get out there. The way we see it, we got nothin' to lose. Betajack might just be so happy to get you he'll leave me an' Kearny alone, since we're feedin' you to him, an' all."

Numb with trepidation, Mendenhour climbed to his feet. Tears dribbled down his cheeks. He stared straight off at the horizon that was a purple-black robe threaded with the violently tumbling snowflakes. Somewhere off to his right, a loose shutter hammered against one of the outbuildings. One of the horses stabled in the barn, afraid of the storm, gave a shrill whinny that the prosecutor barely heard beneath the wind.

Sook gave him a violent shove, and he stumbled forward with another groan. He started walking. His legs felt as though two-by-fours had been shoved up his thighs. His calf muscles ached. His heart raced. Sweat broke out on every inch of him beneath his thin layer of clothes.

What was worse than the fear was his sudden awareness of what he thought he'd probably always known about himself—he was a coward. He could afford to act brave because he'd been raised by a tough man who'd loved him and would back him in anything he did. But one thing Wild Bill Mendenhour had not done for his son was allow him to stand independently against adversity, and thus nurture his own courage.

So easy, he vaguely thought now, as he walked stiffly toward that dark horizon, like a man walking a ship's plank to the cold waters of a stormy sea roiling with sharks. So damn easy to harbor the ideals he'd harbored. Not so easy to stand behind them when it was only himself standing there.

And he'd allowed himself the even worse conceit of alienating the one man who might have saved him. Who might have saved them all. Why? Because he, Mendenhour, had taken offense at the way the man had regarded his wife, and how she, quite understandably, had regarded him in return.

When they'd walked out through a crease between the low hills, Kearny said, "That's far enough." Then he walked around Mendenhour, keeping his pistol trained on him, and shouted into the wind: "Beta-jaaaack! Got your man here, Betajack! Hendricks! Got the lawyer here! *Come an' get him!*"

Chapter 25

"Ah, God . . . *please!*" Mendenhour's knees buckled; he dropped to the ground, hanging his head and his shoulders in defeat. "Don't do this. Oh, Christ, don't do this."

Both Kearny and Sook walked around, yelling up and down the wind, yelling for Betajack and Hendricks.

"Please, don't let them take me," Mendenhour said, sobbing, icy tears dribbling down his cheeks to freeze in his beard. "They'll . . . they'll *hang* me!"

"Hold it!" A woman's yell barely audible above the wind.

A vaguely familiar voice though oddly pitched. Mendenhour lifted his head.

"Told you to stay back in the cabin!" Kearny shouted behind Mendenhour, who turned now to see whom he'd shouted at.

"Drop those guns, both of you," Glendolene said, holding her own pistol—Mendenhour's Colt .45—in both hands straight out in front of her.

Mendenhour stared at her, only half able to comprehend his pretty young wife standing before him, wielding a pistol, trying to save his life. For her part, Glendolene didn't comprehend it, either. She merely gave free rein to her impulses as she repeated the order, trying to quell the shaking of her hands holding the gun.

"We're just tryin' to save all our lives," Kearny yelled above the moaning wind and ticking snow at the woman. "Don't be a fool, Mrs. Mendenhour. Put the pistol down."

Glendolene shook her head. "I mean it." She gritted her teeth as she clicked the revolver's hammer back.

"Look at him!" shouted Sook, pointing at Mendenhour. "He ain't worth it. Why, he's been crying like a little girl, beggin' for his life! He's a simpering fool who don't give a damn if he gets us all killed."

Kearny shook his head angrily, desperately, holding his own pistol out to his right side. "Hell, it even sounds like he mighta hanged the *wrong man*!"

"That was just Betajack talking," Glendolene said, shivering, shaking her head. "Lee, get up. Get back to the cabin. I'll cover you!"

Mendenhour just knelt there, looking half dead, his head hanging, shoulders slumped. His lips moved as though he were talking to himself.

Glendolene screamed shrilly, *"Lee!"*

Just then Kearny swung his gun toward her. Glendolene glanced up as she edged the Colt toward him and jerked the trigger. Their guns exploded simultaneously, Kearny's slug screeching past her right ear so closely that she could feel the heat of its passing.

Glendolene gave another shrill scream as the kick of the big Colt sent her stumbling backward at the same time that Kearny staggered back two steps and sat down hard on his butt. Glendolene's right heel kicked a stone, and she twisted around and fell on her right side, dropping the gun.

"Christ!" Sook cried, staring down at Kearny sitting there with a large wet spot growing on the front of his ragged coat, just left of his heart.

Kearny stared expressionlessly at Glendolene, his features slack. He looked down at the hole in his coat through which blood was beginning to dribble, and then he looked at Glendolene again, eyes widening his shock.

"She . . . killed me."

His eyes rolled back in his head. He sagged backward, hitting the ground with a thump, and lay with his legs bent in front of him, his knees quivering. Glendolene stared at him, her ears ringing with a shock similar to Kearny's own. Mendenhour stared dumbly at the dead man, too. Sook stumbled backward, as though from a coiled rattler, then turned toward Glendolene, his face a mask of horror and fury in the darkness.

"You stupid bitch! Now see what you done?"

He swung his pistol toward Glendolene. She screamed, lifted an arm to shield her face, and threw herself belly-down on the ground. At the same time, a gun blasted. The wind tore at it, muffled it. Glendolene jerked, feeling as though a pin had poked her left side.

She lay tense, the shock of her imminent death numbing her. Only half-consciously she was aware of the thud of a body hitting the ground nearby. Several windy seconds passed, and then she realized that the pain in her side wasn't getting any worse. In fact, it was fading. She'd imagined it. She lifted her head and looked to her left.

Sook lay on his back, his head turned toward

Glendolene. His lower jaw hung slack. His vacant eyes blinked rapidly, lips moving quickly, as though he were muttering. His shoulders twitched out of sync with each other. Glendolene frowned when she saw the round hole in his right temple. Something dark stained the snow-dusted ground around his head.

Glendolene stared at the dead Sook. He was just another part of the recent happenings that merely confused her shocked brain. Something moved in the darkness beyond her and Mendenhour, who knelt as before, his head and shoulders down, wind whipping his auburn hair about his head.

The large shadow moved again in the west. It grew larger. Glendolene stared at it, trying to comprehend at least this aspect of the improbable chain of recent events, until her brain told her that several horses were moving toward her.

"Oh, no," she heard herself whisper, another wave of dread washing over her. "Oh, God, no. Here they come."

But then she saw that there were three horses but only one rider. The rider continued riding toward her on a black, blaze-faced horse. The two other horses trailed along behind him. He wore a black hat tied to his head with a gray scarf, and a buckskin mackinaw. He held a rifle straight out from his right hip.

"What the hell?" shouted Yakima Henry as he pulled back on the several sets of reins in his left hand.

He looked around, then dropped the reins, lifted his right boot over his saddle horn, and leaped to the ground. He ran past Mendenhour to Glendolene, squatted beside her.

"You all right?"

She nodded dumbly, glanced from Sook to her husband and then to Kearny. "I . . . don't . . . know. . . ."

"What the hell happened?"

She was deeply confused, but when she finally managed to start speaking, he said, "Never mind. Let's get you inside. Christ, with all that racket I don't doubt Betajack and Hendricks are headed this way!"

He had her on her feet before he'd finished the sentence, quickly looked her over apparently to see if she'd taken a bullet, then ran over to Mendenhour.

"Mendenhour!" he shouted above the wind, holding his rifle in one hand and jerking cautious looks all around them, the wind bending his hat brim and pulling at the ends of the scarf knotted beneath his chin.

Someone shouted to the east, and Yakima swung in that direction, loudly racking a fresh round in his Winchester's breech, holding the rifle up high across his chest. But then he saw a badge flash in the darkness, and Deputy U.S. Marshal Raoul Arenas took shape before him, his long wool coat jostling around his fur-lined, stovepipe boots.

"What the hell's goin' on?" the lawman shouted. "I heard shooting!"

He looked at the two dead men and Mendenhour and the prosecutor's wife, his mustached face a mask of confusion.

"Get 'em inside!" Yakima shouted. "How'd they get out here without you knowin' about it, anyways?"

Arenas gave him an indignant look but, deciding to save the argument for later, lurched forward, grabbed the lawyer's left arm, and jerked the man to his feet. Mendenhour moved stiffly, wobbly-footed, like a man sleepwalking. Arenas scowled at him incredulously, then took Glendolene's arm and began leading her back in the direction of the station house.

Yakima glanced at the two dead men. He'd just been

riding over the top of a low hill to the west when he'd seen Sook aiming the pistol at Glendolene. He'd raised his rifle, aimed, and fired without even thinking about it as his instincts had kicked in. He was glad they had.

He crouched to grab Sook's arm with the intention of throwing him over Wolf's back, but he froze when the horse raised a shrill whinny. He straightened, looking around.

The horse stomped and bobbed its head. Wolf didn't like the smell of blood, but Yakima had a feeling the black had his neck up over something else.

Betajack and Hendricks.

No point in getting bushwhacked out here helping dead men.

He looked around, unable to see much but the gauzy darkness and the tangled brush and sage shrubs blowing in the wind for a distance of about thirty yards in every direction. The hills were faint, cream-limned shadows a little farther away.

Continuing to look around warily, he picked up the reins of the two mounts carrying the dead Kelsey and Demarest, as well as Wolf's reins. He toed a stirrup and swung into the saddle. Holding the Yellowboy straight up from his right thigh, he booted the mount after the others. At the edge of the yard, as he watched Arenas lead the Mendenhours into the station house, he cut away and headed north to the barn, casting one more glance to the west.

Two minutes before, lying near the top of a low hill from where he'd had a good view of the stage passengers' skirmish, Floyd Betajack reached over and shoved Sonny's rifle down. His younger and sole remaining son looked at him, furling his snow-peppered brows. Betajack looked at the half-breed's broad back as the black stallion carried the man off toward the station house.

Betajack shook his head.

"Why not, Pa? Christ, I had him in my sights. Shit, I had 'em all in my sights!"

Claw Hendricks lay on the other side of Sonny. All the men of both gangs, including the two leaders and Sonny Betajack, were spread out shoulder to shoulder along the top of the knoll. Hendricks laughed, knowingly, wagging his head.

"It's too easy, kid," he told Sonny. "Your old man wants 'em all to sweat a little longer."

"They're all shittin' wheel hubs—Mendenhour most of all," Betajack said with satisfaction, hardening his jaw and jutting his chin toward the station house that he could only dimly see through the curtains of light, blowing snow. "Why put 'im out of his misery? I like him miserable. Fact, I wanna keep him miserable for at least another twenty-four hours."

"You got him in a bad place," Hendricks said with satisfaction, wagging his head in appreciation of the older outlaw's tactics. "You got 'em all in a bad place."

"Soon, more'll turn on Mendenhour. Hell, soon they'll likely be turnin' on each other. That breed fella, Henry, he keeps hope alive. And that's just fine with me." Betajack spat a wad of chew to one side. "'Cause when I'm good an' ready, I'm gonna take it away. And then that'll be the end of Mendenhour and every last one of them people, includin' Yakima Henry."

"Except the woman," Hendricks said. "No point in killin' a nice little piece of work like that, Betajack."

Betajack looked at him from beneath the bending brim of his hat. "You want her?"

"Yeah, I'd like to have her. Of course." Hendricks grinned devilishly. The man beyond him was grinning over his shoulder, showing white teeth in the darkness. "Why not?"

Sonny snickered.

"All right, then." Betajack gave a grunt and heaved himself to his feet. "You want her so goddamn bad, she's yours. Come on, fellas. Let's get back to camp and get some sleep. Big day tomorrow!"

Chapter 26

Yakima opened the barn doors and led the three horses inside. He found a lantern, lit it, hung it from the post he'd found it on, then went back and closed the doors, having to pull hard against the wind.

When he got the doors latched, he went over and began unsaddling the black that stood tossing his head as though still bedeviled by something he'd seen or smelled outside in the hills. Yakima had just removed the saddle and set it over a stall partition when he heard the scrape of the barn doors opening.

He whipped around, the Colt in his fist instantly. The hammer clicked back as he aimed the piece at the three-foot gap between the doors.

"Hold on," said the lawman, Arenas, stopping and glowering through the lamp's amber, flickering light at the half-breed.

Yakima depressed the Colt's hammer, holstered the piece, then walked over to remove his saddlebags from Wolf's back. Arenas closed the barn doors, and then, turning toward Yakima, he said, "What in the hell happened out there?"

"Hell, you got there about one minute after I did."

"Well, what did you see in that minute?" Arenas said, scowling belligerently.

"I saw them two drummers trying to throw Mendenhour to the wolves. His wife took offense, apparently, and Sook turned a gun on her. That's when I rode in and gave him an extra ear hole."

Arenas stared at Yakima, who draped his saddlebags over the stall partition with his saddle and then removed Wolf's bridle and started rubbing the stallion down with a scrap of burlap. Meanwhile, Arenas snorted and walked over to the other two horses. While Yakima worked on the black, giving him a good rubdown, tending the horse with his usual care, Arenas squatted to get a good look at his partner, Kelsey.

He gave a disgusted chuff and then he looked over at the other man whose red hair pegged him as Major Demarest. Arenas whipped his hard gaze back to Yakima, tightening his hand around the neck of his Winchester's rear stock.

Yakima glanced at him. "Yeah, I killed 'em and hauled 'em back here because I got nothin' better to do with my time." He gave a caustic snort as he continued rubbing the burlap across Wolf's hindquarters and left rear leg.

He could feel Arenas's eyes on him. Finally, the lawman lowered the rifle. He leaned it against a stall partition and began lifting Kelsey off his horse. When he had both dead men lying side by side in a pile of straw, he doffed his hat, ran a hand through his wavy black hair streaked with gray.

"What the hell's goin' on here?" he said, pondering the dead men before turning his befuddled gaze to Yakima.

"Didn't you get it explained to you clear enough?"

"Mendenhour told me Betajack and Hendricks were after him for hangin' Betajack's boy."

"There you have it."

"But"—Arenas returned his perplexed brown eyes back to the dead men staring up at him dumbly— "this. . . ."

"It's a bitch on high red wheels, ain't it?"

Arenas walked over to Kelsey's horse, reached under its belly, and unbuckled the latigo straps. "What's your piece of this, breed? Why're you here?"

"Because I'm a damn fool."

"Where you headed?"

"Same place the Mendenhours are headed."

"Belle Fourche?"

Yakima tossed the burlap onto his saddle and then walked toward a water barrel near the front doors.

"What you got in Belle Fourche?"

Yakima pulled a hatchet off a nail in the wall and used it to break the ice off the top of the water barrel. "Private business." He dunked a wooden pale in the barrel and set it down in front of Wolf, who lowered his head to suspiciously sniff the rim before loudly drawing water.

"Look," Arenas said as he unsaddled Demarest's horse, "I was out of line."

Yakima glanced at him, a brow arched in surprise.

Arenas looked at him as he set the second saddle over a stall partition, and canted his head toward the two dead men. "About those two."

"How so? I am a killer, ain't I? I mean, you've seen paper on me."

"What I'm tryin' to say," the lawman said, squaring his shoulders as he faced Yakima and hooking his thumbs in the pockets of his fleece-lined wool coat, "is it looks like we're ridin' together. With the stage. If you're still headin' to Belle Fourche, that is."

Yakima studied him. He had an instinctive dislike for men of authority. Lawmen, most of all. Arenas had moderated his tone only because he needed his help, but that didn't mean Yakima liked the man any better than he had a few hours ago. Or that he trusted him.

But he supposed he needed the lawmen's help getting the stage to Belle Fourche as much as Arenas needed him.

"I reckon that's where I'm headed, all right."

"I reckon we'd best figure out a plan to get there alive, then. The way I see it, we can't stay here."

"No," Yakima said, shaking his head as he edged a cautious look through a crack in the barn doors, "they could burn us out."

"We might be able to get help in Broken Jaw. They got a new sheriff, Brian McAllister. A good man. Not a drunkard like Hal Dempsey was. McAllister's got two good deputies he recruited off one of the big ranches. Damn tough, fair men. One's my cousin, Hector."

"Well, that's three."

"Must be a few more we can recruit to ride along with the stage. Hell, winter's coming on. Lots of out-of-work punchers around."

"All right, that'll be the plan," Yakima said, grabbing his rifle from where he'd leaned it against the stall partition. "Now, I reckon we'd best both keep watch tonight. My horse was skittish as hell in them buttes just west. I have a feeling Betajack and Hendricks are near."

He started through the doors.

Behind him, Arenas said, "I'll tend these horses and be out in a few minutes."

Yakima looked around the windy, snow-murky night and then turned to close the doors. Arenas looked at him, his face only partly lit by the lantern hanging on the ceiling joist. "Mendenhour—he didn't look too good."

"I reckon he met someone he wasn't expecting to meet tonight."

The lawman frowned. "Who's that?"

"Himself."

Yakima closed the doors.

The wind blew, the snow fell, and the night passed.

Yakima and Arenas took turns walking the perimeter of the station yard. Neither man saw the slightest sign of the stalkers. While that was a relief, it was also perplexing, nerve-racking. They had to be out there somewhere. As long as Mendenhour was alive, they'd be stalking the stage.

At dawn, the station's two hostlers—twin Norwegians named Olaf and Oscar—headed out to the barn to prepare the horses. Oscar's woman, a stove-up but still-able Lakota named Wilomena Fire Stick, made breakfast while the passengers roused from their beds, none looking as though they'd slept much after the skirmish in the buttes and the deaths of the two drummers.

Yakima stood outside near the stage horses, cradling the Yellowboy, as the passengers filed out of the station. The prosecutor, ushering his wife off the veranda and into the waiting coach, looked especially pale and drawn. He said nothing to Glendolene or to anyone, and his face was as expressionless as stone.

They rode out at what Yakima assumed was sunrise, though it was hard to tell because a heavy ceiling of low clouds completely closed off the sky from horizon to horizon. It was a gray, wintry world. As he trotted Wolf ahead of the stage while Adlard drove and Arenas rode shotgun, Yakima raked his gaze all around and from far to near.

Still, there was no sign of the stalkers. Not even any tracks in the thin layer of fresh snow along the trail, though if they'd been made overnight, the wind likely would have obscured them.

Now the air was still but cold. A few flakes fell, but they drifted like goose down, swirling slightly before settling on the sage, piñons, bunchgrass, and frequent granite escarpments thrusting up along both sides of the trail. The only movement was an occasional rabbit venturing out of its burrow, twitching its ears and working its nose and then scrambling back to its hole when it heard or saw the lurching, clamoring stage.

Yakima stayed ahead of the stage, scouting the trail, stopping when Adlard stopped the coach, usually at the top of steep grades, to rest and water the horses. Between the Hawk's Bluff Station and Broken Jaw was only twenty miles, so there were no relay stations between. They were on their own.

The country was all buttes and mesas, with the Big Horns rising beyond the gauzy screen of falling snow in the north. The graded stage trail rose and fell over mostly low hills and around butte shoulders. Escarpments and thickets and clusters of pines and firs provided ample cover for any possible ambush, and Yakima scouted these carefully, well ahead of the stage.

Occasionally, he rode to the crest of a bluff and

scrutinized the surrounding country through his field glasses. There was no movement out there anywhere except a small herd of elk heading from the high country to the low country for winter. Once, he spied a few cattle grazing between snow-mantled hogbacks, but there were no punchers with them. No other men out here whatsoever.

At least, that was how it appeared.

He knew better. The knowledge kept the hair under the collar of his buckskin shirt standing on end.

During one short stop to rest the horses, Mendenhour suggested they build a fire. "The women are cold," he told Arenas.

It was the first time that Yakima had heard the man speak since his embarrassing show of cowardice the night before. He looked better than he'd looked that morning, as though he'd somehow come to terms with his actions. Or inactions, as the case were. Still, he spoke in a wooden, peculiarly emotionless tone.

"Best not," Arenas said, glancing at Yakima sitting the black stallion on a small rise just ahead of the stage. "Best not stay anywhere very long. Besides, Broken Jaw should be just over that next rise."

"Broken Jaw, yes," the prosecutor said, nodding once, grimly. "I'll be getting off there." He looked at Glendolene. "Permanently."

The other passengers—the Rands, Lori O'Reilly, and old Elijah Weatherford, who was smoking his ubiquitous quirley—all glanced around at each other. The Rands looked relieved. The others merely looked puzzled.

Glendolene, who'd been standing near a fir tree with her hands stuffed into a fox-fur muffler in front of her, said softly, "But . . . how will we get back to Wolfville?"

"Not we," he told his wife, taking her arm in one of his hands. "Just me. I'm sending you along with the others. When it's safe to come home, I'll send for you."

The Mendenhours stared at each other. The others stared at them, including Yakima. So Mendenhour had had enough of his own cowardice. The half-breed approved of his decision; it would likely save the others besides making his own trip a hell of a lot easier. But part of him hated that Betajack and Hendricks would win their grisly game.

Most likely, despite the best efforts of the Broken Jaw lawmen, they'd find a way to follow through with their intentions. Unless Mendenhour wanted to remain in protective custody, locked in a jail cell, till Betajack died of old age and Hendricks lost interest.

But it was better they got him alone than with his wife and the other innocent stage passengers.

"We'll stop for an hour or so in Broken Jaw," Charlie Adlard said, standing with the horses, running a mittened hand down the neck of the near wheeler but looking wearily, warily off toward the west. "The station there'll be warm, and they'll have a good lunch with plenty of coffee. And"—he gave Arenas a wry look—"I hope something stronger."

Arenas said, "We'll get help from the new sheriff there, as well. Best climb aboard, folks."

Lori O'Reilly looked at Yakima. "Any sign of them, Mr. Henry?"

"Nope, all clear," he said, offering what he hoped was a hopeful smile.

He glanced at Glendolene. She returned the look.

The prosecutor looked at him then, too. Mendenhour turned abruptly away, as though he could read the unspoken words in the gaze his wife shared with the half-breed, and guided her over to the waiting coach.

He knew, Yakima thought. Somehow, the man's instinct had told him what had happened between Yakima and his wife. Yakima made a mental note to watch his back. Cuckolded men—even cowardly cuckolded men—could be every bit as dangerous as the killers trailing them.

Chapter 27

As Yakima rounded a long curve in the trail around the base of a rocky-topped butte, the little town of Broken Jaw spread out ahead and below him, along a deep bowl in the high-desert prairie.

The town wasn't much—maybe thirty, thirty-five log and mud-brick shacks ringing a business section of half a dozen bulky frame, false-fronted trade shops. Just now the sun had slipped down beneath the cap of pewter clouds, and it spread a fiery salmon glow across the humble dwellings nestling there in the four or five inches of new-fallen snow, with blond prairie grass and sage spiking above its icy crust.

The fading light colored the snow a dusty rose. The buildings were copper. The smoke issuing from their chimneys was charcoal threaded with salmon. Gradually, the colors deepened as the sun fell behind the Wind River Mountains in the west.

As he continued walking Wolf along the trail and starting down the long grade toward the town, Yakima glanced behind. The stage appeared around a shoulder of the bluff. Adlard had the team galloping, his

bearded face painted yellow by the western sun, Arenas looking grim beside him, holding his Winchester
barrel-up on his right thigh. The deputy U.S. marshal
had his broad-brimmed tan hat tipped low against the
light. Old Elijah Weatherford just then poked his head
out of the coach's right side, looking around Yakima at
the town beyond him, and his own wizened, bib-
bearded face acquired a relieved expression.

Yakima heeled Wolf into a lope, keeping ahead of
the stage. As he dropped down the hill, corrals and
stock pens pushed up on both sides of him. Beyond,
the stage trail became the town's main street. It wasn't
yet dark, but no one appeared to be out. He couldn't
even see any horses tied in front of the town's two
saloons that he could recognize from having pulled
through here a few times in the past.

He glanced to his left. An old man in coveralls and a
wool-lined coat was forking hay to a couple of mules in
a pole corral. A log shack stood about fifty yards to the
right of the corral. An old woman in a long gray dress,
bulky coat, and red scarf had been beating a rug with a
broom, but now she was turning slowly, heavily toward
Yakima, shading her eyes as she gazed at the stage rattling and lurching around down the hill behind him.

A German shepherd had been running around near
the old woman, dashing from one side of a woodpile to
another, obviously hunting a mouse or a rabbit, but
now the dog turned toward the stage, as well. It raised
its tail and started barking, showing its fangs.

As Yakima approached, following a horseshoe
curve in the trail as it leveled out in the bowl, the old
woman turned toward the old man in the corral and
yelled something in what sounded like German. The
old man responded in the same tongue.

The old woman turned her pale, pinched-up face toward Yakima and the stage again, moved her mouth in apparent disgust, then turned and shuffled hurriedly toward the log shack. She called to the dog, who stopped barking instantly, then wheeled and followed the old woman into the cabin.

The old man stood leaning on his pitchfork handle, staring grimly over a hay pile toward the stage. Yakima stared back at him and then, as he trotted Wolf on past the cabin and into the town, the hair under his collar stood up taller and straighter. The old man's and the old woman's reactions told him something was wrong.

He glanced behind.

It was too late to reroute the stage. Adlard was only just now slowing it as the lunging team hit level ground and drove to within forty yards of Yakima, entering the edge of the Broken Jaw business district and continuing forward, the team walking and blowing and snorting, shaking their heads, ready for hay and oats and a warm barn.

Yakima's face was a stony mask of apprehension as he continued forward, the tall, false-fronted buildings rising around him, casting purple shadows over the broad, hard-rutted, lightly snow-dusted main drag. He scanned the boardwalks and porches and rooflines on both sides of the street, not liking how still and quiet everything was. The stores appeared as though they'd been closed for some time, curtains drawn over their windows. Only a few had smoke lifting from their chimneys.

Even the two saloons—one nearby on the right side of the street, the other farther up and on the left—appeared shut down. The oil pots on their verandas had not been lit against the growing darkness. The

stage depot was on the left on Yakima's side of the
second saloon. It was a long, low, wood-frame building
with a signboard over the shake-shingled front porch
announcing Andrews & Meechum Stage Line.

The place sat on a broad lot; it was flanked by a barn
and three corrals. The depot's windows were curtained. A CLOSED sign hung in the front door on the far
right side of the porch. Behind it, the barn was closed
up. Horses milled in one of the corrals, all looking
attentively toward the main street.

Yakima stopped Wolf in front of the depot. He
reached forward and pulled the Yellowboy from its boot
and racked a shell one-handed before planting the
brass butt plate on his right thigh.

They're here.

Behind him, the stage clattered to a stop, Adlard
yelling, "Whoahhh!" at the tops of his lungs, standing
in the driver's boot and holding the ribbons up close
against his chest.

The driver and Arenas looked around gravely, suspiciously. Neither one said anything. They could tell
something was wrong. Yakima kept turning his head
from left to right and back again, hipping around in
his saddle to cast his anxious gaze behind him and the
coach, squinting against the dust cloud now catching
up to the stage. The top of the cloud was tinged with
the coppery light of the setting sun. Below, it was purple-
gray.

The street was as quiet as a cemetery at midnight.
Even the spent team was silent, looking around, sens-
ing trouble.

Yakima turned his head toward the right. On that
side of the street sat the county sheriff's office—a low
stone building fronted by a wooden veranda. Three

rocking chairs sat atop the veranda, one with a bobcat hide hanging down the back. A small shingle nailed to a porch post announced in red letters against a green background: SHERIFF B. W. McALLISTER.

The office's deeply recessed windows were dark. Yakima had just scrutinized them when the half-closed curtain in the window just right of the front door moved slightly. From inside the building came the muffled scrape of a boot heel. The door burst open and a big man wearing a five-pointed star on his leather vest bolted through it and onto the porch, his face red, eyes bright with exasperation as he shouted, *"Ambush, Charlie! Ambush!"*

He'd gotten as far as the veranda's top step when something exploded inside the office behind him. The buckshot blasting through the open door caused his chest to blossom like a bloodred rose; it lifted him a foot off the porch and hurled him ten feet into the street. He hit the ground and rolled, flopping his beefy arms.

Yakima snapped the Yellowboy to his shoulder and aimed at the open door beyond which a shadow moved. Just then, another shadow rose above the slightly peaked roof of the jailhouse. Yakima raised the Yellowboy higher and fired twice, hearing the yell amidst the Winchester's explosions as the shooter flung his rifle out to one side and flew back out of sight behind the roofline.

"Hi-yahhhhh!" Adlard shrieked, flicking the ribbons across the backs of his six-horse hitch. *"Mooove*, you mangy cusses. We're pullin' *fooooottttttt!"*

The stage bolted forward so quickly that Arenas, who'd just fired at the roof to the right of the jailhouse's, was caught off guard. The lawman slammed back against his seat with a surprised wail and then rolled down the far side of the stage from Yakima. Amidst a sudden cannonade of guns opening up all around him, Yakima heard the crunching thud of the law-man's body hitting the street.

The stage thundered past him as Yakima whipped his head around to see smoke puffing and flames stab-bing from alley mouths and rooftops up and down the street. Arenas was in the middle of the street, rolling onto his side and wincing, his hat lying beside him, a wing of his thick salt-and-pepper hair flopping over his forehead.

Yakima picked out two shooters and fired, one bul-let merely hammering the rain barrel behind which one killer crouched, but he managed to punch a .44 slug through the knee of his other target standing on the rooftop of the Old Blue Hound Saloon. At the same time, he rode over to where Arenas was just now gain-ing his feet and firing his Winchester from his hip while several slugs blew up dust around his feet.

Yakima winced as a slug sliced across his ear while another kissed nap from his hat brim, and flung a hand out to the lawman. *"Here!"*

Arenas lunged toward him, taking his carbine in his left hand and throwing his right one at Yakima. The half-breed grabbed the man's wrist. Wolf pitched as Arenas leaped against the horse's right hip, not hav-ing enough spring in his leap to gain the horse's back. Yakima triggered his own Winchester with his left hand as he tried to pull the lawman onto the horse behind him.

Arenas jerked forward with a groan, blood spraying from his upper-right chest. He bounced off Yakima's right leg and dropped to his knees in the street. "Forget it," he wailed. "Go! Save the others!"

Yakima hipped around in his saddle, using both hands now to fire and lever, fire and lever, but Wolf was sidestepping crazily, and all his lead flew wide. He turned back to Arenas, who was down on both knees. Just then another bullet slammed into the back of his head, finishing him, and Yakima cursed loudly and ground his heels into the black's flanks.

Horse and rider galloped off down the street, Yakima snaking his rifle behind him to squeeze off two parting shots. As he headed for the town's other end and the stage jouncing in front of a roiling tan dust cloud about a hundred yards away, several slugs screeched through the air around his head and slammed into hitch racks and tore through window glass.

Then the town fell back and he passed a couple of shanties, a windmill, and a tipped-over wagon grown up with weeds that had probably served as a barricade against the town's last Indian attack. He dropped down a grade into open country just as the sun sank below the western horizon.

The air instantly cooled. The sky turned to spruce, and a vast purple stretched over the earth.

He felt as though the sun and all the stars had burned out and he was riding through a dead world. He kept seeing the bullet hammering into Arenas's head, blowing out his right eye in a wash of blood, brains, and bone, and, while the air continued to cool, Yakima felt the heat of a calm, killing fury gradually intensify.

He galloped Wolf down the grade and then up a slight rise through scattered pines between buttes. The trail turned between mesas. Ahead, the coach had slowed as it climbed another rise. Yakima caught up to it, rode up to the driver's boot. Adlard stared down at him anxiously. "What happened to Arenas?"

"He's dead."

"Shit!"

"How far's the next relay station?"

"Almost thirty miles. We'll never make it. These hosses is blown!"

Old Elijah Weatherford poked his head out the stage window. "Bottom of the second rise, swing into the canyon there. There's only a horse trail but it's wide enough for the stage. I know an old ranch-stead there burned out by the Sioux about twelve years ago. Far as I know, no one's moved back."

Yakima looked at Adlard. "Do it. I'll meet you there later."

Yakima stopped Wolf, began to swing the horse back around. Adlard said, "Hey, where you goin'?"

"Back to Broken Jaw." Yakima pressed heels to the black's loins. "Unfinished business!"

He and the reluctant stallion galloped back toward town.

Chapter 28

There was only a rose and periwinkle blue wash of color in the western sky when Yakima rode back into the outskirts of Broken Jaw. He checked Wolf down to a walk, staring ahead into the misty darkness and listening. Faintly, he heard the sounds of revelry likely emanating from one of the saloons.

He hadn't figured the gang would come after him and the stage in the dark. Betajack and Hendricks were in no hurry. They were enjoying themselves. Besides, they knew that the stage with its hitch of blown horses couldn't travel much farther, anyway.

He figured they'd be content to wait until morning to resume stalking Mendenhour. Judging by the sounds, Yakima had been right.

He continued ahead for a few more steps. Then Wolf stopped. Yakima felt the horse tensing its muscles, and knowing from experience what was coming, he lunged forward to wrap his right hand over the horse's snout, forestalling a warning whinny.

Ahead, against a faint wash of light from the main street's left side, a shadow moved. Yakima caught a brief glimpse of the silhouetted outline of a horse and rider. Instantly, he reined Wolf down the trail's left side and into some brush where a few of the town's original cabins humped darkly, the bases of their stone foundations showing the whiteness of wind-drifted snow. He rode to the far side of one of the cabins and stopped, pricking his ears to listen.

A breeze stirred. On it was carried the slow clomps of an approaching horse. The sounds grew gradually louder. A sage or juniper branch made a soft snick as it scraped a stirrup fender. The man had apparently seen Yakima and was moving into the brush to investigate.

Yakima reined Wolf away from the cabin and rode slowly south through the brush and boulders and the remains of several stock pens, privies, and cabins. He drew rein behind a falling-down chicken coop, the door of which the slight, chill breeze nudged against its frame with whispery scrapes.

Yakima swung down from the leather. Holding one hand over Wolf's snout, he shucked his rifle with the other. He gave the horse a hard look, commanding the stallion to keep quiet, and then edged a glance around the back of the chicken coop. Horse and rider were moving toward him. He could see the man's broad-brimmed hat with a cord swinging down beneath his chin, and the ambient light silvering his fur jacket.

Yakima jerked his head back behind the chicken coop. The slow hoof clomps continued. They stopped. A short silence, and then, softly: "Hey, Clesh—that you over there? It's Sonny."

Yakima tensed, waiting, breathing regularly through parted lips. He stooped to pick up a small rotted board that had fallen off the chicken coop, and tossed it over Wolf. It bounced off the side of a dilapidated corral about thirty yards away.

There was another short silence, and then the near killer said louder, "Clesh?"

The hoof thuds started again. They were drifting away. Yakima edged another look out around the chicken coop in time to see the tail of Sonny's horse just before it disappeared behind the coop's far side. On tiptoes, he moved out around the rear of the little building and came up behind Sonny. The man's horse had just started to lurch when the half-breed reached up and jerked sharply back on the man's coat.

Sonny grunted and fell back across his saddle cantle, boots stuck in his stirrup. The man's wild eyes and mouth opened wide. His scraggly little mustache pushed up against his long, almost feminine nose. Just before he could scream, Yakima smashed his Yellowboy's brass butt plate against Sonny's forehead with a solid *smack!*

Sonny's tense body slackened. His hat fell off his head to hang across his shoulder by the chin thong, a messy tangle of greasy, blond hair drooping down the horse's hip. The horse gave a surprised nicker as it bolted off around the front of the chicken coop, Sonny flopping unconscious, possibly dead, across his blanket roll and saddlebags.

Yakima paused, standing tense, squeezing the repeater in his hands, listening. There was only the casual sigh of the wind, the dwindling thuds of Sonny's horse, and the muffled sounds of revelry emanating from the Old Blue Dog Saloon. Yakima went back to where Wolf stood nervously staring toward where Sonny's horse had disappeared to the south.

"Easy, boy," the half-breed whispered as he swung up into the leather.

He rode out around the chicken coop and across the trail where it entered town. He made a slow, quiet, cautious circle, weaving amongst shacks and stock pens, and then rode back toward the main street and the saloon from the north. He stopped Wolf well back from the main street, tied him to the tongue of a hay wagon, in the shadow of a large woodshed, and walked south until he was staring straight across the street at the Old Blue Dog from an alley mouth. Left of the saloon sat the dark stone sheriff's office. The local lawman remained in the street where he'd been thrown by the buckshot—a dark, twisted hump in the darkness. Light from the oil pots flickering on the saloon porch shone red on his upturned cheek.

The Blue Dog had three stories. Yakima remembered that the two upper floors were rented out and that customers who'd first rented one of the girls from downstairs were given a discount. A couple of the second- and third-story windows were lit, as were the two large plate-glass windows on either side of the halved-log front door.

Yakima could see the indistinct images of men moving around inside the place, one dancing arm in arm with a woman while another danced by himself and several others clapped and someone played a raucous mandolin. When the dancing man spun the dancing woman toward the front of the place, Yakima could see that she wasn't smiling but had a nervous, tense expression.

There were no lights on in any of the other buildings up and down the street. The rest of the house, knowing it was under siege by Betajack and Hendricks, whose reputations had likely preceded them even this far north of their usual stomping grounds, were likely huddled behind locked doors, clutching shotguns and pistols, awaiting the Grim Reaper.

He waited ten minutes, making sure no other scouts were anywhere near the outside of the saloon, then ran across the street and into the break between the saloon and the sheriff's office. Slowly, he mounted the veranda, stepping over one of the oil pots, whose warmth felt good against his cold legs, and crouched beside the big window left of the door.

Just then, the dancers—a young blonde in a green dress, a tall man in a wolf-skin cape and with a long-barrel silver pistol holstered on his thigh, and a short blond gent with long, braided chin whiskers—stopped dancing. The woman looked relieved. The taller man staggered to a table and tipped a bottle back, taking a long pull. The shorter man ambled to the bar. Most of the gang appeared to be here in the Old Blue Dog, spread out across seven or eight tables. They were a motley crew—savage-looking with their sneering, self-satisfied faces and all manner of armament bristling off them. The chubby barman stood behind the mahogany looking as edgy as the girl who'd been dancing with Hendricks's tall killer.

The mandolin player appeared to be one of them—a stocky, sharp-chinned Mexican with thick brown hair and fringed deerskin leggings tricked out with silver conchos, ivory-gripped bowie knives sheathed on both calves. He had what appeared to be a hawk tattooed on his broad forehead. Now, as he laughed and started playing the mandolin again, bobbing his head and stomping his foot, Yakima saw that he was missing his two front teeth.

Yakima saw Claw Hendricks in his rose-colored glasses and top hat sitting on a couch against the back wall, a girl on his knee. Betajack sat on the opposite end of the couch from Hendricks. He appeared the only one not enjoying himself; he seemed to just be sitting there and staring toward the front, his hat on his knee, his lower jaw slack. He looked worn out, as would figure for a man his age.

They all appeared well distracted by whiskey, women, and the mandolin player. A few were playing cards. They were not suspecting what Yakima intended—to walk in as casually as possible and to shoot as many as he could, including Betajack and Hendricks, and then to get the hell out of there before any of the survivors could get their guns out. He wouldn't be able to get them all, but if he was cool and efficient about it, he could possibly deplete their numbers by half and essentially decapitate the gang by killing its two leaders.

He started to rise and rack a fresh round into the Yellowboy's breech but froze when, at the back of the room, he saw Betajack heave himself up from the couch. Yakima dropped back down to a knee and stared through a clear patch in the frosted window glass as Betajack donned his hat, bent slightly back on his hips, sticking one arm out, stretching, and moved his mouth, speaking to his partner. Hendricks said something in return to Betajack and then continued nuzzling the neck of the uninterested, bare-breasted girl on his knee.

Betajack turned his head forward and Yakima heard him yell above the crowd's low roar, "You men get to bed soon. We're gonna get us an early start tomorrow, finish this thing once and for all!"

Betajack donned his hat and walked to the stairs rising to the second-story rooms.

Yakima squeezed the Winchester in his gloved hands. *Damn.* He blinked. Another thought occurred to him. Quickly, he leaped down the steps at the end of the porch and jogged into the alley between the saloon and the jailhouse. He slowed after kicking a can and stole up quietly to the rear of the place, edging a look around the corner.

No one appeared out here. Rickety-looking stairs rose along the rear wall, with landings on both the second and third stories. Yakima walked over to the stairs and began climbing, pausing and wincing when a board squawked loudly beneath his weight. He didn't use the rail because, it being wobbly, he was afraid he'd rip it off and cause a racket.

Finally, he gained the second story and stepped through the unlocked door. Instantly, he pressed his back against the door and sucked a startled breath. Down the hall to his left, a thick figure turned from the hall into a room. The room's door closed behind the figure with a thump and a click of the latch.

Yakima took a breath, feeling optimistic. Could he have lucked into finding Betajack's room this quickly? He hadn't gotten a good look at the man heading to bed, but he had to bet it was old Betajack himself. Looking around, making sure he was now alone in the hall, he walked on the balls of his feet to the door that had just closed. Heart thudding, he stared down at the knob.

If the old man had locked his door, Yakima would have to go back to his original plan. He wrapped his hand around the knob, twisted. It turned. The latch clicked. Yakima stepped quickly into the room and closed the door behind him.

The old man had just sat down on the bed to kick out of his boots. He stared up at Yakima now, his eyes wide and rheumy, the domelike top of his head red and freckled under thin strands of gray hair combed from right to left. His face swelled between thick, roached muttonchops of the same color, and his eyes and nostrils flared with outrage.

"Why . . . *you* . . . !"

Yakima aimed the Winchester from his hip at the old man's freckled forehead and clicked the hammer back. "You wanna die right here, right now, go ahead and yell."

Yakima stared at him, waiting. Part of him wanted the man to yell. On the other hand, killing only Beta-jack would likely not keep the rest of the gang from going after him and the stage. Hendricks would want revenge at least for making him and the other men look like fools, having crept in here under their noses.

At the very least, taking Betajack would rock Hendricks back on his heels.

"Isn't that what you're here for?" the old man said raspily, his chest rising and falling sharply. He'd removed his coat and was wearing a smoke-stained deerskin tunic over a heavy wool sweater and a thick, blue scarf.

"Get your coat on."

"Huh?"

"You heard me. We're goin' for a ride."

The old man showed his yellow teeth through an incredulous smile. "You crazy? I stomp my boot on the floor here, and you'll have all the men from downstairs up here faster'n you can sneeze."

"Like I said, if you wanna die right here, right now, go ahead. If you wanna live, get your coat on."

The old man stared at him speculatively, the corner of his left eye twitching. Deep back in both eyes, Yakima saw a flicker of fear. Betajack was old, his older boy dead. But he wasn't ready for that long ride over the last divide yet himself.

The old man sighed. He heaved his big-bellied, broad-shouldered bulk off the bed and reached for his coat.

Chapter 29

Aiming the Yellowboy at Betajack's belly that bulged behind his long buffalo coat, Yakima slowly opened the door. Boots and voices thundered from the direction of the stairs. He closed the door quickly, wincing, and looked at Betajack. The old man gave him a foxy grin.

"You're gonna die tonight, you dog-eatin' son of a bitch."

"Maybe, but I'm takin' you with me. Gut-shot."

Yakima waited until the voices and the footsteps had died. Opening the door again, he poked his head out into the hall. In the corner of his eye, he saw Betajack lurch toward him. The old man froze when Yakima smiled at him and glanced at the end of the Yellowboy's barrel. Then he stepped aside, drew the door wide, and waved the barrel at the opening.

Betajack stepped through. Yakima followed him out, drew the door closed behind him, and shoved the Yellowboy against the old man's back, prodding him over to the outside door. He could hear a few men still celebrating downstairs though the mandolin player was now drunkenly raking out a mournful tune. A girl was saying, "Stop," over and over again in a tired, pleading tone.

As Yakima stepped in front of Betajack to open the outside door, a man's voice rose from downstairs: "For chrissakes, can't you see she's had enough? Put that goddamn knife away, you crazy son of a bitch!"

Boom! Boom!

The explosions reverberated through the floor under Yakima's moccasins. All was quiet for about two seconds, and then a girl screamed. There was the heavy thud of a body—that of the big barman, most likely— hitting the floor.

Again, the girl screamed sharply. A man laughed.

Betajack looked at Yakima and a smile stretched his lips with that dark, leering grin. Yakima hardened his jaw, pressed the Winchester's barrel against the underside of the man's chin, and pushed him out onto the landing. Betajack snarled and grunted painfully, tipping his head away from the rifle. Yakima gave him another savage prod, tearing the skin beneath his chin, until the old killer was stumbling, half falling down the stairs, holding on to the railing and causing it to wobble wildly. Yakima was sure it would fall off, but by now the killers inside were all too drunk or happy to pay much attention. He didn't much care if Betajack fell over the side and broke his neck.

He'd had enough of the man and his curly wolves.

Once to the bottom of the stairs, Betajack looked harried. He was breathing hard, his face swollen and red. Yakima could see that even in the darkness.

Yakima poked the gun into his back to get him stumbling off down the alley behind the jailhouse. When he finally had the old man on the east end of town, he stopped suddenly. A horse stood before him, off in the shadows of a dark frame house, about thirty yards ahead. He could see starlight reflected in the horse's eyes, the vapor of its breath jetting around its head. Something lay on the horse's back. Then he remembered Sonny.

Yakima placed his hand on the back of Betajack's neck, forcing him to his knees.

"Stay there."

Then he walked slowly toward the horse, holding his hands out placatingly. The horse snorted and nickered and started to turn away just as Yakima grabbed its reins. He led the horse over to where Betajack knelt, kicked Sonny's boots out of the stirrup, and pulled the kid out of the saddle.

Sonny hit the ground and lay still, head turned to one side. Blood oozed from the deep gash in his forehead that had turned pasty blue in death.

Betajack looked at Yakima. "You're a real tough son of a bitch, aren't you?"

"I do all right. Climb up there."

"We'll see how tough you are when my men come lookin' for me."

Yakima grabbed him by the back of his neck again and thrust him against Sonny's pinto. Cursing, Betajack grabbed the horn and swung heavily into the leather. Yakima led the horse slowly back and in a roundabout way to where Wolf waited across the main street from the saloon. Ten minutes later he and the outlaw leader were a quarter mile east of town, Yakima leading Betajack's horse by its bridle reins.

Betajack laughed as he clung to the horn with both hands. "You're crazy. I don't know what the hell you think you're doin', but if you think this is gonna keep my boys and Hendricks from comin' after me, you're dumber than you look."

Yakima didn't say anything.

"I asked you what you think you're doin'," Betajack repeated, louder.

"Shut up," Yakima said as he continued trotting Wolf along the trail that shone like blue-tinged quicksilver in the light of a rising quarter moon.

"I'm your hostage—that it? Ha! You see, I just don't care if I die, as long as the gutless son of a yellow-livered bitch dies with me!"

It was easy for Yakima to see where the stage had swung off the trail's right side and into the mouth of a narrow canyon. He followed the tracks through the canyon, knowing that it would be easy for Betajack's men to follow, too. A quarter mile up the canyon, it doglegged to the east. The low, left sandstone wall disappeared, and lights appeared in a clearing.

Yakima drew rein, staring straight ahead into the clearing backed by boulder-strewn escarpments. The lights came from the windows of what appeared a long, low shack sitting to the right of a darker, smaller shack. Yakima drew a breath to call out to the lit cabin, but a slug blasted into a rock just ahead and to his left. The rifle wail echoed loudly off the canyon's rock walls.

"Who the hell's out there, goddamn it?" came Charlie Adlard's shout. "One more step and I'll send you to Glory!"

"Stop shootin', goddamn it—it's Henry!"

"Henry who?"

"The Henry who's gonna run that rifle up your ass if you shoot it again!"

"Who you got with you?"

"Betajack."

Yakima rode forward as a bulky, bandy-legged shadow moved out from behind a rock sheathed in cedars and junipers about fifty yards ahead and to the right. Adlard cradled his Winchester in his arms, and as Yakima jerked the outlaw leader's horse along behind him, Adlard poked his hat brim off his forehead and said, "I must be gettin' hard o' hearin'. I thought you said that was Betajack."

"I did."

Adlard just stopped and stared, hang-jawed, as Yakima and old Betajack rode past him and on across the clearing and past a corral to the right, to the long building with the lit windows. As he approached the place, Yakima saw that it was a mud-brick bunkhouse with a brush-roofed veranda. Another man stood atop the veranda in front of the door framed by wanly lit windows, holding a rifle in one hand, smoking a cigarette with the other.

Yakima recognized the spindly frame in the wool coat, watch cap, and scarf wound around the man's neck. "Weatherford, it's Yakima."

"Figured." Elijah Weatherford walked up to the edge of the porch, blowing out a thick smoke plume and turning his head slightly to stare sidelong toward Yakima and his prisoner. "Who you got with you?"

"Betajack."

Weatherford gave a raspy chuckle. "Say again?"

Yakima swung down from Wolf's back and stepped back as he aimed the rifle at the bulky outlaw. "Sit and light a spell."

When Betajack had climbed out of the saddle, breathing hard, his wrinkled face showing red in the light from the windows, Weatherford stepped back in shock. Yakima prodded Betajack up the porch steps. Weatherford backed up as though from a rabid bobcat but then lurched forward toward Yakima as the half-breed followed the outlaw onto the porch. "Good Lord, boy, what have you done?"

"I hope bought us a little time."

Stopping in front of the door, Betajack turned a dark look at Yakima, who said, "Well, you been wantin' to see the prosecutor."

Betajack flared his nostrils again in exasperation, then tripped the steel-and-leather latch and thrust the Z-frame, half-logged door open. Its hinge screeched. Yakima shoved Betajack over the threshold, followed him in, and then closed the door behind them.

Yakima looked around. There was a lamp on the wooden table to his left. To his right was a potbellied stove. Glendolene and Mendenhour sat on a steamer trunk angled before it. The Rands sat on a couple of blankets on the floor nearer Yakima and Betajack while Lori O'Reilly sat in a chair beside it, facing the door, her arm still in its sling. They all looked cold and frightened and generally miserable. Now as they all turned to see Betajack, befuddlement wrinkled their foreheads.

"Oh!" said Mrs. O'Reilly, staring at the outlaw leader as though at someone she knew she should know but couldn't quite place.

Mendenhour rose slowly, tensely from his perch on the steamer trunk, lower jaw hanging, eyes sparking brightly as he pointed a gloved hand at Betajack. "You!"

"Yeah, it's me," the old outlaw said with brassy

defiance, nodding his head. "How you doin', Mr. Law-yer? You still pissin' down your leg, are ya, you yellow-livered son of a bitch?"

Mendenhour jerked his gaze at Yakima. "Henry, what in the hell is the meaning of this?"

"Who is he?" asked Sally Rand, fear showing in her wide light brown eyes as she stared at the outlaw, pressing her fingers to her chin.

Lori O'Reilly said in a thin, disbelieving voice, "The man who's been . . . killing us. . . ."

Mendenhour walked stiffly toward Betajack. Behind him, Glendolene rose from the steamer trunk, as well, as befuddled by the outlaw's presence as everyone else in the room.

"Figured ole Betajack here might be a ticket for our free passage the rest of the way to Belle Fourche." Yakima shoved the man toward the far wall cast in shadow. "Go sit down over there. I'm gonna find some rope, tie you up."

Betajack held his ground, however, because Mendenhour stopped in front of him, glaring at his enemy. "You're a cold-blooded killer," he said.

"And you're yellow, Mendenhour. Oh, you can hang a man, sure—especially an *innocent* man—if you got the law behind you. But what about if the law ain't behind you no more?" Betajack laughed raucously and poked a gnarled finger against Mendenhour's chest. "Then you piss down your leg like a hind-tit calf!"

Mendenhour's face swelled and turned nearly as red as Betajack's. "I will not stand here and be insulted by a cold-blooded killer and common stock thief. You're the next Betajack I'll hang, Floyd. As soon as—"

"As soon as what?" Betajack barked, shoving his face right up against Mendenhour's. "As soon as you swear in a couple more law dogs to back your play, or"—he glanced over the prosecutor's shoulder at his wife standing on the other side of the room, looking stricken—"a hefty pair of *balls?*"

Mendenhour clenched his fists at his sides, glaring down at Betajack, who stood about two inches shorter. "I could kill you for that."

"Why don't you try? Hell, you got the breed here to back you." Betajack grinned up at the man in open challenge.

"All right, all right," Yakima said, grabbing Betajack's coat collar. "I didn't bring him here to—"

Just then Mendenhour gave an enraged snarl, jerked his hands up, and wrapped them around the old man's wrinkled, corded neck, driving the outlaw back against the closed door. Betajack laughed, showing his teeth as he jerked both arms up to easily break the prosecutor's hold. Then he wrapped his own hands around Mendenhour's neck and drove him backward, the Rands scrambling to get out of their way.

Yakima remained where he was. Somehow it seemed fitting that the two antagonists should get a shot at each other *mano a mano,* without Betajack having his gang behind him, without Mendenhour having Yakima and the other stage passengers to cower behind. He knew he should intervene. A better man would. But he felt a savage satisfaction in watching the two men going at it with their fists, snarling and mewling like a bear and a bobcat chained to the same rock sled.

Suddenly, the two men were on the floor, punching and wrestling, boots clomping on the rotten floorboards, cursing and spitting and trying to gouge each other's eyes with their fingers. Yakima looked around. The Rands and even Mrs. O'Reilly seemed to be sharing his satisfaction. Only Glendolene was not. She stared at him reprovingly. Finally, she walked over, glared up at him, and said, "You've made your point."

"What's that?"

"That my husband is no better than that old killer."

Yakima looked at the fighting pair. Mendenhour had the prosecutor on his back and was shoving his elbow against the old man's neck while trying to hold the man's other hand flat against the floor. Betajack had a hand clamped over Mendenhour's nose, trying to dig his fingers into the younger man's eyes. Both continued to kick and wheeze and curse under their rasping breaths.

Yakima glanced at Glendolene again, his ears warming with chagrin. He walked over, grabbed Mendenhour's left arm, and pulled him off the man. "That's enough."

"Let me go, goddamn it!" The prosecutor jerked his arm from Yakima's grip but merely rocked back on his heels, breathing hard. He'd had enough. As had Betajack, who lay supine on the floor, limbs slack, his breath rattling in and out of his throat as he stared up at the ceiling.

Mendenhour swept a thick wing of red-brown hair from his eyes and looked at Yakima. "What're we going to do with him?"

"We'll take him with us when we pull out of here tomorrow," the half-breed said, walking over and removing a coil of rope from a nail in a ceiling post. "He should get us through to Belle Fourche without further trouble."

"Won't happen!" Betajack said, wagging his head. He looked up at Glendolene and the other passengers. "You're all gonna die. You're all gonna die slow for givin' refuge to this cowardly killer!" He jerked his knobby chin and fiery eyes at Mendenhour, who merely glared back at him.

Sally Rand turned her face against her husband's chest.

Lori O'Reilly laughed, drawing all eyes to her.

"What're you laughing at, whore?" Betajack shrieked as Yakima grabbed the man's coat collar and pulled him across the floor and back into the shadows toward the ceiling support post. "You think you're any better than me? You spent half your life spreading your legs for dimes till you found a sick old man to support you over in Sweetwater!"

Lori laughed once more at the irony, the unreality of their situation. Then suddenly, tears washed over her pale blue eyes, and her cheeks flushed. She hardened her jaw and then, jerking her wounded arm from its sling, grabbed Yakima's rifle from where he'd leaned it against the door and ran toward Betajack, loudly pumping a cartridge into the breech.

Chapter 30

"Lori!" Glendolene yelled.

"You don't know a goddamn thing about me, you old wolf!" Lori screeched, raising the rifle to her shoulder. "I loved the doc!"

Squatting behind Betajack, where he'd been tying the man's wrists together behind the man's back, Yakima looked up at the middle-aged woman wielding his rifle, and he gave an uneasy chuckle. "Hell, if you want to kill him, at least wait till we get to Belle Fourche."

"Please!" implored Sally Rand, her body pressed taut against her husband's, staring over her shoulder at Lori O'Reilly.

Lori glowered down at Betajack. Yakima could feel the tension in the outlaw's shoulders ease when the woman depressed the Winchester's hammer with a click and raised the barrel. Betajack swallowed. No, he wasn't ready to die any more than the prosecutor was. Lori set the rifle across the table and then sagged into a bunk on the far side of the stove, in the dense shadows, where several bunk beds sat in a willy-nilly arrangement, with a couple of ladder-back chairs and what appeared to be trash and old tack littering the floor.

Mendenhour stood slowly, breathing hard, staring down at Betajack. "Your son stole those horses from Arnie Douglas," he said with quiet defiance.

"If it makes you feel better to believe that, you go ahead. But old Douglas was lyin'. Pres was wantin' to build his own ranch with clean stock, marry a woman from down Denver way. He *earned* the money he paid for them horses, but ole Douglas was just tryin' to get in good with you against me . . . and get his horses back for nothin'." Betajack snorted, spat to one side. "I'm gonna kill him next. And next time the judge pulls through Wolfville, I'm gonna kill him, too."

Mendenhour stared down at him. His expression was hard to read. His brows were ridged, but his eyes were pensive, dubious. Finally, he turned, grabbed his hat off the table, opened the door, and went out quickly. Yakima glanced at Glendolene, who stood staring at the door, and then he cut off a length of the rope to tie Betajack's ankles together. Meanwhile, the Rands remained where they'd been standing, Percy Rand holding his quietly sobbing wife and patting her back while Glendolene sagged slowly down in a chair at the table.

She regarded Betajack levelly. "Are you sure?"

The old outlaw's sharp eyes turned to her. "That your husband's a murderer? Oh, yeah."

She sighed, propped an elbow on the table, and leaned her head against the heel of her hand. Yakima grabbed his rifle off the table, shouldered it, and looked down at her. "You gonna be all right?"

She nodded as she stared down at the table. On the

far side of the table was a cracked window, two faces staring in through the dirt and the frost. Yakima moved to the door and went out. Adlard and Weatherford turned from the window.

"Hell was poppin' in there for sure," noted the jehu, his voice betraying his awe.

Weatherford shook his head slowly, raking his tangled gray bib beard across his chest. A shadow moved off to the west; it was Mendenhour walking away.

"You fellas might as well get some sleep," Yakima said. "I'll keep watch. I think we're safe as long as we got Betajack, but I'll make sure."

Weatherford said, "I put your horse up in the stable out back."

"Obliged."

Yakima stepped down off the veranda and began walking around the bunkhouse's north corner. Behind him, Adlard said, "You think it's true what Betajack said?"

Yakima stopped and glanced back at him standing there in the shadows beneath the brush roof. He could see Glendolene's silhouette still sitting at the table, her back to the window. Yakima shrugged. "Don't know," he said. "Don't care."

He walked off down the side of the bunkhouse to the stable.

What he'd said was true. He'd lived long enough to have acquired what he saw as a realistic view, however cynical, about the ways of men and women. Nothing surprised him anymore. No one disappointed him except himself once in a while, but he did the best that he could. He'd been sorry about cuckolding Mendenhour, but he wasn't that sorry anymore.

He just wanted to get this nasty business out of the way, deliver the gold, and head south.

The gold . . .

The stable sat hunched in some cottonwoods and willows flanking the bunkhouse. There was a corral off each side. Wolf was in the left-side corral; the stage team was in the right side. Old Weatherford was smart about horses.

Wolf nickered as Yakima approached the adobe brick, brush-roofed stable, and walked through the plank-board door that hung from one leather hinge. His gear was inside, draped over a saddletree, the saddlebags with bulging pouch hanging over the saddle. A mouse or chipmunk scratched in the darkness at the stable's rear. Yakima slung the bags off his shoulder—he'd keep them close until he'd delivered them to Delbert Clifton's family in Belle Fourche—then walked back to the front of the bunkhouse.

He stood in the darkness off the front corner, taking a long look around. Hearing nothing but the infrequent yammer of coyotes and the frequent cooing of a near owl, he sat on the edge of the porch, resting the saddlebags on the rotten floor to his left and laying the Yellowboy across his lap. He sat there for a time, trying to clear his mind, staring up at the stars.

The door scraped open. He turned to see Glendolene move out of the bunkhouse. She closed the door, took a step to the side, and leaned against the bunkhouse's front wall, between the door and the window. She wore her long fur coat but no hat or gloves. She crossed her arms on her chest. Yakima studied her.

She stared off into the night without saying anything, probably just needing some air. He tapped his index finger on the Winchester's breech. Footsteps sounded ahead, and he raised the rifle but eased its butt down on his thigh when he recognized the prosecutor's hatted silhouette.

The man walked straight toward the bunkhouse, smoking a cigar. His long coat was unbuttoned and flapping open. When he lifted the cigar to his mouth, the coal glowed in the darkness.

He stopped ten feet in front of the bunkhouse, looked at Glendolene and then at Yakima. He gave a wry chuckle.

"Together again," he said, giving an icy smile. "Isn't that nice?"

Neither Yakima nor Glendolene said anything. Mendenhour mounted the porch steps, paused in front of the door, staring down at his wife, who did not return his gaze, and then walked inside the bunkhouse and closed the door.

Yakima drew a long breath, released it slowly, staring up at the stars. The only sounds were the coyotes and the owl, the very faint rustle of a breeze causing snow to sift down over the edge of the porch roof. It glittered faintly in the starlight.

"You know who I am and where I come from," the woman said at last, pushing off the bunkhouse wall and walking over to the edge of the porch. "I think it's only fair you return the favor."

"I don't see the point."

"What's in those saddlebags you're so attached to?" She sat down at the edge of the porch, about five feet to his left, and leaned forward to glance at the bags on his right. "Is it really gold?"

"Yep."

"I wish you'd told me you had a grubstake. Maybe

I would have run off with you." Glendolene pitched her voice with dry, self-deprecating humor.

"I didn't have it then. Just got it the other day, though, good Christ, it seems like months ago now."

"Why Belle Fourche?"

"The man it belonged to died saving my hide. And my partner's hide. I'm taking it back to his family."

She said nothing. He could feel her eyes on him, studying him. Finally, she gave a pensive chuff and lifted her eyes to stare at the stars.

"Yakima?"

He turned to her. She was staring at him again, her eyes edged with silver. Her lips were parted, as though she were on the verge of saying something. Then she closed her mouth, lifted its corners with a wry smile though her eyes remained thoughtful, faraway. "Heck of a Christmas present."

She rose and turned to the door before stopping and looking back at him. "It's Christmas Eve, I think," she said as though it had just dawned on her.

Yakima wondered if she was right. He'd lost track of the days himself. Nevertheless, he smiled. "Merry Christmas, Glendolene."

"Merry Christmas, Yakima."

She went inside.

Yakima jerked his head up from the table in the bunkhouse. He'd heard something. Now he looked around the room touched with a misty gray light, saw several figures curled in blankets in front of the fire.

He saw Betajack on the floor, with his head against the ceiling post to which he'd been tied, his chin dipped to his chest. He couldn't see the others, but he heard Adlard and Weatherford snoring in bunks they'd bedded down in toward the shack's other end.

Yakima blinked, turned to the window touched with the gray light, saw the lightening sky straight above the clearing through which a dark blue tongue-shaped cloud stretched from east to west. Jesus, he'd fallen asleep around one or two, had only wanted to doze . . .

Shadows moved in the shadowy clearing, beyond the frosted pane.

Yakima leaped to his feet, grabbed his Winchester off the table. Hearing the others stirring, he went to the door, opened it, and stepped out, closing the door and holding the rifle up high across his chest, peering into the clearing before him. The riders sat abreast in a long, semicircular line a hundred yards straight out from the cabin.

Breath steamed around the riders' heads and the heads of their horses. A couple of the mounts tossed their bits or stomped. The riders sat stiffly, all wielding rifles and staring toward the cabin.

It was too dark for Yakima to tell who yelled, "That you, breed?"

"Yeah."

"We're missin' one of our group."

"We got him here. Safe an' sound." Yakima walked forward and stopped at the top of the porch's three steps. "If you boys stay clear, we'll turn him loose in Belle Fourche, an' you can all go an' celebrate Christmas together. Give thanks you're still alive."

Yakima saw the top hat in the middle of the group. That would be Hendricks. The hat moved, and the man gave a rueful laugh. "How in the hell . . . ?" He laughed again, booted his horse slowly forward.

When he'd cut the distance between him and the bunkhouse to half, Yakima leveled his Winchester barrel from his hip and said, "That's far enough."

He could see the rose-colored glasses now and the long horsehide coat. He held a Henry rifle straight up from his right thigh.

"I'm gonna need proof he's still kickin'," Hendricks said. "And I'm gonna need to hear it from him. Hear it from him what he wants to do about the situation."

"I can do that." Yakima smiled stiffly. "You boys sit tight. There's a gun trained on the old man inside. One shot, one wrong move, and he's gonna have a new ear hole."

Hendricks chuckled softly, menacingly.

Yakima turned and went into the bunkhouse. The others were up and gathered in front of the door, looking nervous. Yakima set his rifle on the table and sidled through the group toward where Betajack remained on the floor, tied to the ceiling support post.

"He hasn't stirred," said Mrs. O'Reilly.

The old outlaw sat with his head hanging nearly to his chest. A thin lock of coarse gray hair hung over his forehead. Yakima kicked his boot.

No movement.

Yakima dropped to a knee beside the man and pushed his shoulder back, causing his head to come up slightly. "Betajack."

The man's eyes remained closed. Yakima lifted his chin, pushing his head back against the post. The man's face was pale blue and drawn, lips stretched back from his teeth in a silent snarl.

"Oh, my God," said Glendolene, standing behind Yakima.

"What is it?" asked Sally Rand.

Yakima released the outlaw's head. It sagged to his chest. Yakima rose, staring fatefully down at the man. "He's dead."

"Heart stroke," Lori said, sucking a breath.

Sally Rand sobbed. "What's to become of us now?"

Chapter 31

Yakima walked to the window over the table and looked out.

Claw Hendricks sat near the cabin, waiting, rifle jutting from his thigh. The others waited behind him. One was casually smoking a cigarette, the smoke and the vapor from his breath forming a large cloud around his black bullet-crowned hat. The sky was steadily lightening.

Yakima rubbed his jaw and turned to the others staring at him expectantly. "Well, I reckon what's gonna happen now is you're all going to become fighters. Fierce ones."

He glanced at Charlie Adlard standing on the other side of the table from him, looking warily out. "How many guns we got?"

"Two rifles," said Elijah Weatherford, smoking his ubiquitous, loosely rolled quirley. He had one of the rifles in his hand. He opened his coat to show the worn walnut butts of two old-model Colts protruding from the waistband of his patched duck trousers. "And I got two of these purty old ladies." He smiled around the smoldering quirley.

"We got them five pistols you took off them two wolves you jumped couple nights back," said Adlard, glancing around the room. "So everyone should be armed."

He looked meaningfully at Mendenhour, who stood a ways off by himself, nearest the dead Betajack. He flared his nostrils slightly and said, "I have my own Colt .45 and rifle, thanks. And I'm right handy with both."

Lori O'Reilly retrieved a Winchester from where it rested across the wood box near the stove. She swung around and racked a round in the chamber. "And I have this."

"I can shoot, too," said Glendolene. "I just need a pistol."

"You sure?" her husband asked her.

She turned to him but said nothing.

"Percy has a gun, too," said Sally Rand. "And he taught me how to shoot rattlesnakes back at the ranch."

She stared at Yakima, and he was surprised by the hard confidence that shone in her pale blue eyes. Turning to the jehu, she stuck out her hand. "I'll take one of those pistols, Mr. Adlard."

Percy Rand placed a hand on his wife's shoulder. "Sally, you're . . . why, you're in the family way, and these aren't rattlesnakes."

"That's right," Sally said, accepting a big pistol from Adlard, hefting it in both her hands. "I got our child to protect. And they are rattlesnakes, Percy. The human kind!"

Weatherford chuckled. They all looked nervous but capable, ready.

"So, what's next?" Mendenhour asked Yakima.

Yakima looked around at each of them. "Choose a window. Prepare to knock the glass out and start shooting. You'll know when." He gave a wry look. "Just wait till I'm out of the way."

"What're you going to do?" Glendolene asked him.

"I'm gonna deliver Hendricks's partner to him." Yakima walked over and cut Betajack free of the post. He returned his bowie knife to the well of his right moccasin and then stood and drew the big dead outlaw leader over his shoulder. Turning to the door, he glanced at Adlard. "Follow me out with my Yellowboy. Be ready to throw it fast."

"Ah, hell—this is it, ain't it?" the jehu said, grabbing Yakima's Winchester off the table, taking his own rifle in his other hand.

"I reckon it is."

"Why you gonna take Betajack out there?" Mendenhour wanted to know.

Yakima turned from the door, the big outlaw hanging off his shoulder and down his back. "There's a chance, probably a slight one, that they won't fight so hard when they realize they got nothin' to fight for now—this bein' Betajack's shindig an' all."

He nodded at Adlard, who opened the door for him. On his way out, Yakima said, "And, hell, maybe they'll wanna say a few words over him."

Yakima stepped around Adlard. He inadvertently banged Betajack's head on the doorframe as he went out. It made a dull thud. As Adlard came out behind him, drawing the door closed, Yakima walked down off the porch steps and into the yard. Hendricks glowered at him curiously as he approached and then stopped and dropped his cargo on the ground before Hendricks's cream stallion.

The horse pitched slightly, nickering. Yakima had hoped it would.

"Turns out he expired on me last night," Yakima said matter-of-factly. "I do apologize. Old ticker couldn't take all this, I reckon."

"Christ, you son of a bitch!" Hendricks shouted, staring down at Betajack as though he'd never seen a dead man before, and fumbling to get his rifle aimed.

Yakima turned to Adlard, who tossed him the Yellowboy. Yakima swung back toward Hendricks, pumping a fresh round into the chamber, and aimed at Hendricks's bespectacled face just as the horse curveted on its rear hooves.

Yakima's Winchester thundered, shattering the still morning silence. His bullet merely clipped the narrow brim of Hendricks's opera hat, flipping it off his head just as his horse dropped back down to all four feet. Hendricks gave an angry bellow that turned shrill when Adlard triggered his carbine, punching dust from the upper right arm of Hendricks's coat. Yakima fired again as the horse pitched like a rodeo bronc, and the outlaw leader snarled through gritted teeth and clamped a hand over his upper-left thigh.

At the same time, the other riders began opening up and galloping toward the bunkhouse. Bullets plowed into the ground around Yakima and Adlard, and the jehu yelped and leaped off his left foot as though the limb had been pinked. More bullets hammered the porch support posts and the adobe brick front of the bunkhouse and cracked through the windows.

"Take cover!" Yakima shouted at Adlard, and the man started hopping toward a rain barrel standing off the bunkhouse's north front corner.

Yakima felt a bullet clip his left calf as he ran, legs

and arms pumping, toward the bunkhouse. Two more tore up dead grass at his heels just before he launched himself into the air, careened over the top of the stock trough left of the front steps, and hit the ground behind it and rolled against the stone base of the porch.

There was the screech of more breaking glass, and a quick glance told him the other stage passengers were doing as he'd told them, hammering out the glass to return fire. As a couple of rifles opened up in the bunkhouse behind him, he racked a fresh round in the Yellowboy's beech, snaked the barrel over the top of the stock trough, squinting down the barrel. Hendricks's horse was buck-kicking wildly in the middle of the yard, about forty yards from Yakima, while the man himself, hatless, rose-colored glasses hanging from one ear, ran toward the cover of the stone well, limping on his left leg.

As the other riders were galloping in a shaggy, spread-out line toward the bunkhouse, shooting pistols or rifles—some with guns popping and smoking in both fists—Yakima fired twice more at Hendricks, wanting to cut the head off the gang's second snake. One bullet tore up dust and snow off Hendricks's heels as he dove behind the well coping, while the second drilled the coping itself, ricocheting loudly.

Bullets hammered the far side of the stock trough, flinging wood slivers in all directions. The riders were within twenty yards now, and Yakima started firing. He knocked one straight back off his saddle, drilled a round through the left cheek of another. Just then, pistols and rifles began blasting behind him, and the entire gang, to a man, hung their lower jaws in shock while jerking back hard on their horses' reins. They hadn't been expecting resistance from any more of the stage's party outside of Yakima himself.

The horse of one stopped so suddenly that the coyote dun flew forward, knees buckling. It hit the ground on its right wither and flung its rider over its head. The man landed hard and rolled, throwing his arms up, amazingly still holding his carbine. As he staggered backward, getting his land legs, he swung his rifle toward Yakima, who drilled him through the dead center of his quilted elk-skin coat half a second before a shot from the cabin snapped his head back sharply. Bright red blood oozed out from where his left eye had been.

The guns in the cabin erupted in a cannonade. Ejecting his last spent cartridge, which bounced off the porch behind him, Yakima smiled. Two more of Hendricks's killers were blown off their mounts, spewing blood and screaming. Their horses screamed, as well, and trampled their fallen riders as they wheeled and headed back in the opposite direction, buck-kicking angrily.

One of the few remaining killers galloped toward Yakima. The half-breed aimed and fired, but his Winchester pinged on an empty chamber. Half a second later, the rider's own carbine clicked empty, and then he hurled himself off the side of his desperately, dustily curveting horse. He slammed into Yakima with a wild yell, the eagle tattoo on his cheek fairly glowing now in the growing morning light.

He threw Yakima onto his back and raised a big Green River knife with a carved horn handle. Screaming like a gut-shot coyote, he thrust the knife toward Yakima's neck. The half-breed released his empty rifle and shoved his left hand up, wrapping it around the killer's wrist when the point of the long knife was six inches from his throat. He gave a grunt and, gritting his teeth and hardening his jaw, tossed the lighter, weaker man over onto his back.

The attacker screamed again, widening his mouth and his dark eyes and nostrils, as Yakima twisted his wrist until it broke with a grinding crack. He gave another grunt as he shoved the man's own knife up through the underside of his chin, hammering the end of the knife with the heel of his hand until the blade ground into his brain.

Blood rushed from the gaping wound like hot water from a gut flask, sopping the front of his heavy, quilted blanket coat.

Yakima pulled his hand away, let the man drop dead to the ground.

He jerked his head toward the open yard, not startled by sound and movement but by its sudden lack. The only ones standing out there were the few horses that hadn't run off. All the killers were down—a few lying still in bloody piles. A few writhing and groaning.

The shooting had stopped.

Yakima glanced behind him. Sally and Percy Rand stood in the broken-out window left of the door. They each held a rifle or smoking pistol and they were looking around cautiously. Mendenhour and Weatherford stood in the window on the door's other side, old Elijah holding a bloody white handkerchief to his forehead.

"Everybody all right?" Yakima called.

Weatherford nodded. "I took a ricochet. Don't think anyone else in here's hit." He darted a bright glance past Yakima. "Look there!"

A man was on a knee about halfway down the side of a burned-out shed ahead and right of Yakima. A gun flashed and barked, the bullet hammering the porch behind the half-breed. The man rose heavily, awkwardly, and ran limping toward a horse standing nearby, reins dangling straight down to the ground.

Yakima recognized Claw Hendricks's long horse-hair coat. He palmed his Colt and, rising to a crouch, fired twice. Both shots blew up dust and gravel just behind the outlaw leader. And then he was in the saddle and ramming his heels against the pinto's flanks, galloping south toward the canyon. His image in the still dull light grew quickly smaller.

He was out of range for Yakima's Colt.

The half-breed cursed. He picked up his rifle and walked out from behind the stock trough, looking around carefully. All the downed men lay still except for one about twenty yards straight ahead. He lay on his back, grinding his spurs into the ground. Blood poured from a hole in his neck and several more in his wolf coat. He was speaking in oddly dulcet tones as though to his Maker in the sky.

Yakima heard the thumps of boots behind him. The others were filing through the bunkhouse door while Adlard limped out from behind his rain barrel. They all held pistols and rifles and they were glassy-eyed, cautious, a little amazed by what they had done and, likely, that they were all still alive to tell about it.

Yakima continued walking slowly forward, looking around at the dead and dying around him, and then he stared off toward Hendricks's dwindling figure. Mendenhour came down the porch steps and walked into the clearing. Glendolene walked out of the bunkhouse with the others, and they all spread out in the yard in front of the porch. Mendenhour continued toward Yakima.

"They all dead?" he asked.

"Pretty much. Hendricks is lightin' a shuck."

"Likely bleed to death—won't he?"

"Probably."

Yakima stared toward Hendricks's jouncing figure just now heading into the canyon. In the corner of his eye, he saw Mendenhour raise his rifle, heard the nasty scrape of a cartridge being levered into the chamber. He wheeled to see the man aiming the rifle at him from his shoulder.

"Thanks for the help, Henry. But I understand you're wanted dead or alive." The prosecutor smiled grimly as he squinted down the Winchester's barrel.

Behind him, Lori O'Reilly gasped.

A gun blasted. Mendenhour's head jerked forward.

He staggered toward Yakima, lowering his rifle and triggering it into the ground near his feet. He stopped, looked at Yakima with a dazed look, blood pumping from the back of his neck. As though drunk, he pivoted, stumbling again, and saw his wife standing six feet behind him, aiming a smoking Remington .44 at him in both her gloved hands.

Her eyes were hard, her mouth straight.

"You son of a bitch," she said softly. "Why did you have to go and make me do that?"

A single tear rolled out from the corner of her right eye and started dropping down her cheek. She lowered the pistol slowly.

"Ah, hell," the prosecutor said through a long, weary sigh.

He dropped to his knees and then to his side, his hands and his brown leather half boots quivering slightly as he died.

Chapter 32

The hovel sat at the edge of Belle Fourche, along the steep, narrow bank of Hay Creek.

Yakima couldn't see the place very well until Wolf had clomped across the creek via a plank bridge buried in new-fallen snow. The wind blew snow through the gauzy twilight, obscuring what appeared to be a very small ranch-stead with a log barn little larger than most cabins, a single corral, and a shack that was little more than vertical boards over which tar paper had been tacked. It had a second story with a steeply slanting east-side roof and a single unlit window. The roof did not appear to be shingled under the snow mantling it.

The torn edges of the tar paper rattled in the strong wind that blew the snow against the house and the barn, causing the hovel's rickety frame to creak precariously. There was a small lean-to stable off the cabin's right side and what appeared to be a chicken coop behind that. The door was on the stable side of the cabin.

Yakima urged Wolf up to the shack. Its windows

were lit with flickering candles, and they laid a vague yellow light on the snowy ground before it. A pine Christmas wreath was nailed to the front door, and it flipped and flapped in the wind.

Yakima swung heavily down from the saddle, wincing against the snow and the wind blasting him. He walked back to his saddlebags and pulled the gold sack out of the left pouch. He hefted the pouch and looked at the cabin. His heart felt heavier in his chest than the gold felt in his hands.

Letting Wolf's reins droop to the ground, the wind jostling them, Yakima walked up to the front door. It consisted of five six-foot-long vertical pine boards and a wooden handle. He knocked on the door. He had to knock once more; a few minutes later, a woman's silhouetted head appeared in the window right of the door, looking out.

She pulled her head back. Yakima thought that, seeing a big half-breed out here in this weather, she'd likely shotgun him through the door. But then the door scraped open a few inches, and the woman's chocolate-colored face appeared in the crack.

"I have something for you, Mrs. Clifton," he said loudly so she could hear him above the wind. He bounced the gold lightly in his hands. "It's from your husband."

She stared at him. He saw her eyes widen slightly. Slowly, she opened the door and stepped back, drawing the door half-open, beckoning with one hand. Yakima stepped into the cabin, and she closed the door quickly, having to ram a shoulder against it to latch it. Then she stepped back away from him, staring up at him warily, spreading a dark hand against her chest.

She was a slight black woman in a relatively clean

gray dress that was older than the decorative green and
red stitching she'd added to the high-buttoned neck
and the sleeves. Her kinky hair was pulled straight
back and secured behind her head. A fine-boned, handsome woman of around thirty, Yakima thought.

"From . . . Delbert . . . ?" she said, dropping her eyes
to the sack in the half-breed's hands.

"Yes, ma'am," he said grimly.

They were in the kitchen crudely furnished with
pine shelves, a small black range, and a square eating
table that had turned silver from scrubbing. The table
was set with simple tin plates, cups, and wooden-
handled forks and knives. A large iron pot bubbled on
the stove, filling the room with the smell of rabbit stew.
Behind a wall partition to his left, hushed voices rose.
A pair of dark eyes appeared around the edge of the
wall. They widened when they found Yakima, and the
boy drew his head back, muttering to someone else in
that part of the shack with him.

"And Delbert . . . ?" The corner of the woman's eyes
were wrinkled with trepidation.

She knew even before Yakima said it in the best way
he could—simply and clearly. "He's dead, ma'am."

Those eyes held his as though beseeching and at the
same time defying him to continue. They turned
golden with a thin sheen of tears.

"He died saving my life and the life of my partner.
He was on his way home . . . with this." Yakima walked
over and placed the sack on the table. "That's when he
died. This here is yours. Probably more money than
you'll know what to do with at first, but"—he glanced
around the humble dwelling, feeling the cold air seep-
ing through cracks between the vertical wall boards—
"you'll figure it out."

Mrs. Clifton stood staring at him, silently sobbing.

Yakima walked over and wrapped his arms around her. He held her tightly for several minutes. Her silent crying racked her. When he pulled away from her, she sniffed, wiped tears from her cheeks with the backs of her hands, and said, "Can you stay for supper, sir?"

"No." Yakima squeezed her arms reassuringly. He glanced behind him, saw a little boy around ten and a girl of about twelve, both dressed in ragged dungarees and patched socks, staring at him from the entrance to the shack's little parlor area. Behind them was a tree only slightly taller and fuller than a sage shrub. It held three candles and a short string of popcorn.

"Your daddy saved my life. Don't ever forget him."

He pinched his hat brim to the children and walked to the door. As he opened it and started out, Mrs. Clifton said, "Sir?"

Yakima stopped.

She frowned, tears still streaming down her cheeks from her glistening eyes, lips trembling. "What's your name?"

"I'm Yakima Henry."

He went out, mounted up, and rode back across the bridge. He rode back through Belle Fourche, through the chill wind pelting him with snow. His heart still felt heavy, but it was getting lighter. He wished the same for the Cliftons, but that might take months, maybe years.

He rode down the little settlement's main street, heading south. The Butte County Hotel was on his right. It was the only business establishment in town with lit windows. A decorated Christmas tree stood inside the large front window of the three-story flophouse. Shadows moved around it. He could hear the jubilant strains of a fiddle and a banjo.

Pausing in the street, staring into the hotel, he could see the Rands dancing in front of the tree, near a popping fire in the hotel dining room's massive stone hearth. Mrs. O'Reilly was dancing with Elijah Weatherford. Charlie Adlard sat on a deep leather sofa, his injured ankle propped on a stool. Adlard had his hair greased and combed, and he wore a string tie over a checked shirt, and a corduroy jacket.

Yakima thought he looked fine. He thought they all looked fine. Vaguely, he wondered where Glendolene was. He hadn't said anything to her after he'd driven the stage into town, trailing his horse. He'd helped them all inside out of the building storm, and then he'd mounted Wolf and ridden over to the Clifton place, completing his mission.

He turned forward and started to boot Wolf again, but looked back at the hotel when he saw the front door open. Glendolene stepped out. She wore a red silk dress. The wind tossed it richly against her long legs. Around her slim neck was a bejeweled choker. Her hair was down, blowing in the wind. It shone in the light from the windows flanking her.

"Yakima?" she said, crossing her arms as she stopped at the edge of the broad front veranda. "Aren't you coming in?"

He shook his head. "I'm riding on."

His heart was too heavy for Christmas. He'd flop in a sheltered ravine, continue heading south when the storm had blown itself out. He hoped the storm in himself would blow itself out soon, too. He doubted it. Despite the gold, Delbert Clifton's family weighed heavy on his shoulders.

"Yakima," she called above the wind, leaning beseechingly over the porch rail, "this is no night to be out. Come on in and join us. It's Christmas!"

"I'll be riding on. Good luck to you, Glendolene. I'm sorry about all of it."

He booted Wolf ahead. Halfway down the street, he kicked the stallion into a gallop. The large, dark buildings on both sides of the street slid past him. So did the lit cabins where families celebrated around food-laden tables and roaring fires. The stormy night swept him up and embraced him.

He heard the faint cry behind him: *"Yakima!"*

But he did not hear what followed: *"The child is yours!"*

He rode farther and farther into the cold, snowy night.

He did not look back.

ABOUT THE AUTHOR

Frank Leslie is the pseudonym of a prolific and acclaimed writer who has penned more than sixty fast-action Western novels. He lives in Colorado.

Also available from
Frank Leslie

THE BELLS OF EL DIABLO

A pair of Confederate soldiers go AWOL and head for Denver, where a tale of treasure in Mexico takes them on an adventure.

THE LAST RIDE OF JED STRANGE

Colter Farrow is forced to kill a soldier in self-defense, sending him to Mexico where he helps the wild Bethel Strange find her missing father. But there's an outlaw on their trail, and the next ones to go missing just might be them...

DEAD RIVER KILLER

Bad luck has driven Yakima Henry into the town of Dead River during a severe mountain winter—where Yakima must weather a killer who's hell-bent on making the town as dead as its name.

REVENGE AT HATCHET CREEK

Yakima Henry has been ambushed and badly injured. Luckily, Aubrey Coffin drags him to safety—but as he heals, lawless desperados circle closer to finish the job...

BULLET FOR A HALF-BREED

Yakima Henry won't tolerate incivility toward a lady, especially the former widow Beth Holgate. If her new husband won't stop giving her hell, Yakima may make her a widow all over again.

THE KILLERS OF CIMARRON

After outlaws murder his friend and take a woman hostage, Colter Farrow is back on the vengeance trail, determined to bring her back alive—and send the killers straight to hell.

S0096